BLOOD COVENANT

ALAN BAXTER

Cemetery Dance Publications
Baltimore
2024

Blood Covenant

Trade Paperback Edition

ISBN:
978-1-58767-976-6

Cemetery Dance Publications
132B Industry Lane, Unit #7
Forest Hill, MD 21050
www.cemeterydance.com

PAUL

BLOOD everywhere.

Slick across the bright white tiles of the bank's floor, arced up the equally pristine wall behind him, a warm spray across his eyes. Paul Glenn's boot sucked against the ground and left a perfect red impression of its sole as he staggered back a step. Screams and wails punctuated the air, the entire thing gone to shit in seconds.

"What now?" he screamed at his brother.

James Glenn's eyes were wide and white, the only part of his face visible, the rest concealed by a thick black ski mask. But those eyes were wild with excitement more than shock. He looked pleased. Paul imagined his teeth bared in a manic grin behind the wool.

"Cops'll be here in seconds," Deanna McKeirnan said. "We gotta bounce. Right now." Her face was tight with shock, hands trembling where she gripped her shotgun, but she remained stoic even as Paul felt his mind threatening to spiral away.

He stood halfway between the door and the body of the old bank guard who had tried to be a hero. Andrew, according to one of the staff who had yelled his name as James Glenn's shotgun reduced his head to burger mince and blood. So much blood.

"We have to go!" Paul said, sobs threatening his voice.

"Not until we have the money, or what the fuck is all this for?" James spat. "Let's move, get them to open the safe."

Rick Dawson remained by the door, his eyes as white as James's, shotgun at port arms. "He's right, man." His voice was level, calm, and Paul was glad of the support. Rick seemed the only one still his normal self. Something about that made Paul's teeth itch.

Sirens wailed in the distance.

"We really fucked this up," Deanna said. Kind of her to say 'we' when it had all been James. "Let's go, try again another time. Or we'll all go down."

"FUCK!" James's body vibrated, rock hard in frustration.

Bank customers cowered on the floor, some sobbed, one man's grey pants had darkened with a wide spread of piss as he lay spattered with the guard's blood and brains. A stark white shard of bone was caught in his hair. *Must be the guard's skull*, Paul thought stupidly. Tellers and staff behind the glass had gone into shutdown, obviously someone already tripped the alarm. Paul looked left and right, his legs twitching with a barely suppressed urge to bolt. Should he run, leave them all and make a break for his own safety? *No one will get hurt*, James had said. *The guns will scare everyone, we'll take the cash and run. Small town banks have big money and little security.* They'd driven for hours from western Sydney to this particular one, chosen after so much deliberation, if James were to be believed. He claimed he'd studied their position, size, number of customers, estimated their value.

And now it was all over in an instant, James's shotgun barking murder. Paul tried to blink the guard's blood from his eyes, his ski mask must be soaked in it. He'd been standing not three feet from the man, yelling at him to put down the gun. Outnumbered four to one, the old man had refused and James had stepped up to within a metre, levelled two barrels, and fired. Almost like he'd wanted to kill someone today more than he'd wanted the money. Paul derailed the thought when pictures of Imogen and the little boy rose in his mind's eye. He couldn't think about that now. But maybe... He looked at his brother's wild eyes and cursed. Was *all* this a reaction to Imogen?

“Those sirens are getting nearer,” Deanna said, her voice iron hard. She stared at James with an intensity that made Paul’s skin crawl. He wanted so badly to run.

“Drop your weapons!”

They spun around. Two uniformed cops in the doorway, both with service pistols levelled, panning quickly left and right, trying to cover them all. Glock 22s, Paul thought dumbly. New South Wales Police carry Glock 22 pistols. He had no idea why or how he knew that. He froze. They must be street cops, just passing. Just lucky. Now they stood between him and freedom. Shit had turned to shitter. How could this day get any worse? *Never think that*, a tiny voice said in his mind, and he pushed it away.

Time slowed as Paul realised the police were watching him, James and Deanna. They hadn’t seen Rick yet, still by the door.

Rick, raising his shotgun, slowly like he was underwater. His eyes widening through the letterbox of his ski mask.

Paul’s mouth started to form the word “No!”

Someone on the floor yelled, “Beside you!”

Rick’s shotgun boomed and the nearest cop’s neck and shoulder exploded in blood and flesh, stark white bone suddenly, horrifyingly visible, as he jerked sideways into his partner. The first cop slumped, ragdoll dead, as his partner turned and fired. More screams punched the air, Rick Dawson grunted in pain and shock, one hand slapping to his gut as he sat down heavily, and James’s shotgun exploded again. The second cop flew backwards out the door, slamming into the pavement in a spray of blood. People outside flying away in a sudden frenzy, like a startled flock of birds.

“We’re out!” James yelled and ran, jumping over the dead cop and pulling open the door of their stolen car parked right outside. Deanna was behind him, but Rick struggled, had only managed to rise onto one knee, scarlet leaking between the fingers of the hand he pressed to his stomach.

“Fucker got me,” he said weakly.

Paul grabbed him around the back with his free arm and hauled him up. “Come on, man, come on!” Rick was a big guy, tall and heavy. It was some effort to move him. Paul's guts were water, a sharp headache of panic speared between his eyes.

They stagger-ran out the door, Rick's grunts of pain muffled through clenched teeth. The sirens were nearer, James yelling at them to *Get in, get in!*

Deanna, in the front passenger seat, leaned over and pushed open the back door. Paul drove Rick forward, into the seat, scrambled in behind him. James peeled out, Paul's boot toes skipping against the asphalt as he nearly fell right back out again. Deanna grabbed his waistband over the back of the seat, Rick somehow held onto his arm, and he hauled himself in. The door slammed as James swerved the old dark blue Ford Fairlane sedan across honking oncoming traffic, through a red light, and away. Paul turned on one knee, looked out the back window. People ran back and forth. The cop outside lay in a widening pool of blood, stark against the pale grey footpath. But no police cars appeared as James swerved again, took a turn, and started putting buildings and distance between them and the debacle of a job that was supposed to be a cakewalk.

LEIGH

LEIGH Moore caught Rueben's eye in the rear view mirror as she drove, rolled her eyes towards her husband, Grant, in the passenger seat. Her son smiled, shook his head. Such a grown-up gesture, her little boy a teenager now. How could he be thirteen? He had even started to look like a man, hints of adult physique showing through, a slight narrowing of the face, thickening of the shoulders. She missed her little boy so much, even while she was proud of the young man he was becoming.

"That joke wasn't funny the first four hundred and nineteen times, Dad," Rueben said, smirking.

"You people don't understand good comedy," Grant said. "Do they, Dad?"

Clay sat forward from his seat beside Rueben. "Son, I'm gonna be honest with you. As a dad, I think it's my duty. You aren't any good at the jokes."

Grant barked a laugh. "That was *your* joke, Dad!"

"Yeah, and when I tell it, it's funny. Stick to hotel management, son."

"Says the retired hotel manager."

Clay sat back. "I gave it all to you for a reason. Might be I'll start up my comedy career any time now. Hey, I could do a Friday night slot in the bar once we open up!"

Leigh, Grant, and Rueben all made noises of amusement and horror.

"Gramps, I'll admit you're funnier than Dad, but you're no comedian either."

Clay mocked a hurt look as Grant said, "Hey!"

"Don't miss the turn now," Clay said, pointing.

The sign for the turnoff had become half overgrown with blue gum tree branches, but Leigh would know the way in the dark or fog or any other conditions, as would Grant. He'd been coming up here since he was born, when Clay ran the place with Molly. Leigh had been coming for the past eighteen years, since she and Grant had been together. Fifteen years since their marriage in the hotel they all called their home.

At least, their most-of-the-year home. "It's not worth opening in the real winter," Clay had explained decades before. "Too far from the snowfields for the ski tourism and not enough regular trade in the cold months to pay the bills. Better financial sense to take a break in the city." Molly had never liked going back to the city, but she did it for Clay. And Grant had enjoyed it as a kid too. Now it was valuable for Rueben to spend some time away from the hotel.

But so quickly the time passed. Perhaps it was Molly's death that made Leigh maudlin, the first time back since Clay's wife fell to breast cancer six months before. But they were all young and hale, even Clay himself a powerful seventy-one years old. Like the trees they drove past he still stood strong, even if he did complain a lot about his arthritic hip. She couldn't ever imagine him going, but she'd felt the same way about her mother-in-law, and how quickly that had changed. She chanced a glance at Grant, wondering again how he was really coping with his mother's death. Like his father. Clay and Grant were equally closed books emotionally.

She made the turn and started up a narrower road, the journey into the deeper bush starting to take shape. Still more than another hour to go, but it always felt like the home stretch when they left the highway behind not far from Enden and headed up into the steep hills of the National Park.

Rueben keyed his walkie-talkie. "Hey, Uncle Simon, you copy."

"Go ahead, Nephew One."

Leigh smiled. Her brother and Marcus might be childless, but they were great with her son. They would make great dads one day, perhaps.

She'd asked once if they planned that and Simon had been circumspect. She thought perhaps he was keen, but Marcus maybe needed convincing. She wouldn't interfere, it was their business. Regardless, she hoped.

"Who's funnier, Dad or Gramps?"

"Well, that's a tough one, champ." Simon made some noises of thought.

Leigh glanced up in the mirror as a curve in the road started to obscure the highway and saw Simon's bronze Toyota turn in and follow them up the hill. She could just make out Marcus behind the wheel, Simon holding the walkie talkie in front of his mouth.

"You know, it's like asking which is tastier, cabbage or broccoli," Simon said, his voice tinny over the small speaker. "I mean, they aren't either a good steak or a tasty donut, you know what I mean?"

Rueben laughed and Clay and Grant both made noises of outrage.

"He does have a good point," Leigh said, grinning at her husband. Grant just shook his head.

"Maybe don't distract those two back there," Clay said. "Maybe they'll take a wrong turn."

"They're right behind us and it's one road all the way now!" Leigh said. "Besides, they've both been coming up here almost as long as us."

"Yeah, but your brother is easily distracted." Clay smiled at her, waiting for the baited hook to catch.

Leigh shook her head. "Enough, Clay. Remember how we just established you're not funny? Leave him alone." One slip-up, years ago, and Clay wouldn't let it go. Rueben was right, the old man was no comedian, if for no other reason than he never updated his jokes. The ones he had were all as old and rusty as garden tools left in the rain. It was kind of endearing, in its own infuriating way, but it was still infuriating. "Besides, Marcus is driving."

"Simon left that hose running one time," Grant said, and Leigh was grateful for his support. "The water damage wasn't even that bad."

"The tank was empty though, and it took half a season to refill."

"And Simon hardly showered for a month in contrition!" Leigh said.

"I remember the smell," Grant said. "You all remember? Oh man, we made sure he did all the outside work that season."

Clay grinned and sat back into the seat. Leigh shook her head, but couldn't suppress a smile. Smug bastard, he loved to stir for no reason other than the sport of it. But he never bullied, she reflected. She was grateful for that. It was an important distinction. Rueben had been dealing with bullies and it was a contributing factor to him being home-schooled, though the main reason would always be their divided life. Spending most of the year at the hotel, remote from anything, made accessing an education difficult. Rueben seemed to be dealing with it well, but Leigh struggled with the guilt of his isolation. It was on them, her and Grant, that Rueben's life was so far removed from that of most kids. He spent almost his whole life in the company of this same small band of adults, and the constantly revolving sets of guests. Still, a lot of them brought kids along and Rueben assured them he loved the life. She needed to talk to Grant about it again. Rueben needed to spend more time among his peers, especially now. He wasn't a kid any more, things changed. She and Grant had argued about it again and again, but her husband refused to be swayed. Roo should be at high school, surrounded by teens like himself. But then there was the bullying. She shook her head, once again lost for a good answer.

The car sank into a silence, the whirr of tyres on asphalt and a gentle hum from the engine the only sounds. The four of them could never agree on what music to play, so no music was the democratic decision. Leigh appreciated the meditative result. It was good to spend time with only your thoughts, healthy for the mind. She hoped the others got the same benefit, whether they realised it or not.

The road climbed, the trees becoming greener as winter slowly gave up its grip begrudgingly to spring. Green leaf and bud would start to burst forth within the next few weeks, hikers and fishers would arrive. The Hotel did a good trade in walking and fishing tourists. Eagle Hotel was a family-friendly, holiday-oriented place. They got a lot of couples looking for romantic getaways in "the most remote hotel in New South Wales."

A bold, and largely spurious claim. Several places around the state tried to hold the title for themselves, and it was a blatant lie, probably for most of them. But Leigh was comfortable enough with the tag line. They were definitely in the top ten. Maybe.

"Hey, Nephew One, copy."

"I hear you, Uncle Si."

"Marcus said he wants to teach you to make proper Chinese spring rolls this year."

Marcus's voice came over. "My old Grandma Cheng taught me and I want to teach you. That okay?"

Rueben looked up, caught Leigh's eye in the mirror and grinned. "Sure thing!" he said into the walkie-talkie. "But why now?"

"I've been trying to get that recipe out of him for years!" Leigh said.

"Marcus said he just wants to piss off my sister," Simon said.

"Hey!" Marcus's voice was muffled and there was a scuffling sound, then his voice came over stronger. "Leigh, I know you want my recipe, but I gave you most of my stuff already. And you watch me cook at the hotel all the time. Roo, this is something special, my gift to you, okay? I wanna make sure someone has it for the next generation, and I want you to have something special from my grandma. That's how we do things."

"Give me that back." Simon's voice came back clearer. "So yeah, that *and* it'll piss off my sister. That's okay, right, champ?"

"Everyone's happy!" Rueben said with a laugh, reaching forward to squeeze his mum's shoulder. Leigh shook her head.

"And *I'm* going to teach you how to fix the engine in that old truck up there," Simon said. "You want to learn about motors?"

"Hell, yeah!"

"It's all home schooling, right, Sis?"

Rueben reached through from the back, his thumb depressed on the talk button. "Yes, I suppose it is," Leigh said into the walkie. "Now you both concentrate on driving, we don't want any accidents in the last few kilometres."

"Check, check, over and out, rubber duck, ten-four!"

Rueben pulled the walkie-talkie back. "Uncle Si, cut it out! You sound old when you do that."

"Holy crap, really? I don't want to sound like your dad!"

"Hey!" Grant barked.

"You people are all crazy," Clay said.

"Signing off," Rueben said, and pocketed the walkie-talkie. He leaned forward between the seats. "I'm hungry."

"All that talk of spring rolls. We're out of snacks, sweetie. The rest of the supplies are in the trailer with Simon and Marcus, so you'll have to wait."

"We could pull over."

Leigh laughed. "We're only half an hour away. I know you have a metabolism like a race car right now, but you'll live."

"Sure, fine. I'll just waste away back here."

He slumped back into his seat, but gave her a crooked grin in the mirror. She caught sight of Clay digging in his jacket pocket and he slipped Rueben something. Her son's eyes brightened and he shared a quick hushed conversation with his grandfather, then started into the candy bar the old man had given him. Leigh pretended not to notice, her heart warm at the closeness Clay and Rueben shared. She and Grant got on well with their son for the most part even if they did have their own differences, but Clay had a special connection with his grandson. He had since the boy was born, some spark secret to them that she and Grant would never really understand, let alone share. Part of her was jealous of it, but a larger part remained happy. For all his life among adults instead of others his own age, he had something there with Clay most kids would never know.

She realised with all the chatter that she'd driven right by the Hickman's place, and silently cursed. She'd meant to swing in and let them know the family was back, as she'd forgotten to call before they left. The Hickmans always watched the place in the off-season, as much as the weather would allow at least. Never mind, she'd call them later, or maybe in the morning. There was no rush.

Before long the sign for the hotel appeared, the 2 km marker. Grant made sure everyone had noticed before drawing a deep breath.

"Dad, come on," Rueben said.

"*Two* kilometres, why is it so far?" Grant asked proudly.

"Every damn time." Rueben looked at Clay. "You used to do this to him, right? This is called the cycle of abuse."

"Yeah, but like I said, it was funny when I did it."

Grant laughed along with them. "It really wasn't, Dad. Even I'll admit that's never funny after a drive this long."

Minutes later Leigh turned in through the carved gates of the hotel and up a long winding, well-maintained dirt driveway. As the hotel came into view, a strange sensation settled in her stomach. The excitement of coming back was there as she'd expected, but something else too. Something greasy and disquieting squirmed inside her. The tyres crunched on gravel as they drove into the grounds proper.

Leigh smiled despite the mild discomfort. The sight of Eagle Hotel always warmed her. It stood tall and proud, surrounded by bush on all sides, the centre a double-height atrium lounge room with wide verandas front and back, the steep gabled roof pointing into the slate cloudy sky. Either side, two stories stretched out like arms with perpendicular roofs, on the right the fourteen guest rooms, six below, eight above, each with their own bathroom. On the left, the large dining room and kitchen on the ground level with the Moore family private quarters above. Simon and Marcus stayed in the small single-bedroom guest cottage across the driveway from the kitchen, backed up into the gum trees there. It was a good arrangement.

The hotel was dark, but at first glance seemed to have weathered the winter well, no obvious signs of damage. A full inspection would be the first job after they'd eaten. The weathered wooden walls, dark tiled roofs, windows each with a small gable of their own, seemed warm despite the obvious lack of occupancy. That was familiarity at work, she knew. Once they'd got the heating on and the lights on and the fireplaces blazing, the place would be like a giant house-shaped hug in the wilderness. If only Leigh could shake off the sudden concern, inexplicable but present, that sat in her gut.

She drove between the hotel and the small guest cottage, crunching across gravel to park in the space behind the kitchen, in front of a huge triple garage of wooden weatherboard and shingled roof. Simon and Marcus had caught up and pulled in right behind them. They'd put the cars into the garages after unloading the trailers, and then Grant would fire up the old pick-up and head an hour and a bit back the way they'd come for more supplies in Enden once a quick assessment had been done. Then a couple of weeks of airing out and fixing damage before the handful of local staff arrived, and guests soon after that.

As the six of them emerged from the cars and stretched, breath clouding in the frosty air, smiling at each other, Leigh said, "Simon, just grab the green bag for now. We can all have a late lunch first, then get to work."

"I'll get it," Marcus said, and leaned back into the Toyota.

Leigh unlocked the back door and they went into the huge kitchen, smells of metal and polish, dust and cold, plus the indefinable familiar scent of the hotel, wrapping them up immediately.

"I'll get some sandwiches made," Leigh said. "Roo, will you wash out the pot and get some coffee on? Run the water first, check it comes clean from the tanks. Your dad can check the bore later."

"Sure, Mum. And when we've eaten I want to go and check out the tree house, okay?"

"You can help us unload the cars first."

"Awwww, Mum…"

Before she could insist, Grant put a hand on her shoulder. "The lad's been cooped up in the car for hours. He's too young for that. Let him go run and exercise. We can manage the unloading."

Rueben whooped and ran across the kitchen to the coffee pot.

"You're too soft on him," Leigh said.

Grant kissed her cheek. "Sure, *I'm* the softie."

"Go and turn the water and power on."

"Sure."

"Stop the canoodling and get with the sandwich-making!" Clay said. "I'm too old to wait this long for lunch. I might keel over dead while you two neck."

Leigh smiled, taking bread from the bag. "Calm your farm, Clay. No one's dying today."

CLAY

1

"YOU okay, old sword?"

Clay smiled. Only Molly ever called him that, had since they first met. That party a lifetime ago and he'd seen the brunette beauty in the gingham dress and said hi, asked her name.

I'm Molly Taylor. You?

Clarence Moore, but my friends call me Clay.

She'd laughed, high and fresh. *Claymore? Like the Scottish sword?*

I guess. He hadn't known what she was talking about, but looked it up later.

There she stood in the Eagle Hotel kitchen, near the door to the big dining room, hands on her hips, head tilted like always when she was about to dispense some wisdom whether you liked it or not. Clay smiled, stood up to stroll toward her.

"I'm gonna stretch my legs, look over the downstairs," he said.

Leigh didn't turn around from the counter. "I'll holler when lunch is ready."

Clay walked past Molly, heard Grant banging around in the utility room as he passed the door. He strolled through into the dining room. It was still and dark, curtains all drawn, chairs upended on tables. It smelled dusty. He began pulling open the curtains, flooding the big space with wan late-winter light, automatically checking for signs of leaks, broken glass, like he had so many times before. The winter in the mountains could be harsh.

"I'm okay," he said softly. He knew she wasn't really there, but he had the sight. He saw… things. She'd had it too, in life. It had cemented their relationship.

"You are not okay, my love. You could rarely lie to me before. You sure as hell can't now."

Clay laughed, reaching for another curtain, then winced. He put a hand to his hip. Damn his aging body, the vagaries of time. His mind remained young and vibrant, his desires and dreams lived on, but there was a hole in his life where Molly had been, and a dozen aches and pains permanently reminding him he probably wasn't far behind her. "I miss you, is all."

"And?"

He turned to her. How he wanted to hold her, feel her, smell her, again. Tears filled his lower lids. "I do miss you so."

"I know. I miss you too. But you're scared of something else."

"You gonna make me say it?"

She smiled at him, head tilted again. She had aged so well, fine features, brunette turned iron grey, still formidable. He was pleased she appeared this way, not like at the end, when breast cancer had reduced her to bones and tears.

"Dammit, woman." He grinned, but his insides were ice water, had been since they'd pulled in and he'd seen the old place again. The first time without her. "We took such a risk buying this place."

"But we made it wonderful."

"And now you're gone."

"But you're still here."

Clay shook his head. "I'm not enough."

"You've always been enough. More than enough."

"It was you, Molly. Always you. You're the strength."

She smiled. "My sweet, sharp sword. You know better."

"I'm scared it'll happen again."

"How can it? That was then, one horrible time, and we sent him away."

"But he might come back."

"He hasn't for what? Fifty years? He's gone, I promise."

Clay nodded, stared at the floor. He was gone, true. But Clay had always feared the thing that night was a symptom, not the cause. With Molly around, he felt he had a way to fight anything that might come along. With her gone, he felt vulnerable. Alone.

"It's been half a century, old sword. You just miss me, that's all. Don't try to make it about something else."

He sighed, wandered through the dining room, past the stairs leading up to the family's private quarters, the door closed at the top. He stared into the empty, cold stones of the massive dining room hearth. "It was bad."

She stood at his shoulder, so close, but an infinity away. "Yes. It was bad. But we fixed it no problem, remember? We finished it, easily enough in the end, and completely."

He walked past the hearth, through the wide double doors into the huge, high-ceilinged main lounge. The counterpart of the dining hearth stood equally cold and dark on this side. Sheets like ghosts lay over all the couches and armchairs. Photographs of the area, historical and modern, adorned the walls, fans hung inert from the dark wooden cross beams high above. Two wood columns, each some two feet square, evenly spaced in the centre of the room, added structural strength to the high, wide atrium roof. Clay stared up between them, remembering a night with terrible shadows. He shook himself. Molly was right, he'd lived here almost fifty seasons since with not a care. Maybe it was just grief.

Light poured in through tall gable windows above the small box of the reception office at the front, where the main doors led in. He pulled open the curtains below them, next to the office, revealing sliding doors that let out onto the large front veranda. They'd remove all the covers, open the doors and windows, go into the other wing and air out all the bedrooms soon enough. Maybe it would seem less daunting when it was freshened, warmed. When it had emerged from its winter stasis to be a home again. A welcoming hotel. Ready for people. He dimly registered the green exit signs lighting up as Grant put the power on.

He went to the bar along the back wall of the big room, sat on one of the stools in front of dark, polished wood. His eyes fell, as they always did, on a large black and white photo. He and Molly so young, so long ago, when they had opened that first day. A brass plaque underneath read *Clay and Molly Moore welcome you to Eagle Hotel.* Nearly fifty years ago. They were so very young, and already they'd endured so much. And beaten it. They were valiant, invincible, eternal. Now an invisible corruption of cells had taken Molly away, and time itself ate his bones.

"What do I do, Molly? If something starts again?"

"It won't."

"You're not here. And Grant's never had the sight, he can't help."

"Perhaps you should call Cindy if you're so concerned?"

Clay smiled sadly, shook his head. "Grant's sister has the sight and could help, but she still won't admit it."

"She came when I was sick. And to my funeral."

"Yes. But she won't come here, you know that. Never here again. She hated the hotel, the home-schooling. She felt the history of this place. What happened even before we came. Even though it was so long before she was born."

Molly nodded, looked at the ground. "She always said this place was bad."

"We tried to prove to her it was fine."

"I wish we could have found some common ground with her over that."

Clay nodded. "Our daughter will talk to me occasionally on the phone, but that's all."

"Even now I'm gone?"

Clay laughed softly. "I think perhaps we're *more* estranged now you're gone."

"I talk to her sometimes, but she pretends she can't hear me. Can't see me."

"I guess I'm not surprised."

Molly sat on the stool beside him, reached out one hand that could never touch him. "Maybe Rueben..."

"I hope so. It sometimes skips a generation, you said. Never two?"

"I wouldn't say never, but I only ever heard of it skipping one. It missed Grant, but not Cindy, so who knows. Rueben's around the right age."

"I've been watching. Haven't seen anything yet."

Molly nodded softly. "Me too. But soon, I'm sure. He'll need your guidance."

Clay shook his head. "Even so, the boy is thirteen. Too young for that kind of responsibility. Too young to fight."

Molly smiled. "We weren't so much older. And you won't have to fight again, no more than we ever did in the years since. Keep the love in sight, be here for each other. The hotel is okay now, has been since before Grant was born. You just miss me, is all. And I miss you too, old sword."

"It was you who kept the peace here, Moll. I don't know if I can do it. I tried so hard to convince Grant and Leigh to sell up after you..." He swallowed.

"Died. Say it, my love."

He nodded, breath stuck behind the grief in his throat. Tears trickled over his wrinkled cheeks. At last he gasped in. "After you died," he said, the words bitter. "But they wouldn't listen. They put it down to grief."

"They've been building a life here for a long time now. They plan to go on with that, like we did. And they will. They'll be okay. One day Rueben will run this place."

"I hope you're right." He looked up, saw her smile, and his heart cleaved again. "I miss you so much, my Molly."

"I love you."

"Clay! Lunch!" Leigh's voice bounced through the big rooms and Clay startled, glanced back over his shoulder.

When he turned back, Molly was gone. If she'd ever been there. Was he really talking to her ghost? Or her memory? Was there even a difference? The sight could be opaque sometimes, despite its clarity. One of the many dichotomies of life.

“Coming!” he called out, and slipped off the stool, wincing again at the deep pain in his hip and an accompanying stab in his knee. “God damn this aging carcass.”

DEANNA

JAMES'S knuckles were white on the wheel, his teeth clenched in a grimace of fury. Of determination. Paul's fast, panicked breaths in the back seat were not loud enough to cover Rick's laboured ones, his grunts of pain. Traffic noise outside the careening car, horns blaring, tyres hissing on the asphalt, screeching on the bends. Who would be the first to say something, anything, to burst the thick tension between them. Did they even want to break it? What might happen if the brittle glass of panic shattered?

Deanna looked back over her shoulder. Rick's hands were slick with blood, his clothing soaked black by it from below the waistband of his pants right up to his chest. His face shone, glittered with sweat, skin the colour of ash. The whites of his eyes showed and his breathing began to hitch.

"James, fuck!" Deanna's concerns about talking vanished like smoke in a gale at the sight of Rick.

"Shut up, let me drive."

"No, it's Rick. He's dying, James. Really fucking dying. We have to get him to a hospital."

Paul sat beside Rick, his face white from shock, eyes wide. The shaking in his hands visible even over the vibrations of the speeding car. The kid was too young for this, what was he, not even 18 yet? James should never have involved his little brother. The blood spray across his eyes, an oval in the pale moon of his face now the ski mask had been pulled off, looked like some crazy face painting. He looked from her to Rick and back again, shook his head, clearly on the verge of tears.

"No fucking hospitals, are you crazy?"

She whipped her attention back to James. "He's dying! Right there in the back of this car, James. He's covered in blood!"

James rocked back and forth as he drove, tiny movements that betrayed an edge of madness. His jaw worked as he ground his teeth, eyes unblinking. With a sudden screech, he wrenched the wheel and skidded across another junction, heading for the highway out of town.

"James!" Deanna hated the high fear in her voice.

He shook his head. "If we go to a hospital, we're busted. Rick knew the risks."

"No, he didn't! None of us did. The guns will scare the locals, you said. Easy payday. That's what we signed on for." She buried the memory of James shooting that security guard. Almost gleeful.

James barked a laugh. "Sure, that was the plan. But plans have a habit of getting fucked up. You might put years into something only to have it ripped away from you."

Deanna frowned as realization pushed through. Was he talking about this or about Imogen? About James Junior?

"If there are guns, they might get used. What are you, seven years old?" James swerved again, then pulled back into a straight run. "This is the real world, Deanna. Besides, it was that idiot security guard. He fucked us, not me. He was gonna shoot me." He barked a laugh. "You see that fucker's head? Boom! It was just *gone.* And we smoked two fucking cops. You and me, Rick. We finished those fuckers, like they deserved. Like all those pigs deserve. One eight motherfucking one!"

Deanna saw the madness glittering in James's eyes, the bloodlust. He was rushing on the memory, riding some kind of adrenaline high that didn't look like it would ever end. "This is not the bad streets of America, James! None of that is what we agreed to."

"It wasn't me!" James shot her a venomous look. "That idiot guard caused it all!"

Deanna sucked in a breath. "No one is blaming you, James. Okay? But this is bad. Really fucking bad. We have to get Rick to a hospital."

"No hospitals!"

"He'll die!"

James turned his head, his eyes wild as he pinned her with his gaze. She felt driven back into her seat. "So. Be. It."

Short, gasping sobs came from behind the driver's seat, Rick clearly conscious enough to hear every word. Paul's shallow, terrified breathing increased, he sounded like a dog after a long sprint. A foul stench permeated the air, blood and sweat and shit. Tears breached Paul's eyes and he dragged a sleeve across his face, even now scared to let his older brother see him cry. The spackling of blood smeared into a mask. He sniffed.

Deanna's mind whirled. She had to agree with James to some degree. She didn't want to get busted. They would all go down for sure. For a long time. But she'd known Rick for years, they came through high school together. Hell, they'd fucked a couple of times and it hadn't been too bad. James had known him even longer. They couldn't just let him die. He was one of them, chosen family.

"Okay," she said. "How about this? We go by the hospital, and just tip him out on the sidewalk, then drive the fuck away. Blare the horn, make people notice, but we leave. At least he has a chance."

A wet, rasping came from the back and Deanna looked around. Rick nodded, making "yeah, yeah" noises that sounded like he was underwater. She looked back to James, her eyebrows high.

James shook his head. "They see him, they know it's from the bank. That means they investigate known associates. That puts all of us in the frame."

"James–"

"No! Right now they have no idea who pulled that job. The best they have is footage of us with our faces covered and this car leaving. They don't know where we're going, this car is boosted, and there's no way to trace it to any of us. We get the fuck out of here, torch this car, and we're clear. If we go anywhere near a hospital, we're busted."

"Won't… talk…" Rick managed, the words carried on gasps of pain. "Tell… them… other… names… not… you…"

James's voice became surprisingly soft. "I know, man. I know you won't talk. I know you'll do anything to direct the heat somewhere else. But it doesn't matter. They know we hang together. They'll follow up all known associates. They'll learn we weren't home at the time of the job. One way or another, they'll track it to us. They can't know now who was involved, and we're all hours from home. That's why we came all the way down here. We get away now, clean up, torch this car and find a new one, sneak back home, and we're all clear. We'll plan a new robbery, somewhere else."

Deanna stared at him. How could he be talking so casually about future plans while Rick drowned in his own blood right behind the seat?

"James…" Rick's voice became further muffled by sobs. "I'm… dying… bro…"

James nodded. "I know, dude. I know."

Rick sank into muffled crying, his breath more shallow than ever. Paul's trembling increased as he looked from one person to the next, almost as if he were trying to find a way out of the car. Deanna shared his thinking. If there was a way out of this now, she'd take it. If James pulled up at a junction or stop sign for even a moment, she'd be out the door and rolling across the tarmac. She just wanted out, to get the fuck away from all of this. The stench, the fear, the hatred, the panic. She wanted to close her eyes and make everything go away.

She sucked in a breath and gave herself a mental slap, then twisted and pushed through between the front seats. "Pauly, help me. Take off your shirt."

"My… my shirt?"

"You have a tee on underneath, right? Give me your top shirt." She put one hand briefly against Rick's cheek, held his eyes for a moment and nodded, then moved his hands aside. The clothing underneath was sopping with blood. She tore it open as Paul struggled out of his shirt and handed it to her. She mopped at Rick's belly, wincing at the small hole in his gut only a couple of inches below the rib cage. It was a little to the left and she desperately tried to remember anatomy. The liver was on the right, the stomach on the left. All the intestines between and below. Was that right? So this bullet might have taken out his stomach, maybe just some guts. What about the spleen, where the fuck was that? And what did it even do? If his organs were mostly intact, he could survive if he didn't lose all his blood. Keep him going for a while. Maybe James had something. If they could get rid of this car, get another, go back home, then find a hospital and claim it was an accident with their own gun or something. But they were hours from any city, let alone the Sydney suburbs they called home. And right now James was heading further away instead of back.

"This is gonna hurt," she told Rick, then, gritting her teeth, used her pinkie to jam some of Paul's shirt material down into the bullet hole before he had a chance to think or ask any questions. He screamed, arched up against her. She gathered some more cotton and forced it into the hole, then wadded up the shirt on top, pressed down hard. "Rick, hold it in place." He gasped, shaking, barely conscious.

"Pauly, you do it. Press down on this, don't let it move. Be firm."

As he complied, dumbfounded, she put a hand behind Rick's neck and hauled him forward, pulled up the back of his shirt. His flesh there was starkly clean and white, unblemished. Unmarred by a bullet hole. An exit wound. She cursed. Would it be better if the bullet had gone right through? An exit wound would have been big and ugly, but the round still inside was bad for infection, wasn't it? Or perhaps it was safer in there, less injury. Infection would take a lot longer than blood loss, so maybe they had more time this way. Unless the slug had rattled around, glanced off a bone and turned half his internal organs to soup. And the blood he'd already lost? But he was a big guy, tough as hell.

He was alive right now, any injury couldn't be too catastrophic. Could it? She leaned him back, his eyelids fluttered. Probably for the best he'd passed out, it would free him from pain and panic at least for a little while. She had to convince James to drive hard and fast, get to another town and make up a story. Get Rick some kind of help, somehow.

She drew breath to state her case, but James spoke first. He'd obviously been thinking while she worked on Rick.

"We need to be rid of all this evidence," he said. "We have to find somewhere to dump this car and burn it, and find a new one. That's the first priority. And we have to get out of these clothes, burn them too, and clean up and get new clothes. Then we have to keep moving, far the fuck away from that town. There'll be an all points out for this car by now, we have to assume that. Security was low, but I bet the bank or some traffic camera got a shot of us running and this car will be hot as fuck."

Deanna deflated. No way would he consider anything else before they'd done those things. If she was honest, perhaps he was the only one really thinking clearly. If they wanted to stay out of jail, they had to get clean. Which meant Rick would almost certainly die.

"So how do we achieve all that?" she asked.

James nodded forward at a sign that said that read *Eagle Hotel, the most remote accommodation in NSW.* More details underneath about fishing, weddings, romantic getaways.

"Hardly remote up here compared to the outback," Deanna said.

"That's just marketing. See the bit underneath? Says it's not open until next month. There'll be no one there. We can break in and find some supplies, and I bet they keep an old truck or something in a garage I can hotwire. Maybe some overalls or something somewhere. I'm sure we can find clothes there, even if we end up looking homeless for a while. We dump all this, set a good old cleansing blaze going, clean ourselves up, and get away again. It'll be weeks before anyone even knows we've been there. Perfect."

RUEBEN

MAYBE it had been long enough. He'd eaten, then washed the dishes, without being asked. The adults were starting to get things organized for the unloading and unpacking, and the big annual check for leaks and frost damage would soon start.

"Mum–"

"Yes, go on! But wear your jacket and be back before dark."

"Yes!" Rueben headed for the door.

"Roo, you hear me?"

He turned back, his momentum interrupted. "What?"

His mum pointed to the jacket hanging on the back of a chair.

"It's not cold out."

"It *is* cold, and it'll get quickly colder as the afternoon moves on, you know that. And it gets dark early still. So wear your jacket and be back before it *starts* to get dark, okay?"

"Muuu-uum..."

Dad turned with a smile, some small inexplicable bit of machinery in hand. "Mind your mother, son. It is still cold, the nights are below freezing probably. We've only just got here, there are months ahead of us. Take your jacket and don't be more than an hour or two, okay?"

Uncle Simon stepped over, put one hand on Rueben's shoulder. He needed to lean down to whisper, but not much. Rueben would be as tall as Uncle Si before long. Then maybe even taller. "You wanna know a secret, champ?"

"What?"

"If you do everything they say now, early on, they'll relax. Set a good foundation, then you can get away with more later. If you act up now, they'll watch you closely for weeks."

Rueben looked up, saw the sincerity in Uncle Si's brown eyes, shadowed under a mop of sandy curls. He saw humour there too. "I guess you're right."

"Of course I am." Simon smiled. "When am I ever anything else?"

"What are you two whispering about," his mum called out, eyes narrowed.

"Nothing!" Rueben grinned at Uncle Simon, saw Uncle Marcus flick him a sly wink from under his too long jet black fringe. They were good uncles. He grabbed the jacket and slipped it on. "See you before dark!" he said, then bolted before anyone could come up with anything else.

The air was colder than he had expected, though he only grudgingly admitted that to himself. The temperature had dropped while they ate and the afternoon drew on. Uncle Si was right, there were months ahead. And home-schooling was a breeze, just a few hours a day to keep up with the curriculum, then all the rest of the time to play and explore. Going to school, all those wasted hours, was a mug's game.

"Hey, Roo."

He paused, looked back. His dad came across the gravel drive. "I've got my jacket!"

"I know, son. Just..." His dad smiled crookedly.

Rueben braced. His father was a stoic man, rarely given to outpourings of emotion. *So uptight, if you put coal in his arse, he'd shit out a diamond*, Grandpa Clay had said once. Rueben had mentioned that to his mum and she'd laughed. Told him it was mean, but not entirely untrue. So it was always apparent when his dad was warming up to be sentimental. "What's up, Dad?"

"I just wanted to say that I know this is hard for you sometimes. Traipsing up here with us."

"Mum been bugging you again? *She* thinks I should got to high school. I like coming here."

Dad smiled. "I'm glad. And I'm glad your uncles have plans for you this season. But I want *us* to do some stuff too, yeah? You're growing up so fast, I'm so proud of the young man you've become."

"I'm sure I can disappoint you yet."

His father winced. "Don't make light of it, mate. I'm serious. I love you so much. And I've got things I want to teach you too. We'll make time this season, okay?"

"Sure."

"I'm telling you as much to keep myself honest, Roo. I know I get busy and distracted. Not this year."

Rueben smiled. This was more honest than his father had been in living memory. Maybe Mum's influence was rubbing off. Truth was, Rueben had enormous respect for his father despite frequent frustrations. "I love you too, Dad." He gathered the man in a hug, enjoyed the aroma of aftershave and soap that was so quintessentially *Dad.*

As they broke the hug, father and son held each other's eye for a moment. Then his father nodded once and winked. "Don't be out too late."

Rueben rolled his eyes. "See you in a bit."

He turned and jogged over gravel past the garages and then hung a right, straight as the crow flies across the wide back lawn. As he approached the tree line, he spotted patches of unthawed frost in the shadows turning icy, glittering in the lowering sun. It gave him a shudder of anticipation, but he looked forward to spring, when everything would come back with new life, new vigour. The days would grow warmer and longer, the bush alive with the buzz of insects and the rustle of chatter of wildlife. Nowhere better in the world as far as he was concerned.

The deeper shadows between trees sucked the temperature down again and he was glad of the jacket. "Shut up, Mum," he muttered with a grin, and jogged on.

He picked his way through the edge of the woods, eyes wary for wildlife or half-covered roots that might grab an ankle. He drew a deep breath in, exalting in the chill, the damp, the earthy loam aromas and hints of fungus. Some patches of fallen leaves were still frosty, crackling under foot. He knew his way so well, paid little attention as he ducked along the narrow path that would be all but invisible to a stranger's eye. In truth, it wasn't really a path, just a route he always took, a little more worn if you knew to look for it. Probably a wombat track originally. But a winter of leaf drop and snow and rain and wind had mostly obscured it again. By the time he left in about nine months, it would be trodden clear once more.

A hundred yards into the woods, the trees thickened again as he moved from the edges into the bush proper. He paused, listened to birdsong, the rustle of branches in the soft, cold breeze overhead. With a nod of satisfaction, he walked on, ducked behind a stand of trees that had grown a little since he'd last been here, and there it was. His castle. *His* place, built by his own hand. Well, and Grandpa Clay's. And, if he was honest, Grandpa probably did most of the work, but Rueben had been involved and was instrumental in the construction. He'd borne the cuts and grazes to prove it.

The treehouse was impressive, even if he thought so himself. It hung in a big old snow gum about ten feet off the forest floor, surrounded by a variety of other trees. He'd tried to learn all the local flora, but had trouble getting the names to stick in his mind. He remembered a couple of others as he stared at the treehouse. Flowering gum, silky oak, tree waratah.

The base of the treehouse was dark wood, more or less square, about three metres to a side. The walls of overlapping pine had a window on each side, Perspex grimed with dirt and lichen now, and a door in the front behind a narrow veranda, reached by a rope ladder. At least, it was usually reached by rope ladder. Every year before the family left for the winter, Rueben rolled the ladder up and stored it inside, to protect the rope from the weather. Then he hung from the edge of the veranda between the gnarled balustrades of lashed-together branches, and dropped to the forest floor. When he'd been smaller, the plummet had been terrifying, and he'd taken Grandpa or his dad along to catch him. The last couple of years he'd done it alone.

He turned his back to the treehouse and jumped to grab the low hanging branch of the gum tree above his head. A grunt of strain and he was up, one leg hooked over the limb. His mum would complain about stains on his pants, but that was nothing new. He clambered up, crab-walked along the limb he stood on until he was within about two metres of the tree house veranda, behind him and just a little below. He turned to face it, got a good grip on the thin branch above his head and swung out, tucked his knees and swung again. Once more and he let go, arcing gracefully across the small gap to land as lightly as he could on the veranda, sinking his knees into an almost full crouch to absorb as much impact as possible.

He pulled open the door and ducked inside. It was musty, damp, but fine. The roof of overlapping shingles had survived another winter, no signs of leakage anywhere. His small table and chairs had a layer of dust and the old single bed mattress in the corner was a little damp to the touch, but nothing a day or two of airing out wouldn't fix. Another few weeks and it would start to heat up, the days long and dry. He looked forward to those shorts and t-shirt times of running wild in the bush for hours. Not the snakes and spiders and bugs though. Every season had its pros and cons.

He took the rope ladder out onto the veranda, hooked the two metal rings at the top to sturdy brackets mounted on the edge of the wood and let the ladder drop with a clatter. It unfurled and hung about a foot above the bark and leaf littered ground.

Back inside, he sat in the worn leather armchair he kept in one corner, beside a window. This was his favourite spot in the tree house, maybe in the whole world, where he'd sat for hours consuming books and comics, eating snacks and drinking cola. He would bring his supply down the next day, once the hint of damp had been removed by the moving air. And this year he would spend a few nights out here. This year for sure. He had tried to spend the night in the tree house several times before, but it always freaked him out. As the light failed and the forest fell into darkness, the flickering candles creating writhing shadows on the walls, he would baulk and run. Sprint through the gloom to break into the relative light of dusk in the gardens. His parents and grandparents, Uncle Simon and Uncle Marcus, would all smile and chide him good-naturedly for being chicken, but they were supportive too. They encouraged him, never genuinely mocked him for running home.

"I'll be damned if I'd ever spend the night out there," Uncle Marcus had said once. "The bush out that way is creepy."

"Marcus!" Mum had said, her face stern. "It's a forest, safe as houses, especially ten feet off the ground. Nothing creepy about it."

Well, maybe Uncle Marcus just didn't get the urge. He was a real homebody. He and Uncle Si had taken Rueben camping one summer, higher up the mountain. They'd set up a tent near a sparkling clear stream, Uncle Si had taught Rueben how to fish and Uncle Marcus had cooked their catch over an open fire. It was a glorious time, one of Rueben's most treasured memories, and to this day he and Uncle Si would laugh at the recollection of Uncle Marcus's constant complaining. But with Uncle Si, anywhere they went, he was safe and happy.

Meanwhile, spending the night alone in the tree house was a challenge. A milestone. One day Rueben would do it, and he would be so proud of himself. This year, for sure.

Movement on veranda made him gasp. A shadow shifted out there and he breathed deeply, calmed himself. It wasn't really her. Grandma Molly stood silhouetted in the treehouse doorway. She stepped in, her face soft, smiling. Her mouth moved, but the apparition was silent. She spoke, but he heard nothing. He didn't want to hear anything, she wasn't real. Grandma was dead, six months gone now and he missed her like crazy, but *he* wasn't crazy. Ghosts weren't real. Hallucinations triggered by grief, stuff like that, was common.

He stared at her, refusing to be scared, but also refusing to accept her presence. It was all in his head. Despite himself he smiled, and she smiled back, stopped talking. She nodded once and turned, walked out onto the veranda. The shadows of the branches outside swallowed her up and she was gone.

"Not real, and not crazy," Rueben said aloud. His mantra. "Not real, and not crazy." He got up and found the dustpan and brush he kept in a small cupboard in the corner, along with candles, matches, a few other bits and pieces, and set about dusting and tidying his place.

LEIGH

LEIGH stood in the big kitchen and watched her family bustle about. Clay went through to the dining room again, Simon and Marcus headed for the cars to start unloading the trailers. Grant came back from checking the rainwater tanks. Her family worked well together. The thought of Rueben out in the bush gave a her a kind of cautious warmth too. The caution born of any mother's need to see her child at all times, hold them close constantly; the warmth from the pleasure of seeing him grow, imagining him out there living his life, having experiences. He didn't need to take over here when she and Grant retired, like they had from Clay and Molly. The world was an open book for Rueben to write his own chapters in however he pleased.

"Dad's checking the ground floor bedrooms for leaks," Grant said, stepping up behind her and slipping his arms around her waist. "You want to help with the unloading?"

"Yeah, let's just get everything in here first."

"I might put off going to town until tomorrow. I could get there in time to shop, but no way I'd get back before dark. We've all been a bit slow today. I don't really want to drive at night."

Leigh nodded. "Good idea. We've got enough stuff with us to last a week or so if we need to. Tomorrow is plenty soon enough."

"Did you call Laura Hickman?"

"I forgot before we left. Then I forgot to stop in on the way here. She would have called us if anything cropped up."

Grant stepped around Leigh and headed for the back door. "Would she? Laura and Bob say they keep an eye on the place while we're away, but when they never call, how are we to know?"

Leigh laughed. "They do us a favour, we can't expect much. Anyway, I talked to Laura about two weeks ago. She said the road was impassable for a day or two at the height of winter when a couple of trees came down, but when they were cleared she came up to check and saw nothing untoward. So I guess not much can have happened since. I just forgot to let her know we were coming today. We're a bit earlier than usual, after all."

"It's weird without Mum here."

Leigh went to him, squeezed his hands, immediately glad he'd brought it up. "It is. Molly would be cooking already, with Marcus probably. You okay?"

"I guess so."

"Really? We didn't need to come up an extra two weeks before opening, you know. I mean, what are we going to do up here on our own for a month?"

He put his arms around her, held her close. "I guess I just feel closer to Mum here."

"I get that."

"But it's also really hard to be here now she's gone. I've never been here without her before."

His face crinkled and Leigh pulled him back into a tighter hug. "Me either. It feels somehow empty, huh? She'll always be a hole in our lives, but we'll learn to live with it."

"I read somewhere that grief never gets smaller. Your life just grows bigger around it and it becomes less all-encompassing."

"That's a really fine way to think of it, Grant. I mean, I don't want the grief to go away, do you?"

"No. Grief is love unexpressed, right?"

"So let's make sure we continue to build a life Molly would have been proud of, yeah? You think she's out there somewhere, looking down on us?"

Grant smiled crookedly. "I don't know. Her and Dad have some weird ideas about that stuff. But if she is, I reckon she'd be proud."

"Of course she would. I miss her too, love. So much. But we'll enjoy the peace and quiet before the bookings kick in. The ledger is filling fast already."

"Just as well, we need the cash. You want to invite Laura and Bob over for a drink?"

"Sure, but not tonight. Everyone's tired. I'll call tomorrow morning, let them know we're here, and invite them then. Let's keep it simple for now, it's been a long day already."

"Fair enough. Come on, then."

He turned and headed for the door. For a moment, Leigh watched him go. He frustrated the hell out of her sometimes, but she loved him. He was a closed man so often, but he loved his family and was entirely reliable. That wasn't something to be underestimated. She walked fast to catch up.

As they went out, Marcus passed them coming back in. He turned sideways through the door, straining under the weight of a large box. Leigh recognized it, knew it contained a lot of canned food. When she had mentioned enough stuff to last them a week, she'd meant fresh produce. If they counted the tinned and bottled supplies they could probably last a month if they rationed themselves.

Why was she thinking about surviving an extended period without food? Perhaps the thought of Rueben growing up had her considering change. She wished her family could stay the same as it was forever, there was something fabulous about them all at this stage. Well, she realised, maybe a year ago, when Molly was still alive and well. Hard to believe she'd been robust and hearty twelve months before, but now she was six months in the ground. That had to contribute to her feelings of flux, her desire to freeze her family in time. She shook herself. Melancholy didn't suit her, she didn't like it.

"Si went to open up the cottage," Marcus grunted as he went by. "Said he'd be back in a few minutes."

"Good idea," Grant called back. "Get the place warmed up."

"We should get the fires lit in the main rooms of the hotel," Leigh said.

"Clay's already on it," Grant called from the trailer. "Said he'd get it all up and running while he checked through the downstairs. Said he might as well make himself useful now he's too damn old to lug crates."

"He is not!" Leigh said, aghast. "That old man is still strong as an ox."

"Of course he is." Grant slid out a stack of crates and lifted the top one.

Marcus returned. "I think he's feeling fragile since Molly died."

Leigh raised an eyebrow. "Fragile?"

"Sure. He's grieving, of course, but I think he's had a slap in the face from the hand of mortality. He's older than Molly was by a couple of years."

Leigh nodded, recognizing the truth of that. Marcus was an emotionally aware guy, he often spotted the heart of a person's mood. "We'll have to all make sure we build him up." She looked hard at Grant. "No more old man jokes for a while, okay?"

Grant thought a moment, then nodded. "Yeah. Yeah, okay." His face softened and she knew he was considering mortality too. Having so recently lost his mother, thoughts of his dad going next were only natural.

There was a pause and Leigh felt something unspoken pass between the three of them. Grant glanced back at the house, vaguely in the direction of Clay. Marcus nodded once to Grant, gave him a soft smile, recognising his discomfort, no doubt thinking the same things she was. Her brother's husband would make a good counsellor.

"Just because he's feeling old doesn't mean anything right now," Leigh said, sensing the need to avoid her own melancholy soaking into the others. "He's fit and strong." She meant it too, he really was.

"Yeah, and he'll be around a long time yet," Marcus said.

Grant laughed. "He's too damned stubborn to die. He'll probably outlive all of us."

The laughter spread and Leigh's concern for her family lessened and pulled tighter at the same time. They were good together, but if only it really could last forever. One thing was certain, change was inevitable. "Come on," she said. "Let's get to work."

"Is that an engine?" Marcus said, turning to look past the house. He took one step toward the driveway curving around the large bulk of the kitchen, then paused. The engine revved loudly, gravel crunching under tires.

Grant put down the crate he'd been holding. "Maybe Laura or Bob Hickman saw us come by?"

"Or they're popping up to check anyway, seeing as I forgot to call and let them know we were in today." Leigh bit her lower lip. It didn't sound like Bob's ute. Something tickled the back of her neck, like the touch of ghostly fingers and she shivered, suddenly cold.

A dark blue Ford Fairlane sedan came quickly around the hotel and skidded to a stop. In the front were two people, wide-eyed with shock, a man and a woman. Leigh saw the silhouettes of two more in the back seat. Everything about the group made the hairs on her arms prickle, a weight settling hard in her gut. In no way she could clearly articulate, she knew these people were going to be trouble.

PAUL

JAMES'S shoulders bunched up and Paul instantly recognized his big brother's rage posture. In the past, when James hunched like that, Paul expected an arse-kicking. This time it was likely to be the poor fools staring at them on the receiving end of James's violence.

"Why the fuck are people here?" James growled.

"Keep going!" Deanna said. "Just drive through, we'll go somewhere else."

Paul's guts were watery with fear, with regret, with the certainty this was all going to get worse and worse. The sharp headache between his eyes redoubled, an ice dagger in his brain.

"No way." James reached beside his seat and pulled the shotgun up.

"What are you doing?" Paul barked.

"They've seen us," James said. "They've seen the car. No doubt they've seen the news, or they will, and they'll report us and the fucking cops will know which way we went."

"James, no." Deanna reached out a hand to stop him, but James flung the door open and stood, leveling the shotgun over it.

"Nobody fucking move!"

Paul realised he was panting like a dog, sucking short, shallow breaths that made him giddy. He forced himself to suck in one long deep breath, determined to calm himself, to not freak out. Then he looked over at Rick. The man's face was pale grey, and covered with a sheen of sweat. He was unconscious.

Swallowing, Paul leaned toward him, wondering if he'd died, then saw Rick's chest rise and fall quickly. A couple of seconds later he did it again. Not a good sign, but he was alive at least. For how long was anyone's guess.

"Deanna, Rick's passed out again."

She glanced back over her shoulder. "Fuck me." Grabbing her shotgun, she matched James's posture on her side, aiming over the open door.

"Just calm down," one of the men in the driveway was saying. "Let's all just be cool. What's happening here? You want something? Money?"

"Shut the fuck up!" James walked around his door, sweeping the shotgun slowly side to side to cover them all.

Paul watched through the windscreen, shivering in the cold that blew in through the open front doors. A tall, dark-haired guy in the middle had spoken and now he clammed up, his mouth a flat line. To one side of him stood a woman with a short blonde bob, similar in age. Maybe they were a couple. On his other side was a guy with black hair cut short except for a long fringe swept to one side. Chinese maybe, or Korean. How did you tell? Paul actually had no idea and it didn't matter and he wondered why these random thoughts were rattling past his brain now.

"Who else is here?" James demanded.

The tall guy in the middle raised both hands, palms out. "Now let's just–"

James fired the shotgun straight up into the air, the blast shocking as it shattered the quiet with obscene volume. "Do not fucking tell me to calm down. Do not act like you have any control here. Just answer my fucking questions or I'll kill you."

Paul watched his brother's shoulders tighten and a tear squeezed from one eye. Someone was going to die, he knew it. James had gone into a blind rage, the same as he always did when he didn't know what to do. When a situation was out of control. Never one to think rationally, James always turned to violence to solve problems. He'd done it in the bank and was warming up to it again now. Paul thought again of Imogen, the anger when she left, the coldness that settled into James then. Had he been heading towards this rampage of violence since then?

An old man appeared at the kitchen door, his face shocked. Deanna twisted in place, she must be aiming her gun across the car's roof at the old-timer.

"Dad, don't move!" the tall one said.

"Who else?" James demanded as the old man stood framed by the white-painted doorway, hands raised to shoulder level.

"Just us. Four of us, that's all." The man tried a smile, but it was twisted, a grimace. "I'm Grant, this is Leigh, Marcus, and Clay." He pointed out each in turn. "Now let's–"

"You think telling me your names will help? You think it'll make me care about you?"

Paul tried to lick dry lips, but his tongue was sandpaper. "James..." he croaked. There was no way his brother would hear. Tears streaked his cheeks and he dragged them away with a sleeve, knowing James would whip him for crying like a baby if he saw.

The guy on the left, Marcus, looked up and his eyes widened, then he quickly looked back to James. But Paul had seen it. So he had no doubt James had too. Paul twisted around in the seat and cried out, "No!" at the sight of another man, sandy blond hair and wild eyes, sneaking up behind the car, a pistol stretched out in one hand.

Paul flinched as James's shotgun boomed and the blond man's chest exploded in red. He sailed backwards and skidded across the gravel, twisted onto one side. The screaming started. Paul covered his face with his hands, sobbing. James was yelling, Deanna screaming at everyone to *lay down, lay the fuck down and don't move.* The others, the poor fuckers in the driveway all howling and crying out.

"Get out here, Pauly!" James called. "Right fucking now!"

Paul grit his teeth. He threw open his door and staggered out. The shot man's blood had spread impossibly wide already, a lake of it around his still body, his eyes staring at the cottage beside the hotel that he must have come from. His chest was wide open, purple and grey organs inside that should never see the light of day. Idiot! Paul tore his gaze away and came around the car. The other four were all lying face down on the driveway. Marcus's face twisted in agony as he stared at the fallen man, one hand reaching out, fingers clutching at the air. The woman, Leigh, sobbed face down on her folded arms, while Grant stared white-faced at their attacker. The old man, Clay, lay beside Grant watching the ground, his face hard, impassive.

"Where's your fucking gun?" James said.

"I don't have one! I'm too young, remember?" He'd been the only one without a shotgun. His job to carry the money bags, James had said.

"You should have Rick's, you dumbass! This has gone way beyond our plans, use your fucking brain!"

Paul jumped in place, shocked at his brother's vehemence, then ran back and leaned into the car. Rick's shotgun, slick with the man's blood, lay on the seat beside his unconscious body. Paul grabbed it and ran back.

"Now you stay here and cover these four. Anyone moves, you kill 'em, got it?"

Paul nodded, swallowing, unable to speak.

"I am not playing, little brother. Do you get it?"

"Yeah." The word came out restricted, like it had to cut his throat to get into the day.

"James," Deanna said. When he looked at her, she said, "This is a real mess."

"No shit."

"What are we gonna do?"

"We're gonna take some time to think, that's what." He turned to look at the people lying in front of him. "What the fuck are you people doing here?"

"This our hotel," Grant said, his voice wavering. "We're opening up, getting ready for the season."

"The sign said you don't open for weeks yet."

"We have to get the place prepared, make repairs, do laundry, there's–"

"All right, shut the fuck up, I don't need a lecture." James looked up and around himself, face twisted in thought.

Paul tried to still the shaking in his hands as he pointed his shotgun in the general direction of the people. The hostages. That's what they were now.

What the hell were they going to do with hostages? Could he really shoot them if he had to? He wasn't sure, but he knew he couldn't defy James. He hoped that conundrum never demanded an answer.

His brother's face creased with anger and indecision, his teeth bared in an animal snarl. James was a man fuelled by passion, by violence, but he wasn't stupid. In fact, if their grandpa were to be believed, James was so much trouble *because* he was smart. Because he was never challenged enough by life, growing up poor without the opportunities wealth might have offered him.

But Paul thought maybe that was bullshit, their grandpa trying to rationalize something much simpler. Perhaps the real truth was James happened to be a nasty piece of shit. Not stupid, but nothing special. Just an arsehole. And Paul was an arsehole for following his brother again and again, always leading to something like this. But no, not like this. Never this bad before. The bank guard dead, two cops dead, now that guy lying on the gravel, dead. Paul was pretty sure James had killed before, that one story about Craig Benson he liked to tell at least was true, Paul thought. But things had never been this bad before. This was pretty much as bad as it could get, wasn't it?

Paul realised there was no way he was shooting anyone. Bad enough the situation they were in, but that was a line he refused to cross. He shook his head, hoping he would be able to keep that promise.

"Deanna, go and cut the phone line. We need to be isolated here." She nodded and trotted away. "The rest of you, give me your mobiles."

Grant looked up at him. "There's no service up–"

"Did I fucking ask?" James yelled and the man flinched. "Give me the phones."

They scrabbled in their pockets with shaking hands and put three mobile phones on the ground in front of themselves. Clay remained still.

"Old man?" James said.

"Don't have one. Never have." His face was still hard, defiant. Paul worried for him. That expression would get him killed. The old man lifted his arms out to either side. "I'm not lying, feel free to search me."

"Paul, do it."

Paul startled and hurried over. He crouched and put his shotgun on the ground to start going through Clay's pockets. He saw the old man's eyes stray to the gun, only inches away. "No," he whispered. "He'll kill all of you."

Clay glanced up, caught Paul's eye and stared hard for a moment. Then he nodded once, and it seemed to Paul the man had just agreed to something other than not making a grab for the gun. Like he and Paul had reached some decision Paul himself hadn't caught. Then the old man was looking past Paul, into nowhere, and he nodded subtly again. It was creepy. Marcus and Leigh still sobbed, their anguish cutting through the cold air. Grant remained passive, ashen-faced.

"He's not lying," Paul said, grabbing his gun and standing. "Only a wallet."

"All right, everyone inside."

"What do you think you're going to achieve here?" Clay asked.

"Don't," Paul said quietly, but James had already rounded on the old man.

"You ask no questions. You don't say a fucking word unless you're spoken to. Do you understand?"

The old man stared back at James, his expression hard. Paul's trembling redoubled.

"Do you fucking understand?" James yelled, spit flying from his lips.

"Yeah. I understand."

Clay was cool as hell, frighteningly so. Perhaps the old man had nothing to fear, he was so close to death anyway, but he needed to think about the others. They might survive this yet if Clay didn't fuck it up for them. "Get up!" Paul said, before James and Clay could say any more to each other. "All of you, up!"

They stood and Marcus ran to the fallen man, crying out, "Simon!" as he fell to his knees beside the corpse, cradling the man's head to his chest.

"Marcus, no," Leigh said, her eyes red from tears.

James strode over and hauled Marcus up by his collar and shoved him hard in the back. Marcus staggered away, fell to his knees and quickly scrambled back up. He spun to face James. "You fucking murdered him!"

James's face was strangely calm as he lifted the shotgun and pressed the barrel hard into Marcus's face, twisting the man's nose to one side. Marcus gritted his teeth, but braced his neck, let the weapon stretch his skin.

"Marcus, no!" Leigh shouted again. "Don't!" She looked at James. "Please! It's grief. It's… it's…"

James didn't move the gun, but turned to Leigh. "What is it?"

She looked at the ground, shoulders shaking. "Please don't hurt him. Nobody else."

James turned his attention slowly back to Marcus and lowered the gun. "Get inside."

Marcus walked unsteadily to join the others. James and Paul walked behind, guiding them with prods from the shotguns. They entered a huge kitchen, the smell of fresh coffee overlaying all other aromas. An internal door led into a big dining room, the chairs upended on tables. A fire crackled in a stone hearth in the far wall, just getting under way. Another door led them into a huge, high-ceilinged lounge with photographs on the walls, a bar along the back and couches and armchairs scattered around. Another fireplace burned merrily.

"This'll do it," James said. "We'll keep 'em here. Paul, go find some rope. Check the garages. Once we have these fuckers secure, we'll get Rick in here and find a first aid kit."

Paul nodded, trying to establish some equilibrium. This was not a good situation in any way, but James seemed to have found some calmness. Maybe he felt in control again. Maybe killing someone else had eased his rage. But for how long? "What about the one out there?"

James pursed his lips for a moment. "Drag him into the garage and put him under a tarp or something. Out of sight for now will do. It's cold enough out there." Then he turned back to the others. "Now, you lied to me before, so I'm going to ask one more time. Is there anyone else here?"

"No," Clay said.

Grant and Leigh shook their heads, Marcus sat heavily on the floor, his feet together, knees out to either side, head hanging as he cried.

“Is there anyone else here?” James asked again.

“Just us,” Grant said.

James stepped up and jammed the shotgun against the side of Leigh’s head. She gasped, but sat rigid. “Is there anyone else here?”

“We come up early to open and prepare for the season,” Grant said. “Me and my wife, my father, Leigh’s brother and his husband. You shot Simon, that’s Leigh’s brother, and the rest of us are right here. That’s it. That’s all.”

James stared at them intensely. Clay returned his gaze with obvious malice, Grant and Leigh both looked up, held James’s eye. Marcus continued to cry, oblivious. After a moment, James nodded once and said, “For your sake, you’d better be telling me the truth. Paul, get the fucking rope.”

RUEBEN

RUEBEN crouched behind a tarpaulin-covered pile of firewood beside the large triple garage, shaking. He couldn't stop staring at Uncle Simon, twisted uncannily on the gravel in a dark pool of blood, the hole in his chest glistening. Edges of white bone were visible, shining organs reflecting low afternoon light. Who would teach him about engines now?

Simon was foolish for trying to sneak up like that. Rueben couldn't understand why he hadn't fired from further away. But he'd just kept creeping closer and closer until it was too late. Maybe he didn't trust his aim. Rueben had no idea if Uncle Simon was a good shot or not. He didn't know his uncle even had a gun. *Why* did he have a gun? It didn't matter now. He was dead, and everyone else was trapped inside.

His dad had said no one else was there, just them. Rueben knew he'd said that to protect him, but Rueben had never felt so alone in his life. What should he do? All the time those psychos with the guns didn't know about him, he had a chance to do something, but what? Who were they? Why were they here? Perhaps that didn't matter. They *were* here. Uncle Simon was dead. Oh shit, oh shit, Uncle Simon was *dead*! How could that be real?

The rest of his family were in terrible danger. What could he do? One thing ran through his mind more than anything else. More than watching Uncle Simon get killed, more than seeing Uncle Marcus in such anguish, more than watching his family get marched away at gunpoint: Whatever happened now, it was down to him. That thought, over and over. It was all down to him. He had to save them. He wasn't ready for that.

And then something else came back to him, momentarily lost in the shock of the moment. He'd seen Grandpa Clay look up, past the guy who had searched him, and nod. When Rueben followed his grandfather's gaze he saw Grandma Molly standing there, silently saying something to Clay. And Clay had nodded, like he saw her too. "Not real, and not crazy," Rueben whispered to himself.

But Grandpa had surely seen her. There could be no other explanation for what he'd witnessed there. Tears rolled over Rueben's cheeks, his gut an empty space with nothing but a gale of grief howling through it. What should he do?

The kitchen door opened and the young gunman came out. Paul, the older one had called him. Paul and James, Rueben said to himself as he hunkered down again. Remember that. It might be useful, or important.

Deanna, go and cut the phone line.

That's right, James had called the woman Deanna. So James, Paul, and Deanna. Remember, Rueben told himself. Remember their names.

Paul crunched across the driveway, his face crumpled with confusion, shotgun swinging slack beside his leg. He didn't look all that much older than Rueben himself, maybe not yet even eighteen. He looked like he was trying hard not to cry. What the hell did he have to cry about?

Paul glanced down at Uncle Simon, so still and crooked and wrong, an unbelievable amount of blood pooled around him. Then Paul stepped up to the Blue Fairlane and looked inside. Squinting, Rueben jumped to see there was someone else still in their car, a shadow slumped in the back seat. Paul said something to himself and then turned quickly, striding towards the garages.

Rueben's heart hammered and he scrunched down, desperate not to make a sound as Paul came nearer. He stifled sobs, sure his racing pulse must be audible clear across to the cottage. There was a scrape and bang as Paul pulled one of the garage doors open. They were never locked, unlikely anyone would come this far into the middle of nowhere for old tools. Moments later

Rueben heard the gravel crunching again. He risked leaning out a little, past the back corner of the building, and saw Paul heading towards the hotel with a couple of heavy coils of nylon rope.

They were tying up Rueben's family, that had to be it. He swallowed. If they were tying them up, at least that meant they weren't just going to kill them. At least not yet. He had time to do something.

Again the same thought raced through his mind, looping around and around. *What should I do? What should I do?*

More footsteps and the woman, Deanna, came around the corner, intercepting Paul by the kitchen door.

"What are you doing?"

"James told me to get rope."

"Then what?"

"Tie 'em up."

"Obviously. But I mean, then what? What are we going to do?"

Paul's face folded up again and he shook his head. "Deanna, this is bad. It's more than bad." He gestured back to their car. "Rick is... well, he's breathing but only just."

Rick, Rueben said to himself. He repeated it over and over, making sure he remembered. James and Paul and Deanna and Rick. Remember their names.

Deanna frowned. "I've killed the lines. They had satellite, so I disabled that too. We're isolated for now, and there's no service from mobile phones that I can tell. But whether or not Rick makes it, you and I have to be smart, Pauly."

Paul looked from the Deanna to the house, back to their car. "We have to not make James mad, that's all for right now. Take this to him. I have to move that one."

Deanna looked over at Uncle Simon and nodded. She took the rope and went inside.

Paul turned and stood staring at the body in the driveway. He winced and crouched, took one of Uncle Simon's limp arms in a double grip around the wrist and dragged. Rueben's uncle slid across the gravel, rippling a little over the rough ground. Blood smeared behind him and something wet and shiny fell with a slap. A coil of pink and grey intestine followed it out onto the stones. Rueben clapped hands over his mouth, tears streaming.

"Jesus fuck," Paul muttered. He stopped pulling, stared in disgust. Then he used the toe of one boot to try to nudge the viscera back in. It slipped and slid, going anywhere but where he wanted it. Suddenly Paul staggered back and yelled, "FUCK!" at the sky.

He stomped into the garage and crashed around for a moment, then came back out with an old blue tarpaulin. He tucked it under one side of Uncle Simon and then rolled. The body quickly disappeared into the tight turns of crinkling blue. Paul grabbed the leading edge once the roll was finished and hauled the body into the garage. After a moment more of banging and scraping inside, he came back out and pushed the garage door closed. He stopped at the tap by the kitchen door to wash Uncle Simon's blood off his boot, then went in.

Rueben shook with grief and shock and rage. He had to gather himself, gather his thoughts, and make sure he had a plan. But trembling out here by the garages wasn't the way to do it. The light was falling fast, already twilight. Whatever he might do, it was unlikely to be before the next day. The mountains were dark as pitch at night, no electric lights for miles other than those inside the hotel and the cottage. The temperature fell with the light, already a biting chill nipping through his jacket. So it looked like he would be spending a night in his treehouse this season after all, and right away. But he needed more than the clothes on his back. He had a couple of old blankets and a tatty quilt on the mattress in the treehouse. He might be warm enough. But he remembered lessons from his dad about survival in the wilderness. And lessons from Uncle Simon too. He knew the value of a foil survival blanket in keeping warm when temperatures fell. And he knew there was one in the first aid kit under the driver's seat of their car. What else might be there?

He looked over to the cars in the driveway. The trailers still open, crates standing on the gravel. The crates were plastic, bright colours with ventilated sides and clip on lids. Through the side of the top one nearest him he saw the unmistakable colours and design of the brand of muesli bar he loved, that he insisted his mum always buy. So she bought multi-packs, twenty-four bars to a box. He would need to eat. But could he take the risk of being seen?

He trembled harder at the thought of it, but he needed stuff from the cars. If he stayed low, the cars would be between him and the hotel, so he wouldn't be seen. If they even looked out. And he could keep an eye through the cars for any movements in the windows of the kitchen.

Swallowing hard, feeling like metal spikes blocked his throat, he crept out from around the side of the garage and scuttled to his parents' car. Breathing hard, he pulled open the back passenger door and felt around under the driver's seat until his fingers found the strap of the first aid kit under there. He pulled it free, closed the door as quietly as he could and sat back against it, holding the kit to his chest, heart racing so fast he thought it might burst clear through his ribs. Now to get some food.

The kitchen door banged open and angry voices punched the still, cold air. Rueben's muscles seized in a paralysis of fear.

"I don't want to hear it, we're in it now and we work through it."

"We could still leave, James!" That was the woman, Deanna. "Leave 'em tied up in there and just go."

"Come on, James, please!" That was the young one, Paul. His voice wheedled and even Rueben knew that wouldn't go down well with someone like James.

"Quit it! This is our reality and we're dealing with it. Let's get Rick inside before he freezes to fucking death!"

Rueben willed his legs to work, but where would he go? Pressed up against the car, pinned out in the open. The blue Fairlane belonging to the gang or whatever they were was parked only twenty feet behind the vehicle he sat against. It would only take for one of them to walk around to his side and they'd be looking right at him. He heard the Fairlane door open.

"Fuck, there's blood everywhere."

"Is he already dead?"

"No, he's breathing." That was the woman again, she sounded the most compassionate. And the most calm. The younger one just sounded scared.

James, the leader, sounded crazy and charged, like he was on the mother of all sugar rushes.

There was some scuffling and grunting. "He's in a bad way, James," Deanna said. "Moving him is likely to make it worse. He needs a hospital!"

"Yeah, well we're all he's got. Paul, get around the other side and help turn him. Hold his legs while we lift him out."

A squeak of terror escaped Rueben's lips as feet crunched on gravel again. He felt a desperate need to piss and didn't know if he could stop it.

"What will we do when we get him inside?" Paul asked as he rounded the back of the Fairlane.

He looked over the car as he spoke, presumably at James. One glance to his left and that was it, he'd see Rueben sitting there in his jeans and pale blue jacket, obvious against the gravel. No matter how tightly Rueben scrunched up, knees pressing the first aid kit into his chest, there was simply nowhere to hide. Tears poured over Rueben's cheeks, his lungs screamed for air as he held his breath, blood pulsed in his temples. The trembling had become a vibration, his fingertips numb, teeth chattering if he didn't clamp them shut. He had never been so scared in his life. All he saw was Uncle Simon's chest exploding, that spray of blood, glistening organs, spikes of stark white bone, that shiny thing falling onto the gravel. He would be next.

"Look at me, little brother!"

Paul stopped outside the rear door of the Fairlane, still looking over the roof at James. Brothers, Rueben thought, and despite his fear he filed that away too. Paul wasn't carrying his gun, but that didn't mean much. One of the others would be, surely. *Don't look this way. Don't look this way. Please don't look this way.*

"Rick may die, Pauly. Okay? He might. We'll try to save him, but if he dies, he dies. We go forward from here. Whatever else, this is happening now. We're not going anywhere any time soon. These fucking people, they're a complication, sure. But we're safe here, so here we stay."

"James..."

"Get his legs!" James's voice was a bark, a verbal gunshot.

Paul jumped, one hand scrabbling for the door handle. Rueben clearly saw him wince, his creased face of despair as he pulled the door open and ducked inside. He didn't look. But what about when he came out again?

"That's it, turn him." James grunted, the sound of someone taking weight. "Okay, keep coming, support his legs."

He's going right through the car, Rueben thought. He's not coming back out this side.

"Deanna, go hold the kitchen door open. Keep coming, Pauly, let's get him inside."

Legs like jelly, Rueben forced himself to push up slightly, risk a peek through the side windows of the car. Deanna held the kitchen door and the brothers carried their blood-soaked friend into the hotel. Deanna followed them, closed the door behind her. Rueben watched their shadows pass across the kitchen windows, then keep going as they headed for the dining room. The blue Fairlane stood inert, all four doors open like frozen wings.

With a sob of terrified relief, Rueben tore open the top of the nearest plastic crate and grabbed a box of muesli bars and a ten-pack of juice poppers, tropical fruit. With those and the first aid kit clenched against his chest he felt overloaded. He wanted to search for other things, maybe stuff these in his jacket first. His heart hammered and he decided he'd pushed his luck far enough. He pressed the crate lid back into place and scurried for the cover of the garages again. As he ducked around the corner to get behind the old buildings he yelped in shock to see someone standing there. The piss he'd been holding nearly flooded his leg, but he held it as he realised the figure was Grandma Molly. She reached out beseeching hands, her mouth working with silent words. Rueben stared for several seconds, then shook his head and ran across the lawns in the rapidly darkening twilight, desperate for the safety of his treehouse.

CLAY

"HE'S safe," Molly said, her face twisted in pain, and Clay nodded. "He's scared, but he's resourceful. He still won't hear me." Clay nodded again, not daring to speak.

His back was pressed into one support column in the main lounge of the hotel, which left him facing the doors to the dining room. Legs out in front, arms held back to either side of the dark, hard wood by rope tied too tightly at the wrists, looping behind the column. His shoulders burned. On the opposite side, out of sight but present when their fingers occasionally brushed, Marcus sat in stunned, catatonic silence, similarly tied. Clay glanced to his right. Bound either side of the other column, nearer the bar, sat Grant and Leigh, a mirror image of himself and Marcus.

Clay wanted to tell them Rueben would be okay, but he didn't dare. So many reasons. They would ask how he knew. And no way would he risk those psychopaths overhearing and learning Rueben was out there. As if on cue, their voices and grunts of effort came from the dining room. Clay saw shadows move through the door, but couldn't tell what they were up to.

"Put him up here." That was the main psycho, James. "Near the fireplace. Warm him up."

"He's so cold and grey." The woman, Deanna. "I don't know if he's going to last much longer."

"Get a cushion for his head."

There were sounds of furniture scraping against the floor. The young one, Paul, ran in and threw sheets aside on the couches until he found a cushion, then ran back with it. He didn't spare the four prisoners a glance. Clay's tension ratcheted up.

James appeared in the doorway, face hard. "First aid kit?"

Clay looked at him. "Kitchen. Big cupboard with a red and white cross on it." He wished there was bottle marked medicine that actually had poison in it. Then again, it sounded like their buddy was close to death anyway. He ground his teeth, wishing them all dead. Images of Simon's desecrated body kept flashing through his mind, burned onto his brain like a brand. Why did Simon even have a gun? Why didn't he use it from further away?

Grant, facing the same way as Clay, said, "I think you should take your friend to a hospital. He'll die here."

James scowled. "I don't give a fuck what you think."

"We won't say anything. You've destroyed the phones anyway, right? You could get away, be long gone." Grant's face changed, as he realised something. "Hey, you could trash our cars so we can't get away unless we walked, and then you'd get a real head start."

James laughed. "Why? We're safe here."

"No one else has to die!" Grant's voice became desperate.

"Let me help," Leigh said.

Clay couldn't see her, not even if he craned his neck hard, the wood blocked his view.

"Help what?" James said, taking a few steps forward to see her on the far side of the column behind her husband.

"I trained as a nurse back… before all this. Let me help your friend."

"Leigh, no," Grant said. "Why help them?"

"Like you said, no one else has to die."

Clay willed his son to shut up. He guessed what Leigh was doing, trying to become useful to these people, build trust, mutual need. Who knew what opportunities might arise. It was a far better plan than Grant's exhortations for them to simply leave again.

"You can save him?" James asked.

"I have no idea, but I think I'm probably the best qualified to try. Untie me. Let me see him."

Clay watched James's face run through a series of emotions. Eventually, the psycho gave a tiny nod and Clay let out a held breath of anticipation. James freed the rope from Leigh's wrists, pulled it out where it went around the column behind Grant, and retied it where Leigh had been sitting. Clay noticed Grant tug experimentally against his bonds once Leigh stood, no doubt checking if the change had given him some new slack. It was clear it hadn't. These people knew how to tie folk up.

James kept a tight grip on Leigh's wrist as he led her from the room, saying, "No tricks. I'll kill you if you do anything stupid."

"I won't. And ease up, you're hurting me."

Clay turned his head, caught Grant's eye. His son stared with clenched teeth, furious eyes. "She's smart. Let her do this."

Grant nodded. "Yeah, I'm slow, but I see what she's up to."

"You guys *all* play it cool," Molly said, seen and heard only by Clay. "Stay calm and you can get out of this."

"How?" Clay whispered at his lap, knowing she would hear.

"Rueben can go for help. He can get to Laura and Bob's tomorrow."

"Why tomorrow?"

"It'll be dark soon. He'll go when it's light. He'll tell them, they'll call the police. Just get through the night."

Clay looked up, her words sparking a memory of that night so long ago, when they first took over the hotel. "We just have to get through the night," Molly had said, young and beautiful, so full of vigour but, at that moment, so full of fear. They both had been.

BEFORE

IN SPRING sunshine speared through trees overhanging the newly built hotel, dappling the dirt driveway. Fresh smells of pollen and grasses drifted on a warm breeze, currawongs called in the distance. But still Clay felt a chill to his bones.

"Are you sure, Moll?"

Molly hooked her long brunette hair behind her ears and tipped her head to one side. "You know I am."

The real estate agent stood a respectful distance away but his eyes were alive, hopeful. He knew Molly was convinced and Clay felt the man willing her to pass on her decision. But they were so young to be taking on such a responsibility. Then again, was a person ever really old enough for a decision like this?

"Hey!" Clay called the man over. "Tell me exactly what happened. I mean, this place is cheap as hell with good reason, but I need the details."

The man's eyebrows rose and Molly said, "Do you really?"

"Yeah." Clay turned his attention back to Henry Carrell of Carrell Real Estate, his face a question mark. From the corner of his eye he caught Molly's sardonic half-smile and marvelled again at her beauty. He was a fit young man, decent enough looking, but daily pinched himself. He had no idea how he'd got so lucky.

"Okay," Henry said, nodding to himself. "But it's a grisly story, you know that much already. You sure you want your wife to hear—"

"Let me stop you there," Clay interrupted. "She's made of sterner stuff than you and I put together. Proceed."

"Right." Carrell seemed to deflate, maybe convinced the full story would cost him the sale. "Well, the place had an auspicious start. All these acres of grounds were cleared. You know the title extends twice as far again into the bush behind and on either side too. There's fencing along the back, about two hundred metres into the trees, because the land falls away sharply there. A kind of hollow of loose scree, so that's dangerous even though it's well within the title. But there are so many acres around, it hardly matters. This, though, is the area Cecil Ellery chose to build on. It's almost entirely flat, and that whole area behind was going to be cleared too, for lawns. You can easily see that vision through if you buy the place. He started by clearing the long driveway in and then this area ready to build. The lawns added behind would really make this place something, you should consider that. Pretty easy to clear another acre or two of bush.

"Anyway, Cecil Ellery concentrated first on the hotel. He built the main building, the high central part you see there. Then he built the big kitchen and dining wing, and added his family quarters above that. Then they moved in, lived happily here at first by all accounts, and Ellery began work on the other wing to the right there, with all the guest rooms. That's when the trouble started.

"You see, Cecil was here with his family. He had a wife, Samantha, and three kids. A young son called Trent, who was about fourteen years old, then sixteen year old Wendy, then an elder son, Michael, who was nearly nineteen at the time of… the incident."

"One incident?" Clay asked.

Carrell's lip twisted. "Well, no one knows for sure. It might have taken place over a few days or even weeks. But the bodies were all relatively… well, not especially decomposed."

"But it was in winter," Molly said. "So they'd keep pretty well."

Henry blanched, then nodded. "I guess so. And access, as you've seen, is rough. Takes a while. Anyway, all we really know is what the police pieced together after everything was found and the rough shape of it is like this. Seems the eldest son, Michael, had been going weird for a while. Don't forget, this whole place was built by Cecil and his sons, with occasional help from Cecil's brother, Herbert, and his family who visited a couple of times. They spent the whole of last year doing nothing but building, living in tents behind there until it was habitable. They worked fast, keen to move in before the winter struck. No one would want to be in a tent up here in winter. They did that and were in their quarters before autumn was halfway through, and they built the shell of the guest wing before the first snow.

"But once they moved in, Michael's... I guess you'd call it a psychosis? It started to manifest itself more and more. Cecil's brother—if you read the police transcripts after the event, they interviewed him at some length—anyhow, he said Michael had been getting really strung out all that summer, and went downhill fast as autumn set in. Claimed there was something in the woods and it talked to him at night. Sometimes the family would wake up to find him gone and he'd come back hours or even days later covered in dirt and leaves. They tried to talk to him about it, but he'd have periods of lucidity, then go weird again. Ever more frequently, apparently, as the weather cooled.

"He started drawing these weird designs on things, you can still find a few of 'em inside the guest wing, where the internal walls aren't finished yet. And he said they were sigils to the greater power."

"You seem to know a lot of details," Molly said quietly.

Henry shrugged. "I've been trying to sell this place for a while, so I got interested. And when I realised the police had lots of information from the brother, Michael's uncle Herbert, I asked if I could read up and they had no problem with that. It's pretty fascinating stuff."

"It sure is." Clay looked at Molly, one eyebrow raised.

"You feel any of this?" she asked him, that sardonic smile again.

Despite the story he didn't feel a thing. His sight gave him no clues to the authenticity of the tale, and he wondered how much of the whole thing was twisted fabrication. How much embellishment, like a fish that grows bigger with every telling of the catch.

"I guess not." He turned back to Henry. "Sorry, go on."

Henry looked from Clay to Molly and back again, clearly wondering what these two youngsters were surreptitiously discussing, but shrugged it off. He mopped his brow with a handkerchief, running it back over his wide forehead where his hair had begun to go grey and retreat. "As Cecil and his sons got the guest wing structurally finished, and started on the interior, it seems Michael lost his mind completely. They think Wendy died first." Carrell took a deep breath, then plunged on, talking more quickly. "There were signs he sexually assaulted her, and then he crucified her right here in front of the main doors, left her strung on a big X of branches. She died slow, the coroner reckons, small cuts all over her body to bleed." Henry looked from Clay to Molly once more.

Clay knew his face was hard, but he also knew if he could hear more then Molly surely could. She wanted to buy, she saw a whole new start for them up here in the wilderness, away from cities and people and so many shades that sometimes caused the sight to give her terrible migraines. And truth be known, he was fascinated. He wanted the details too now. He nodded for Henry to continue.

"Okay, so after that, the mother died. She was dismembered and stacked in the big stone hearth in the dining room, all her pieces one atop another. The father, Cecil, was strung up high in the main lounge room and that was the really unexplained killing. The police have no idea how he ended up hanging there, they never found how the deed was done. But he was inverted, ankles tied, one to each of those big wooden columns that hold the roof up in there, so he was hanging like a sort of Y-shape about ten feet up off the ground. At least, his head was ten feet up, his body and legs above that. The ropes were wrapped around his shins and ankles, making sure, I guess, they didn't cut through or just pull his feet off. And his legs were held so wide apart, his pelvis had cracked and broken. Tied to each arm with more loops of rope were two big logs, each one weighed about a hundred pounds. Those huge weights had pulled his arms from the sockets and stretched his body, and the strain from his legs and pelvis had damaged his organs there, and the whole thing just kinda slowly pulled him to pieces inside, held together only by his muscles and skin." Carrell paused and sucked in a deep breath. He seemed simultaneously both appalled and excited by the tale. "There were slices cut under his arms, in his neck and shoulders, none enough to kill him on their own, according to the coroner. The police reckon he got hung up there alive and was left to die by slow by excruciating stretching. Oh, and his eyes was gouged out, before he died, they think. And all those cuts, they just bled him out. But how the hell Michael got him up there, or lifted those huge logs and fastened them on? No one knows. Probably they think, he tied the logs on first, then somehow hoisted his father up."

"Jesus hell," Clay whispered. "Maybe his brother helped? Could the two of them have done that? You haven't mentioned his younger brother yet. Or his uncle?"

"Well, his uncle was gone back to Sydney by then, he had plenty of witnesses to corroborate that. Herbert and his family were long gone when all this went down. Maybe the younger brother helped, but the police don't think so, because they found him out in the woods behind the hotel, in the area Cecil was planning to clear for lawns that I mentioned. He was impaled on a sharpened log. The stake was about eight feet tall, sticking up out of the ground at an angle, and the boy Trent had been jammed onto it from above and forced down its length until the point drove up out of his throat, tipping his head back to stare at the clouds." Carrell paused again, swallowed. "So they don't know how Michael did that either. The police reckon he used the same scaffolds and pulleys and things they'd been using to build the house, and then took everything away afterwards to make the tableau of murder and desecration more impressive to whoever finally discovered it. Or maybe just for his own sick and twisted pleasure. To look upon his works, so to speak."

"Holy shit," Molly breathed. "Michael really went off the deep end, huh."

"Isolation, the police said. A kind of cabin fever. Uncle Herbert said Michael had been a weird kid all along, kept quiet, read a lot and didn't play much with others."

"Being an introvert doesn't make a person a psychopath," Clay said.

"Well, no, I suppose not." Henry shrugged, looked around himself and sighed.

"What about Michael?" Molly asked. "What happened to him?"

"Suicided." Henry pursed his lips, nodded as if to himself. "After all that, maybe the madness drained out of him and he saw what he'd done. Couldn't face it. The police found him in the kitchen, and their best guess is he poisoned himself."

"Best guess?"

"He showed all kinds of signs, mostly asphyxiation, foam around the mouth, discolouration of the skin, stuff like that. They never figured out what he took, but the verdict was suicide by poisoning. All the other signs of violence on his body were also deemed self-inflicted or the marks of his victims struggling against his attacks."

"Sweet lord," Molly said quietly. Clay watched her, wondering if the story might have changed her mind about the place. "That surely is a blood-soaked history."

Henry smiled crookedly. "Well, that's actually perhaps the weirdest thing. One part I didn't mention. There was virtually no blood."

"What?"

"All the bodies were drained of it, dried out. Police said it was probably why they were killed like they were, hung up or dismembered in those ways, so Michael could collect the blood."

"For what purpose?" Clay asked, dismayed.

"We'll never know."

"And the blood wasn't recovered? Found?"

"Nope. No idea what he did with it. Probably best not to think too hard on that particular aspect of the whole debacle. Anyway, I suppose you won't be buying the place after hearing all that." Henry's face was downcast, his entire demeanour sagging. Clay thought the man enjoyed relaying the tale and it had maybe cost him sales before. The story was compelling. And perhaps the burden of knowledge was hard to bear, so he shared it whenever he could.

Clay caught Molly's eye and they stared at each other for a long moment. He saw a flicker of mischief in there, the spark he loved with every atom of his being. Maybe she wasn't cowed by the gruesome yarn after all. She raised one eyebrow slightly. It was true, this place was amazing, and it was cheap as hell. For good reason, but Molly was also right about the vibe. He couldn't feel a thing, no cold presence, no restless spirits, the ghosts of the murdered Ellerys weren't exhorting him for some kind of vengeance or peace. Would the history prevent people from wanting to come and stay here? If they didn't make too much of it, maybe no one would know. Maybe those who did know would come because of it, some kind of macabre murder tourists.

He looked up at the neat, finely-made building. It was a beautiful hotel in a beautiful place, far from the maddening crowds of modern life. They could truly start something magical here if they gave it their all, a business and a place to live that would cost them next to nothing. It wouldn't be easy, but then again, whatever was that was worth having?

"I don't know, Henry," he said with a smile. "I think maybe we'll make you an offer, but it might be a little lower than the asking price."

"The asking price is already rock bottom," Henry said, brightening.

"True, but that story? The things that happened here? I think that's worth at least another ten percent off."

LEIGH

LEIGH'S hands shook as she stared at the pale face of the man in the dining room, lying across two tables pushed together. James and his pals had pulled the tables up close to the crackling hearth. The man's abdomen was black with half-congealed blood. More dotted the floors through the kitchen and dining room where they'd carried him in. His hands were red with it where they lay pressed loosely against his midriff. Leigh's mind skipped and stuttered as she tried to think. Images of Simon flashed past her mind's eye, her brother flying back, his body blown open to the cold, grey sky. The boom of that shotgun blast kept filling her mind. Grief threatened to overflow like a dam breaking, but she knew if she let it out, it would consume her. Hard to believe though it was, this situation was real. This stuff was happening. Had happened. Simon was dead. She gasped, swallowed hard and pushed that thought away. *Dead dead dead...* Tears breached her lower lids and she blinked her eyes clear.

More than anything else, she had to protect Rueben. And the only way she could do that was to buy him time. He must have seen what was happening and decided to remain hidden. No way could he have missed the shotgun blast, his treehouse was less than two hundred metres into the bush. Surely he would have come to investigate, and thankfully managed to remain unseen when he did. She held onto that thought like a shipwrecked sailor in rough seas holds onto the one spar of broken wood they've found. Rueben was a smart kid. He would wait, find a safe time. Maybe wait for light, it was already darkening outside. It was a single twisting road back down the hill, impossible to get wrong, but dangerous at night. Yes, he'd go first thing, surely. Laura could call the police in from Enden or Monkton and they'd only take an hour or two, maybe a bit more, to reach the hotel. *Wait for daylight, Roo,* she thought to herself, over and over again. *Then run for help.*

She glanced around, wondering if any opportunity might present itself for her family to escape. But three of them, heavily armed, against one of her, was suicide. Build trust, get them to relax a little, and something might present itself. But even if it didn't, Roo would come through. *Come on, my big brave boy.*

For now, keep these lunatics calm. No more dying. Though the scumbags were clearly the worst of humanity, she wanted no more deaths, not even theirs. Not now.

"Well?" James snapped.

Leigh startled, realised she'd been dithering, lost in thought. She was more scared than she'd ever been. "I don't know. Let me look." She drew on her old training, back when she thought being a nurse and helping people was her calling. If she hadn't met Grant, maybe it would have been. She'd have made a good nurse, she knew that. Maybe even a doctor by now. But youthful infatuation changed her plans, and she bore no ill will to anyone for that. They had a good life, the hotel, their family. Until now. "I need more light."

The hotel was warming up slowly, partly from the large fires Clay had lit in the dining room and lounge, partly from heating system slowly kicking in, but the edge of a chill still lingered. It would for days yet, Leigh knew. The place took a while to shake off its winter indolence.

Paul dragged a standard lamp over from one side of the room and plugged it in right beside the hearth. He tipped the shade back to act as a spotlight for her. Its glow turned the blackness across Rick's body to deep crimson. Leigh reached for the first aid kit the invaders had retrieved from the kitchen and opened it on the table beside her. There were more supplies in the cupboard if she needed them. She had a feeling she would.

She turned to James. "On the other side of the lounge, there's a door next to the reception office. It leads through to the guest rooms. Right after that door, before the rooms start, is a staircase to the left leading to the upstairs rooms, and a storage closet on the right. In the closet are linens and stuff. I'm going to need a decent pillow and plenty of blankets. If you're going to keep him here, we need to make him more comfortable, and warm. Give him a chance to recover. And I need to cut off these clothes."

James pointed to Paul. "Go."

As the younger man left, Leigh took trauma shears from the first aid kit and drew in a deep breath. "Okay, let's see how bad this is." James and Deanna moved closer for a better view as she opened Rick's shirt and then cut the t-shirt underneath. The makeshift plug bandage jammed into the wound was sodden through then half-dried, stuck to the skin. Leigh wished they hadn't done that. All around it, Rick's flesh was swollen and white as marble, except for an angry red that marked the outline of the actual bullet hole spreading out a couple of inches like some obscene bloom.

Leigh looked up. "Exit wound?"

Deanna shook her head.

"So the bullet's still in there?"

"Must be."

"Jesus." She stared at the mess, wondering how to proceed. "I'll need hot water and towels. And water to drink. Rainwater from the taps is safe."

Deanna turned away without needing James to order her. Leigh watched the woman leave, wondering if there might be more of an ally in her than the others. Something about Deanna's face, the way she shot quick, acid glances at James. Maybe there was a wedge to be driven there, keep the bastards focused on each other rather than her family.

When Deanna returned with the water, Leigh soaked the wounded area then, holding her breath, pulled the wadded up shirt free. Blood welled instantly in the deep, round wound. She had needle and sutures ready, unsure what else she could do but patch up the hole and treat the man for shock. Maybe feed him antibiotics somehow. There was nothing to be done about the blood loss, and no way she knew enough about surgery to go after the bullet. It could be anywhere inside him, could have caused untold damage. The thought of cutting him open made her knees weak.

Unsure what to do with the blood-soaked shirt, she looked left and right, desperate to not be holding it any more, staining her hands red. With a small cry of disgust, she threw it into the hearth behind her. It hissed against red hot logs for a moment and Leigh watched the blood drip through, imagined it spattering the hearth stone under the andirons, only to hiss there and burn up.

Then all of them, including Paul with an armful of linens just returned from the guest wing, gasped in shock. While the shirt sat blackening, the flames suddenly leaped and danced a bright, virulent green and, despite the surge in strength of the fire, the temperature dipped, a gust of chill washing over them. The verdant flames danced again, leaping thick and high, shooting up the chimney with a rush of sound like air sucked through an open window.

"What the fuck?" James said, the only one able to squeeze words past his shock.

A distant howl sounded softly, seeming to come from outside the hotel and inside the hearth at the same time. Then the flames died down, the heat of the fire returned, the shirt crisped and blackened, falling apart among the thick logs and sticks.

"Was that the blood burning?" Deanna asked.

There was silence for a moment as they all stared.

"Probably the fabric," James said eventually. "Some cheap shitty nylon or something."

Leigh looked from the fire to James but decided to keep her peace. She was pretty sure that shirt had been cotton. And whatever just happened hadn't felt like something as simple as cheap fabric burning. Despite the returned warmth, a chill remained with her.

"Did you hear that howl?" Paul asked.

"Dingo," James said.

"Here?"

Leigh shared Paul's scepticism, but remained silent. She turned her attention back to Rick, mopping up the fresh blood and cleaning the wound with saline as best she could. Then she set to stitching him closed.

"I can seal this, stop him losing any more blood. But there's a strong risk of infection. I have some antibiotics if we can get him to swallow them. I have no idea if they're strong enough. He needs a hospital."

"Too bad," James said.

"Well, it's antibiotics and pain relief then. There's nothing I can do for the blood he's already lost." She looked up, caught James eye. "And he's lost a lot."

James shrugged. "Too bad."

Leigh held the man's eyes for second, then looked away. She saw madness there. Cold, relentless viciousness. But she saw something else too. Some kind of pain, some primal hurt. She thought of an animal, biting in fear when someone tried to help it. James had a feral look about him and whatever had happened before this day was deeply embedded. But this day had changed him, she thought. Maybe tipped him over some edge he'd been teetering on for years. The way Deanna and Paul cast furtive glances at him, like they didn't quite recognise him any more, made her only more confident in her theory. "Well, he needs something for his strength, besides meds. And we all need to eat. I've got all the ingredients for a big soup, so if you let me and Marcus work in the kitchen we can feed everyone. And then we can strain off the broth and give it to Rick here. Help me sit him up a little."

Paul and Deanna moved to lift Rick's shoulders while James stared, immobile. Rick moaned weakly as they moved him, but Leigh took that as a good enough sign that he wasn't dead yet. She broke up a couple of antibiotics and analgesics into rough dust and tipped them into his mouth, then lifted a glass of water to force him to drink. His throat pulsed convulsively and he spluttered, moaned again and grimaced. She made him drink more and he swallowed more easily the second time. Deanna reached for a pillow, brushing the couch cushion aside. They settled him and Leigh pulled off his boots, then removed the rest of his blood-soaked clothes, including his jeans that were wet down to halfway along the thigh with piss and blood, and his shit-stained underwear. Leigh cleaned him up as well as she could, then covered him with fresh blankets. "He should be in a bed, but I don't want to move him any more than necessary. Maybe bring a mattress through from one of the guest rooms?"

"He's fine like that," James said. "You've done enough."

Deanna caught Leigh's eye and mouthed, *Thank you.*

Leigh nodded. She'd stitched a hole that was probably the least of the man's problems. She'd be surprised if he lasted the night. "So will you let me feed everyone?" she asked James.

"Just you, not the other guy. He stays tied up. Deanna and Paul, you watch every move she makes. No knives. Any chopping, you do it, Deanna."

Leigh sighed. Well, so much for slipping a blade into her sleeve like she'd planned. But they did all need to eat and feeding people would keep them on an even keel. She glanced to the window, saw full night had fallen. *Come on, Roo,* she thought to herself again. *Don't be scared, darling. Rest, stay safe, then go get us help!*

RUEBEN

IN THE treehouse door was closed, the rope ladder rolled up inside it. The mattress he sat on had an edge of dampness to it still, a musty smell like subtle rot and fungus permeated the air. It usually took a couple or three days to air out the place each year, but he didn't have that luxury. Darkness closed in on the forest, inky stains between the trees spreading like mould. And inside the treehouse it was almost pitch, just the weakest light from a tiny sliver of moon edging out the black. But he didn't dare light one of the candles he had nearby, or the oil lamp Uncle Simon had given him two years ago. He swallowed hard at the memory of his Uncle, blown open, and pushed his thoughts in another direction.

He desperately wanted light, the darkness seemed to reach out and take hold of him with cold hands that brushed and caressed, then began to squeeze. But he imagined even the tiniest light in the treehouse like a beacon to the hotel. He knew, almost one hundred per cent knew for certain, that the trees were more than thick enough to mask any glow. He couldn't see the lights in the hotel, after all. Even if someone came outside and stood on the grass looking into the bush, they wouldn't sese a small candle burning. He knew that. But he didn't dare. He simply couldn't take the risk he might be wrong.

Fear made his stomach glassy. He had forced down a muesli bar that tasted like cardboard and stuck in his throat, and a juice box that tasted far too sweet, and both now sat like an icy rock in his gut. With all the panic, he hadn't secured any water and he wondered if that might be his biggest mistake yet. A person could survive a few days without water if they had to. His dad and Uncle Simon had both told him that. Surely the juice would be liquid enough. He just had to last overnight.

He pulled the space blanket from the first aid kit, its glittering foil rustling noisily in the night. Along with the darkness, cold had fallen like a shroud. His breath puffed clouds in front of his face. His eyes had adjusted as much as they ever would, and everything remained shadowed lumps, varying shades of grey and charcoal black, but his breath looked white as snow. He pulled the foil blanket around his shoulders, tucked it in under his crossed legs and held it tightly at his chest. He stared out the window by the closed door, branches like broken bones of blackness against the deep indigo of the night sky. It wasn't quite full dark yet, but would be any time. Would his vision fail completely then? The sliver of a moon would surely save him from total blindness as long as clouds didn't cover the sky entirely.

He remembered camping with his uncles, lying on the ground by a dying fires, red embers in the darkness, staring up at the blanket of stars across the firmament. Marcus had pointed out constellations, joked about how different the western names were from the Chinese ones his grandmother had taught him. The night sky then had been a celebration of light, sparkling and entrancing, mesmerizing and magical. So different to the deathly dark that embraced him now.

Sounds echoed through the trees. Bird screeches that sounded like ghost wails, scratching in the leaf litter that might be wombats or wallabies or werewolves or lumbering, rotting corpses, reaching up for the treehouse. He looked again at the ladder rolled up, pulled in for safety. He was high above the ground, nothing could get him here. Except those people, of course. If they found him they'd get in as easily as he had. More easily, as they were bigger. Grown-ups. He had been so excited opening up, getting ready for another full season at the hotel. Before everything had turned to terror so quickly. Before Uncle Simon had died. Before those awful people had carried that big, blood-soaked man inside, who was surely dead by now. Rueben had never seen so much blood in his life.

He looked up again, out of the window towards the hotel. In the distance, high up, something glowed briefly a bright, unnatural green. He frowned, staring through the thick branches, but it was gone. Had he really seen that? A distant howl rose from far behind him and set his hairs on end, his gut quaking. The sound was wolf-like but not, somehow deeper, more primal. His mouth went dry, his pulse raced. And then a voice, or something close to it, whispering through the trees. Almost like a breeze, words formed and slipped around him, but not words he could understand. Was it a different language? Or English blurred and slurred too much to comprehend? He leaned forward, subconsciously stretching toward the window as if to absorb the words more easily.

He cried out at movement right outside, a person standing at the window. The space blanket was a sudden riot of noise as he scrambled back on the bed, until he hit the wall behind himself.

Grandma Molly leaned in through the window. Through the closed window. Then she leaked through the wall and stood before him, a soft glow surrounding her. Her face was twisted in pain and longing, her hands reaching for him like when she wanted a hug. And in life he would have run into those arms, felt her heavy, soft warmth embrace him, smelled her lavender and cinnamon scent, the enveloping of her love. He wanted more than ever to be in Grandma Molly's arms again, but she was gone. This wasn't real. He squeezed his eyes shut, sobbing, tears pushing out. He had never felt so alone in his life.

He sensed a presence close by him, refused to open his eyes and look. Trembling wracked his body, his toes and fingertips were numb. The presence became more insistent. What if it was one of them? What if he opened his eyes now and saw that bastard James staring down at him, shotgun levelled at his chest? What if James was about to fire and turn Rueben's chest into a wet, glistening hole like Uncle Simon's?

"No!" Rueben yelled and forced his eyes open.

Grandma Molly crouched right in front of him, her eyes imploring, her mouth working soundlessly. He saw his name formed on her lips, over and over again, and the word *Please!* over and over with it.

He shook his head. No, no, no. "Not real, and not crazy." His voice was weak, whisper-thin and cracked. "Not real, and not crazy."

The howl echoed again, louder by a tiny amount, obviously nearer. Nothing in the Australian bush howled like that. It seemed to have echoes of something slavering in it, the might of something huge and the hunger of something ancient. More of those slippery, whispering words fluttered around him like summer bugs.

Grandma Molly tried to smile, he saw her lips forming *It's okay! It's all okay!* But he knew she wasn't real. He knew that maybe it wasn't all okay. After all, everything else *was* real. Those people had his family. They *had* killed Uncle Simon. Whatever he heard in the distance of the far woods was a thing he hoped never to see, never to know more about than its distant sound, which was already far too much knowledge. But it was real. He *heard* it clearly. All those terrible things were real and enough to threaten his sanity. His mind stretched and warped against the pressure of his thoughts and he wondered if part of him might snap or burst or rupture, taking his sanity and then his life with it. Was this what it was like to be literally scared to death? His chest constricted, his heart smashed into his ribs. His breath was fast and shallow, desperate gasps and he felt as though he were drowning.

All that stuff was real, and the only thing he really wanted, Grandma Molly's love and embrace, was the only thing right now that wasn't. Of course not, being the thing he wanted most. It couldn't be real, because she was dead. As dead as Uncle Simon. That was real life. It happened despite what you wanted. His muscles tightened, dragging on his bones like he might curl up so tight every part of him snapped.

He squeezed his eyes shut again, turned onto his side on the damp mattress and pulled the foil blanket tight around himself. He had started to warm up inside it before, and he needed to be warm at least. He reached out and hauled up the two ratty blankets and the threadbare quilt, pulled it all up over his head and body, cocooning himself within the dank confines of its dubious safety.

He just had to get through the night, stay warm and ignore everything. He forced one deeper breath, then another. There was nothing else he could do but wait. He didn't think for a moment he would sleep, but that didn't matter. He only needed to make it until dawn. As soon as there was light he would sneak back out. Stay in the trees but keep the hotel in sight, skirt around it and not get lost in the bush. Then he could run alongside the long driveway, he'd be able to see that in the dawn light too, but there was no risk of those intruders seeing him if he stayed in the trees. Then a long walk down the road to Laura and Bob's place. It might take him hours, half the day even, to get there, but that didn't matter either. That was a plan. It was the tiniest spark of hope in the otherwise stygian blackness of his fear.

He just had to make it through the night.

BEFORE

"I still can't believe we've done this." Molly's face was alive with excitement and Clay had never loved her more.

He held his reservations still, but the purchase was finalized, the new future stretching out before them like a blank page, ready to be written. Her excitement infected him and he grinned, grabbed her up in a hug and spun her around. "Can you imagine our parents doing something like this, *ever*, let alone at our age?"

She laughed, kissed him. "Not at all. Honestly, I can't imagine us doing it at our age, but we're grown-ups now, Clay. And we did it! So let's get our bags inside and figure out where to start. We have a lot of work to do."

The rest of the day was filled with a frenzy of tidying, organizing, list making. By the time the oil lamps and candles were lit and they had settled down for a late dinner, both were exhausted. But a warm sense of achievement pervaded them.

Then Molly stiffened and Clay felt it a moment later.

Their ability to occasionally see the dead, what Molly's grandmother had called the sight, was as natural to them as hearing or touch, even if Molly's ability far outshone his own mediocre talent. They knew it to be rare, unusual, nothing to discuss in popular company. They agreed some people used their sight for gain, the mediums and séance holders, but it was a nebulous and untrustworthy ability, not to be relied upon. Certainly not to be used as gospel fact for paying, grieving strangers. And most of the mediums didn't have the sight anyway. The vast majority were charlatans, grifters and con-merchants, cold reading for dollars.

Now and then one or other of them would nod surreptitiously to a shade lurking in a room or on a street corner, and that shade would smile in acknowledgement, or duck away, shocked to have been seen. *Most are used to loneliness*, Molly had told him, and he thought perhaps that was the saddest thing he'd ever heard.

There had been a strangely malevolent entity near a park one night and, on discussing it later, Molly had assured Clay it was simply an angry and vengeful spirit, nothing more. As her sight was clearer than his, he accepted her word. But Clay had thought for sure that particular entity had been something else, something non-human and malicious. He was glad to have never seen it again.

When they looked around the hotel with Henry of Carrell Real Estate they had been alert, whispering to each other of the trauma encountered here, before Henry had given them the details. And both had agreed there was no trace of the killings. No restless spirits trapped inside or looking for revenge. It was unusual, Molly had told Clay years ago, for spirits to linger. Most had no grip on the mortal realm after death and those who did, well, who could even be certain they were genuinely ghosts? It could be a shape worn by some other lifeforce, or an echo with no real soul or intellect behind it, or sometimes perhaps a memory conjured by the grief of those left behind. "Whatever the truth of it," Molly had said one quiet night while sipping wine and staring in to the flickering flames of their fire, "all ghosts are grief. All are memories. They can't touch us."

"They speak to us, though," Clay had said. "Like your grandmother. Don't forget, she told you how nice I am. She approves of me."

Molly's laugh bubbled gently out. "So she did. But perhaps that was simply my projection of what I want to believe."

So knowing the hotel they had just moved into to be free of spirits after their detailed inspection, the presence and chill that permeated the air suddenly as they sat with their dinner was disconcerting in the extreme. It reminded Clay of that time in the park.

"What is it?" Clay whispered, the hairs on his neck and arms bristling.

Molly shook her head, expression dark, lips pressed into a thin line.

"We looked hard," Clay said, scanning the kitchen as candles made shadows dance on the walls. Out the window, a half-moon sheened everything pale silver, stars a glittering shroud above the trees.

A half-smile tugged at Molly's mouth. "I think someone was hiding from us. I didn't know they could do that." She pushed her chair back from the rough pine table and stood, turned a slow circle. "Hello? You can come out, there's nothing to fear."

A wet, slavering voice slipped out of the darkness near the large sinks. "Oh really? I think you might soon revise that opinion."

Molly stepped back as Clay jumped up to stand beside her. The sensation of presence intensified, the kind of psychic pressure someone with the sight would never have missed. How could they possibly have not felt this before, especially as they had so actively looked for it?

"Michael?" Molly said. "Michael Ellery, yes? What is it you need?"

"Need?" A figure formed from shadow and extended into the dancing candlelight. As it moved, it slipped and ebbed and slowly stretched into a thin young man. He stood over six feet tall, wiry and angular, with long dark hair in greasy tails that sat on his shoulders. His face was sallow, cheekbones high and sharp, eyes black as night. "Isn't that a strange concept? One *needs* air to breath, food to eat, shelter, I suppose. Well, the living need those things. What do I need? Nothing. None of those things. What do I *want*? Well, there's a question."

"I think you need to leave, Michael." Molly took a step forward and Clay reached out a hand to stop her. This felt wrong. Volatile.

Molly had mentioned before that ghosts could be moved on. Sometimes it was as simple as telling them they were dead and it was time to go. The realisation was enough, and they'd fade away. She had done it before, apparently. It seemed she thought she might do it again now.

Michael hissed laughter, like air escaping underwater. "You think you're safe, don't you?" He gestured and Molly staggered back, hands clutched to her head. A sound of shock and pain slipped between her clenched teeth.

"How..?"

Michael laughed again and strode forward. "You didn't know I could choose not to be found. You're children facing eternity and you think you know everything about it. You have no idea."

Clay grabbed Molly and pulled her from the kitchen, through into the large dining room. The space was shrouded in gloom, mostly empty, dining furniture on the long list of things they needed to acquire. The large hearth in far wall stood cold and dark as Clay hauled Molly with him.

"Where are we going?" she demanded.

"How did he hurt you?"

"I don't know. It's like the migraines I get from seeing too many ghosts, like in the city sometimes. Only worse! I don't know how he did that, how he triggered it. I've never felt a ghost as strong before. Have you?"

Clay thought briefly of the malevolent entity by the park, but though the sensation was similar, it wasn't the same. "No. I don't know what he is."

"So I ask again. Where are we going?"

Before Clay could answer, the darkened hearth burst into bright light, flames and smoke, thick, unnatural and tinged a deep scarlet. Dark, long shadows whipped out, flickering at the air like enormous snake's tongues. The room lit with writhing crimson lights and swirling shadows.

"What's that?" Clay yelled as a wave of coldness swept over him.

"It's not real!" Molly shouted.

Gravity hauled at Clay's gut. He staggered as the floor seemed to shift and undulate. Michael Ellery strode into the room, laughing. He reached out towards them, palms forward in a kind of supplication.

"Don't look in there!" Molly shouted, now pulling at Clay as he had dragged at her before. Despite her words, he caught a glimpse of the deeply red burning hearth and saw body parts in there, stacked like winter wood. He tore his gaze away and together they staggered through into the high-ceilinged lounge.

"Help me!" The voice was rasping with agony, thin and strained. Shadows moved above, a drawn silhouette suspended in the darkness between the tall wooden columns.

"Don't look!" Molly said again, pulling Clay through. "We have to get to somewhere he hasn't been, or at least, where he hasn't killed. He's too powerful here."

Clay glanced back, saw the red glow whipping around the doorway between the lounge and dining room, questing up into the darkness above the lounge. Then he let Molly drag him through the opposite door, between a staircase and a large supply closet. The guest wing was framework and external walls only, no internal build started yet. It smelled of freshly sawed wood and turpentine. They stumbled all the way to the far end and into an unfinished room where they fell against the outer wall, shrouded in darkness, trembling, holding tightly to each other.

"What is happening?" Clay asked. "What was that, in the hearth?"

"Hell, maybe?"

He turned to look at his wife, but she was lost in shadows, her face unreadable. "Hell?"

"Or its equivalent. I don't know. Wherever Michael should have gone, because of the things he did here? Did you see the way it reached for him?"

"It seemed to reach for us too."

"Yes, but it yearned for Michael. You didn't feel that? I think he's resisting it. It's where he needs to go."

"Can we help with that?"

He felt Molly nod in the darkness. "Ghosts are strong at night, but their power wanes in the day. My grandmother was powerful in the cunning ways and she taught me a lot. I never thought I would need those skills, not in the modern age, but here we are."

"And are we safe here?"

"I'm not sure, but we're safer, I think. Michael's power is tied to where he committed his sins. Perhaps he can find us here, harangue us, cause me pain, but we can try to ignore him. We certainly don't want to be drawn back to… to whatever is happening back there. Not at night." She pressed a hand to her head, still wincing.

Clay swallowed hard. "You think you can do something about it?"

"We have to send Michael on his way. Maybe in the dining room hearth? I don't know why it's there. Perhaps because that was where he left his mother. He's tied to that spot emotionally, more strongly than anywhere else."

"And you can send him away?"

"I know ways. I think."

"You think?"

Michael's voice came to them, cursing them, uttering the foulest epithets. His form, more gossamer here, wavered in front of them, his face a mask of fury.

Molly winced, pressed one hand to her temple, squeezed Clay's arm with her other. "Ignore him!" She pressed her head against his shoulder and he felt her trembling. "We just have to get through the night."

LEIGH

LEIGH stared at the large pot on the stove top, the gas down low to let it simmer. She visualized grabbing the two handles at the top and spinning around with it, dousing Paul and Deanna with boiling soup and hot lumps of vegetable. But it was a fantasy. She might get one or the other, not both. And James loitered around, moving between the kitchen and the dining room, stalking like an impatient big cat in a zoo.

They'd chopped up a variety of vegetables while a large bacon bone boiled along with herbs and spices and stock. The pot would make plenty of hearty soup for the eight of them. Leigh pressed down her emotions at the thought of Rueben out there somewhere in the cold, scared and hungry. She guessed he would have retreated to his treehouse, where there would be shelter and he had blankets at least. Would it be enough? Perhaps he might come up to the garages or the cottage, but that thought terrified her. *Stay well away from these murderous bastards, my boy*, she thought to herself.

The soup broth was thick and hearty, the vegetables softening. She added tins of lentils, stirred slowly.

Paul moved over to the kitchen door, looked through into the dining room. Watching his brother, Leigh presumed. The young man, little more than a kid himself, was nervous, twitchy. Where James was a caged tiger, Paul was a nervous house cat, skittish and apt to bolt or react badly at the slightest provocation. Deanna seemed to be the only stable one among the three, but she was cold, holding her nerves in check with arrogant will.

"You think he's got a plan?" Leigh asked, as the woman leaned on the countertop beside her, watching casually.

"Best you don't talk to me."

Leigh nodded, pursed her lips. She took up a piece of potato, blew on it gently and then tested it with her teeth. Maybe another ten minutes. Truth was, a soup like this was best left to simmer for a few hours, but there wasn't the opportunity for that.

"Your friend Rick is going to die."

"I know."

Leigh glanced over, Deanna shrugged.

"I know you give a shit," Leigh said.

Deanna's face crumpled slightly, then she looked away. "Of course I give a shit. He's my friend."

"If you got him to a hospital, soon, he might live."

Deanna nodded gently, looking at the floor. "Not gonna happen."

"What did you guys do?"

There was silence for a while and Leigh thought Deanna wasn't going to answer. She tried to think of something else to say, desperate to get the woman talking, establish some common humanity between them.

"It was a bank robbery. It went… bad."

"How many?"

Deanna looked up, one eyebrow raised. "How many what?"

"How many did you kill before Rick got shot? Before you got away."

Deanna sighed. "A guard and two cops."

Leigh blew air out of her cheeks, looked back to the soup and resumed stirring. No wonder there was no chance James would risk a hospital. Bad enough to end up caught for bank robbery, but murder as well? Three murders, two of them police, these guys would never see freedom again. Unless… After a moment, she asked, "James killed them?"

Deanna stared for a moment. Thoughts flickered by behind her eyes, perhaps wondering how much she should say. Perhaps thinking it might be nice to unburden herself. *Come on,* Leigh thought. *Talk to me.*

Deanna sniffed in a quick breath. "James killed the guard first. Then Rick killed the first cop and James the second."

Leigh nodded. "So you and Paul didn't kill anyone?"

"No."

"You could use that."

Deanna frowned. "What do you mean?"

Leigh put the spoon down against the edge of the pot and turned to face the other woman. "This doesn't have to keep getting worse. You can end it. You and Paul are both armed. Two of you, one of him. Shoot James. Or demand he do what you say and shoot him if he doesn't." Leigh saw her brother again, flying backwards, his chest opened to the cold air. She desperately wanted James dead, despite her earlier determination to see no more killing. She pressed the thought away, took a deep breath. She needed to be the calm one. The rational one. Deanna was shaking her head, so Leigh plunged on. "Think about it. You didn't kill anyone. You got dragged into this by James. First chance you got, you took control, you didn't want any killing, you had to stop him. You could cut us free and just head to a hospital. Rick might live. Hand James in, get yourself and Paul a better chance."

Deanna huffed a laugh and shook her head. "A better chance at what? You have no idea how this stuff works for people like us, lady. We're poor, we're scum, we have records. No judge would give a fuck whether we pulled the trigger or not. We'd get the maximum for robbery, we'd get the max for murder or accessory. Blowing James away now won't ease our sentences any. We're not rich, lawyered-up folk."

"You think James is going to calm down and leave? Find a way out for you all?"

Deanna nodded. "That's what I'm hoping. Once everything calms down a bit, we'll get away, find a new life. This went bad, but it doesn't have to get worse."

"It probably will though."

"Enough chatter!" James strode into the kitchen and roughly shouldered Leigh away from Deanna.

"Hey!"

He turned, raised a hand as if to slap her and she cringed away, hating herself for it even as she did so. For a moment she imagined James raising a hand to Deanna like this, and the woman standing there, staring, ready to be hit. A blush of shame rose in her cheeks, but James had already turned his attention to the pot of soup.

"This ready?" he asked.

"Yeah, probably."

"Let's get some liquid in Rick first," he said to Deanna. "Then we'll serve up bowls for everyone else. Paul, find some bread. Deanna, tie this bitch up again and we'll do it ourselves from here."

Deanna shrugged at Leigh, offered a half-smile. She reached out to take Leigh's upper arm and guide her, but Leigh shook her off.

"I can find my own way, thanks."

As they went through the dining room, past the too-still, too-grey Rick, Deanna said, "Just be chill, okay? No trouble. I'll convince James to leave as soon as I can. Just be good through the night, yeah?"

BEFORE

THE night was long and neither of them slept. Michael visited their spot of refuge numerous times, cajoling them, cursing them, saying the most depraved and appalling things. But it was evident to Clay that Molly had been right. He could harangue them, but had no real power. Molly winced at the pain he caused in her head, but nothing more. He was stronger where he'd killed. He tried numerous ploys to get them back out into the main hotel but they remained resolute, not moving.

"Could he do more out there?" Clay asked.

"Let's not find out," Molly said. She regularly covered her eyes, pressed fingers against her temples, but assured him the headache was nothing compared to what had hit her in the kitchen.

The pale pink smudge of dawn that eventually crept through the glassless window above them was one of the most beautiful things Clay had ever seen. They waited longer, until full light an hour later, then slowly stretched aching muscles and emerged cautiously back into the main lounge. The high open space between the wooden columns was empty. No writhing black shadows whipped and quested through the air. Everything was mundane, almost boring in its normality.

"Hard to believe any of it was real," Clay said, his voice a low whisper.

"But we know it was." Molly's tone rang stronger and he recognized her determination. "Michael!" she shouted, making Clay wince. "Michael Ellery, show yourself."

Clay sensed a mild shift in the air, but no one became apparent. "You think other people would have seen what we saw last night?" he asked.

"I don't know. I was thinking the same thing. Our sight lets us notice a lot other people don't see, but could anyone *not* have been aware of that gateway in the hearth?"

"Is that what it was?"

"I don't really know. But that's how I plan to treat it. It's clearly a spot of significant emotional resonance for Michael, and that's what we need. My grandmother taught me how to send powerful spirits away. She said sometimes the walls between worlds is thin, often rubbed away by atrocity. She talked about strange things people saw when they were at war. Or in the death camps. She told me a story once of one she dealt with. You know, I never believed that story, not really. But now? I wish I had given it more credence. I think she knew I didn't accept it as truth, but she made sure I listened anyway. Previously when I've nudged ghosts over, I've gently told them they can go, suggested they let go of whatever holds them, and every time they've seemed relieved and drifted away. But Michael, he's different. He's pure fury and hate, tethering himself here against the pull of whatever wants him, so it's reaching for him. He needs to be pushed."

Clay looked around the big, mostly empty hotel. All the promise, all the possibility, had fled in the night as he huddled in the dark. "Moll, I think we should sell up."

"What?"

"This was a mistake."

She turned to look at him, her face soft, but he saw the refusal in her eyes. "What little money we have is now entirely tied up in this place, love."

"So we sell and get it back."

"Remember how hard it was for Henry Carrell to sell this place, with its history? We were the only ones dumb enough to take it on. It's kind of a one way trip, I think."

Clay looked down at the floor, unable to hold her gaze. "Don't say that. It sounds too final."

She laughed. "I meant financially, not existentially!" She stepped forward, tipped his chin up with one finger and put her other hand on his shoulder. "Listen to me, my sweet, sharp sword. Last night was terrifying, but Michael is dead. They're all dead. Let's cast him out. Then it's done. We have the power here, in the day time especially. We are the living and this is the realm of life."

Clay wondered about that, thinking of the things they'd seen the night before. Was Michael all of it, or was there something else? Something beyond Michael, some primeval catalyst? He couldn't articulate the nebulous thoughts. "You're really not scared?"

"Not now, in the light. We take this place back. We'll be done by lunchtime."

And her word was true. She burned sage, she spoke powerfully in a strong and strident voice, insisting any restless spirits leave and stop resisting the call. Clay caught glimpses of shadows moving and melting away. Within a couple of hours the entire hotel felt cleaner, more airy and bright.

"Just Michael then," Molly said. She went to the kitchen, holding Clay's hand, and called to him again.

A wave of rage passed over Clay and he realised it wasn't his. The anger permeated his skin, seemed to swell his cells and forced his heart to race.

"Molly, I–"

"I know. I feel him."

Clay tensed, tried not to crush her hand in his. He clenched his teeth and a soft growl escaped as he resisted the presence.

Molly barked a short phrase in a language Clay had never heard before and he had never sensed such control from her. She was truly powerful. The anger drained out of him like water from a sink with the plug pulled and Michael's shade rose from the floor like smoke. Face twisted in fury, he coalesced into his human form and reached forward, hands clawing as though he meant to throttle Molly. But though his presence was intense, though Molly winced in pain, her free hand pressing to her temple, Michael's presence was nothing like the night before.

"Time to go, you evil little shit!" Molly said.

Michael growled, then tipped his head back and howled, an unnatural, guttural sound.

"You are dead, Michael Ellery, and this is the realm of life. Move on!" A sensation of drag pulled through the air and Molly turned, still holding Clay's hand. "Pull him with us, love."

"How?"

"Just will it."

Clay tried to do just that, imagined an invisible tether tied to Michael's neck like a rope in those old westerns he enjoyed, where the good guy would haul the bad guy into town, stumbling and cursing behind the hero's horse.

"You fucking worms!" Michael hissed. "You fetid abominations, fuck your mothers!"

"Now, now," Molly said, her tone soft, almost conciliatory. "There's no need for that. I know you're sick, Michael. You need peace. You deserve rest. It's too late to correct anything you've done, but you can go now."

They stood before the hearth in the dining room. It emanated cold, like a refrigerator door left open instead of a large square of neatly hewn grey stones.

Molly moved them to one side of the hearth and gestured to it. "In you go, Michael."

"This is not the way of things!" the malevolent shade insisted. "You are weak. You are *meat*!"

Molly's voice rose, loud and strong. "Michael Ellery, I banish you! For your sins, in the name of the light, in the name of the living, I send you forth! Begone!"

"This is not how it is meant to be!" Michael screamed, but he staggered forward as if dragged by unseen hands. "It wants more! I can give it more, even now, like this!" He looked up and around. "You said you would protect me!" he yelled.

"Michael Ellery, I banish you! For your sins, in the name of the light, in the name of the living, I send you forth! Begone!"

Clay's shirt rippled in a sudden, icy breeze. A deep but distant howling rose up from the hearth. His bones were hollowed by it, his heart a frozen shard in his chest.

"You remember my words?" Molly asked him. He nodded. "Together then!"

"Michael Ellery, we banish you!" they yelled together. "For your sins, in the name of the light, in the name of the living, we send you forth! Begone!"

It was all Molly's strength, not his, but he willed her to be right. For this to work. Dark clouds whipped and swirled above the pale stone and Clay looked away. Michael's scream was agonized as his form stretched and warped and curled away into the hearth.

"It needs more bloooood..."

"Push him with your mind," Molly said. "Picture him forced through, never to return. Visualize the land of life forever sealed to him."

Clay did as she asked, and Michael wailed again. The sensation of drag increased and Clay staggered. His foot caught the edge of the hearth stone and he fell, clipped his head against the wide mantle. Pain whined above his eye and blood dripped, but he stood again, ignored the dizziness and concentrated only on Michael being pushed far away. It didn't matter where, just nowhere in the land of the living. He sensed a slamming shut.

Molly was muttering something again, her grandmother's cunning tricks no doubt. The frozen wind eased, the sense of desperate falling lessened.

Molly hurried back into the kitchen, leaving Clay to stare in bemused wonder at the normal, plain stones of the fireplace, one hand pressed against the small cut above his eye. Red spots stood out on the grey stone.

Molly returned with a large pot of rock salt and shook it liberally all around the edge of the hearth's base. Then taking small handfuls she threw them in, muttering more of those strange words. She pulled a small glass bottle from her pocket and began trickling a thick, gentle stream all around the hearth's perimeter, careful to maintain an unbroken line over the scattered salt. "Sage oil," she said to Clay's raised eyebrow. "To make sure he stays gone." It meant nothing to him, but he accepted her greater knowledge.

All was still then for several moments. As Clay opened his mouth to ask if it was done, a sudden, high howl echoed through the bush behind the hotel. It seemed far away, but powerful and unlike any creature he had ever heard before. Unlike anything he had ever considered even. It sounded both agonized and somehow triumphant, almost gleeful. He jumped, turned in the direction of the thick trees.

"What the hell was that?"

"Michael's last fury?" Molly's eyes were narrowed though, like she wasn't entirely sure.

Clay sucked in a long, deep breath. Any sensation of malice had indeed gone. The hotel felt cleaner and clearer than ever. "So it's done?"

"Yes. Like I told you, in the light, we have all the power."

"Moll, was any of that really real?"

She laughed, kissed him. "How real is anything, my love? What is reality?"

"So it's done. It seems too easy."

"It is easy, Clay. We are the living. We have the power. Fear is the strongest weapon of the dead. When we refuse to fear, when we take control, it's simple."

It needs more bloooood...

Clay wondered what Michael had meant. Was there more to this than Michael's furious ghost? "So it's finished?"

Molly smiled, laid a hand against his cheek. "It is."

Clay frowned. "You're sure?"

She squeezed his shoulder. "You worry too much. Can you feel any presence remaining?"

"Well, no. But we couldn't feel him before either."

She shrugged. "Then I guess we'll wait and see. But trust me. It'll be fine."

And for nearly half a century, it was.

PAUL

IN NIGHT in the hotel was quiet and dark. Paul's fear had become a kind of numbness, resigned to the horrible and absurd situation they were in. James had fallen into some kind of furious stability where he would accept no conversation, no suggestion of any other course of action. Like he had become locked on rails and would see this impossible situation through to its destination, though none of them could have any idea what that might be.

They'd given Rick some of the hot broth from the soup, but he'd coughed weakly and almost choked. Paul wasn't sure any of it had actually gone down inside the poor bastard. Certainly not enough to help him recover. Rick was going to die. There could be no other outcome there, surely.

Then they'd freed one hand of each of the family in the lounge and let them spoon soup mechanically into themselves. Except Marcus, who'd sat staring at the floor, unresponsive. Eventually, when the others were finished, James told Deanna to take Marcus's untouched bowl away again. Leigh had cajoled the man to eat, but he'd ignored everyone. His dislocation made Paul uncomfortable.

Then, at James's instruction, he and Deanna had taken each of the hostages, one at a time, to the bathroom at the back of the dining room, before retying them to the thick wooden columns. They had used the pistol that idiot Simon had held as he snuck up on them, kept it pressed against the body of the hostage even as they pissed.

The old man, Clay, had complained about the position he was bound in, asked if he could be secured another way. Paul sympathized, the man's hip and leg were clearly causing him great pain, and his shoulders were stiff. Paul had nearly had to carry the poor bastard and hold him up while he pissed. But James would hear no claims for mercy. And the old man stared daggers at Paul as the knots were retied.

"You'll suffer for this," Clay had whispered to him. "One way or another, you'll suffer horribly. You know that, right? Stand up to James now, before it's too late."

Paul had told the old man to shut the fuck up, even though the truth of the words stung him. Grant had said something similar as he had been tied up again, too. But it wasn't the old timer's admonition that had disturbed him the most. On the way to and from the bathroom, Clay had looked at Rick's body, stretched grey and still on the tables in front of the hearth, and the old man's face had been strange. If Paul had to put a name to it, he would have called it fear. But more than that. Clay looked terrified.

Now the hotel was dark and still. James refused to sleep and sat in the lounge watching over the hostages. Was James thinking of using them to buy their freedom? It could work. Maybe. Or would he kill them and run? Or run and leave them tied up? Whatever, his brother refused to take his eyes off the four of them. And James's gaze had a glassy, feverish sheen that caused Paul no small measure of fear himself.

Deanna and he had been instructed to rest and, despite everything, a deep and dragging fatigue pulled at him as he sat in the dining room. He had wanted to go to one of the bedrooms, it was a hotel after all. An actual bed, some private, quiet space, would have been a blessing. But James refused that too.

"We stay together," his brother had said through teeth clenched in mania. "Go rest in there with Rick. Deanna, you too. Both of you sleep and I'll watch these bastards."

James sat with the dead guy's pistol, his shotgun on the bench in the kitchen. Paul and Deanna kept their shotguns to hand and took seat cushions from a couple of the couches in the lounge to put together makeshift beds on the dining room floor. They stayed near the fireplace, desperate for its warmth as the end of winter cold bit down, but not too near. If they got too close, the death stench of Rick became too strong. The man was barely alive, though his chest did hitch in short, shallow breaths every few seconds. He would moan sometimes, in pain or fear or both they couldn't know.

Paul had tried to look, to see what he might do to make his friend more comfortable, but impotent despair quickly replaced any desire to help. Rick's mouth hung open and slack, his breaths wet and rasping, and foul to smell. The stink of shit and blood clung to him like a shroud, his skin waxy and grey, almost green. Spatters of Rick's blood covered the ground around the table he lay on, and the otherwise clean tiles of the kitchen where they'd carried him through. Despite Leigh's stitches, Paul thought perhaps his wound was still bleeding as well.

One blood-stained hand had slipped from Rick's chest and hung limp off the side of the table, the fingers almost brushing the floor. Paul lifted it, tucked it back in, appalled at the cool clamminess of Rick's skin. But the hand had immediately slipped free and hung down again, like a rag. Paul hadn't wanted to touch it again, and left it.

He tried not to think about it while Deanna snored. Slowly, his eyes drifted closed and agitated sleep carried him along on a rough stream of barely held unconsciousness. He heard Deanna's snores and grunts, the rustle of her restlessness even as he battled his own. He slipped deeper into sleep only for nightmare images to haul him back up again. The bank guard's head, that guy Simon's chest and his glistening organs, Rick's face rotting away even before he died, his breath clouding out, taking form, a cloying stench that wrapped around Paul's throat and tightened, tightened, throttled him.

Paul gasped, bouncing slightly on the cushions as he startled from sleep. At least half a dozen times he sank under only to be ripped back. But his exhaustion was almost all-consuming and he repeatedly fell into dark depths. His brain registered something strange. A rippling, pale red luminescence painting deep crimson shadows across the ceiling. Something black and writhing across the floor beside him, reaching, like an eel sniffing out prey.

Entangled in the woolly threads of sleep, Paul tried to make sense of what he'd seen. Or had he dreamed it? There were subtle wet sounds, like someone eating too loudly. Then a dragging sound, and a heavy thud that he was sure he'd actually felt through the floor boards, made him grumble in his half-asleep state and turn onto his side. His eyes flickered again, and once more he was confused by the redness. He opened his eyes more fully, his back to the fireplace, and stared in confusion at the black rectangle of the doorway through to the kitchen. Wan red light washed the walls around it, like late afternoon sunlight through scarlet curtains. But it was night.

It came from the floor, slightly brighter, rippling, blood red in patches that rose and skittered then scurried away. Paul blinked, tried to place the patterns of the weird movements, then realised they matched where blood had been left across the tiles. Was the blood rising from the floor, lit up inside? He began to shift onto his elbow for a better look, sleep slipping away.

The dragging sound again and a low moan of pain.

Paul took a shuddering breath, wakefulness pushing through ever more quickly, and rolled onto his back. Red light danced across the ceiling and long, wavering tendrils of night writhed through it above him.

"The fuck?"

Deanna snored on and Paul took another breath, trying hard to shake off the deep exhaustion that wanted to pull him back into sleep. He turned to his left and all fatigue washed out of him as adrenaline surged through his body. Rick was on the floor in front of the fireplace, his flesh alive with undulating red. An icy chill pushed towards Paul, made gooseflesh stand up on his skin and his breath catch in his throat. Rick's body rippled, as though tiny things ran back and forth beneath his skin.

Paul sat up with a cry, scrambling back on his hands and heels, mouth agape at the impossible sight. Rick's head tipped back, his eyes wide and beseeching. One pallid hand, weak and grey, lifted and flopped back, reaching for Paul.

"Heeellllpp meeeee..." Rick slurred, his voice a slush of pain and feeble need.

"Rick! Rick, I..." Paul's voice was tight, no words could make any sense of what he saw.

Blood soaked freshly up through the sheet still wrapped around Rick's body and was immediately lit with that foul crimson luminescence. His body arched, teeth gritted in pain, and then fell back. Paul stared in horror as Rick seemed to deflate, his skin pulling tighter to the bones as the red light grew up from him, solidifying into dark, scarlet-black shapes, hard to perceive in the gloom. They scurried towards the kitchen, as though his blood was coming alive in pieces and lumps and running away.

Paul jumped up, staggered back, staring in disbelief. He wanted to stamp on the glowing things like so many cockroaches, but at the same time was terrified to touch them, even with the thick boots he still wore. They glowed and rolled, tiny whipping tendrils flickering out to propel them along. They rushed in a flock towards the kitchen and across the floor, as though heading for the door.

Rick's breath hissed out, his face constricted and agonized and somehow reduced.

"Rick!" Paul cried out, and his friend howled, terrified horror, and fell still.

"RICK!" Paul screamed, as the horrendous lights faded and fled the room.

The weakness of normal flame in the hearth seemed dull as shadow in comparison.

Deanna sat up with a startled cry and James ran in from the lounge next door. The voices of the family, tense and confused, sounded behind him.

"What the hell is happening?" James said, the pistol still live and loaded in his hand.

Paul turned to him. "Rick!" He pointed to the pale and desiccated corpse on the floor.

"What happened?"

"His body was moved by these... I don't know what. They sucked him dry and ran away!"

"The fuck are you talking about? You're dreaming, you idiot."

Paul turned, pointed to where Rick lay. "Look at him!"

CLAY

CLAY wanted more than anything to talk to Molly, but her shade was frustratingly absent. Well, if he were honest, he wanted more than anything to move, to be untied. His right hip was on fire with a bone deep pain and no amount of shifting his weight to the various limited extents of his bonds would ease it. The agony lanced down the outside of his thigh and into his knee, caused a pulsing throb behind his kneecap. And his hands were tingling with pins and needles, his shoulders aflame from being pulled back all night. Surely Grant, Leigh, and Marcus were beginning to feel the discomfort of extended restriction too, even with their young, fit bodies. He hoped it was nothing close to his own. But all that had become secondary to the mayhem. And his fear.

In the heavy darkness of the deep night the tense but somnolent hotel had exploded in shouts and alarm. The injured one, though he was likely almost dead anyway if the whispered conversations with Leigh were to be believed, had been attacked somehow. But not simply attacked, maybe that wasn't the right word. According to a nearly hysterical Paul, he had been sucked dry by moving, wriggling red lights and icy cold winds. He was definitely dead now. On top of everything else, as if the home invasion, the murder of Simon, Rueben alone in the woods, wasn't enough, now this? Were his fears of almost fifty years finally coming around? He and Molly had never learned what set Michael off on his psychopathic rampage. Had it started with something like this?

After they had made the hotel theirs all those years ago, they had slowly put their mark on it. The guest wing was finished, internal walls and fittings put in. Furniture was bought, supplies, personal touches all around. They had found several of the carved sigils Henry Carrell had mentioned, and Clay sanded them all away, then put internal walls over the spots, or painted where the walls were already in. All were simply signs, they decided, of Ellery's psychosis, and best removed and forgotten.

They had cleared the trees in a large swathe behind the hotel, to make the lawns old man Ellery himself had intended. When they took those trees down, there had been strange carvings in many of the trunks too. Sigils and symbols, swirls and crossed lines, some things that looked almost like a language. He and Molly had discussed them at length, especially the ones around the area where they guessed the brother, Trent, had been impaled. They were densest there, and most complicated. Clay had even copied a few down and done some research over the years, but had never managed to decipher them, never matched them to anything. He'd long since thrown away the notes. More of Michael Ellery's psychosis, Molly had assured him, that's all. Finished now. Those trees had been cut and dried and eventually burned in the hearths over the following winters.

There had been a lot more carvings throughout the woods. He'd found several over the years and suspected he hadn't discovered them all. Whenever he did notice one, he desecrated it with a knife or hatchet, ensured it was unrecognizable. There were several scarred trees in the deep bush behind the hotel as a result of his wandering.

The marks went far beyond the not inconsiderable distances he had traversed over the years, though he avoided the loose scree a kilometre or so directly behind the hotel, as Carrell had suggested he do. They maintained the low wire fence back there to ensure guests didn't wander accidentally into the loose fall. He'd ventured to the edges of it once or twice, in the early days, but the shifting rock and barren, stony hollow beyond looked exactly as dangerous as Carrell had suggested, so he was happy to take the man's advice. With so much verdant wilderness all around, it was easy to avoid that part, and they always recommended their guests do the same. Even the trees there were stunted and sick-looking, unable to thrive in the unstable ground. Beyond it, the mountain rose again, thick with vegetation as far as the naked eye could see, but that was well beyond their title.

When he and Grant had worked with Rueben to build the treehouse, the main consideration in its location was the lack of carvings in that particular spot. He had never mentioned this to his son or grandson, of course, but couldn't help wondering now. Perhaps Michael was really gone, but did those symbols, the root of the young man's psychosis, still somehow persist? Michael had insisted on some commanding entity, and Molly had assured him it was all in Michael's head. But what if it wasn't? What if something had simply lain dormant all this time, until now, awaiting some kind of trigger?

He recalled his conversation of the day before. *You worry too much*, Molly had said. His worry, it seemed, had been well-placed. But what was he to tell the others?

As James had screamed at Paul and Deanna, as Paul had promised he wasn't lying, as Deanna had cursed and cajoled, Clay had taken the opportunity to talk to his family.

"You have to listen to me now and not ask questions," he said as they sat in the dark. "This place has a dark and bloody history. Molly and I always kept it to ourselves, and I'll tell you the full story one day, but for now simply know this. Molly and me, we fixed it. Or we thought we did. And for decades it's been just fine. But these people, these events, they've... I don't know, maybe they've started something. Put something in motion."

"What are talking about, Dad?" Grant's face twisted in confusion. "A dark and bloody history?"

"It was easier to keep things secret in those days," Clay said. "No internet messing everything up, I suppose." He paused, thinking along lines he had never considered before. Where did the shade of Michael go? When Clay reached out with his mind, when he stretched the limits of his sight, there was nothing. No spirits, no entities, like he was used to. Nothing except a vaguely cold sensation from the dining room, and that was probably his own bias. His memory. But the sight was ever ambiguous. Gods, how he wanted Molly and her knowledge, her surety.

"Dad! What do you mean they started something?" Grant demanded.

Clay shook his head, grimaced in consternation. "Look, it's not something I can easily explain, okay? But those people are going to be even more irrational now, even more on edge. We have to be careful. Whatever you feel, whatever you think or hear, close your eyes. Just don't look at it."

"Clay," Leigh said, her voice soft, fearful but also concerned. "What do you mean? What happened before?"

Clay sighed, lost for any sane way to explain. His secret, shared only with Molly, ignored by Grant's sister, Cindy, had become a front and centre madness. And the bigger secret they'd kept all these years, the horrific origins of this wonderful hotel that had given them all their lives and their livelihoods, threatened to come hammering back. "Just trust me, please?"

They reluctantly agreed, Grant and Leigh anyway. Marcus remained close to catatonic. He hadn't even used the bathroom, had been unresponsive when Paul suggested it, so they left him alone. Clay hoped he would find a way back soon. At least back to conversing, being with them in this.

James came storming back into the lounge, demanding answers. "What the fuck happened to Rick?"

"How can we know?" Clay said. "We've been tied up here the whole time, you know that. You've been watching us. What's happened?"

"Rick's dead, that's what. But he's sucked dry. He looks like a mummified corpse, dead for centuries."

"What do you mean?" Leigh asked.

"Exactly that. Paul says red lights sucked him dry." James stomped across the room, leaned down to yell into Leigh's face. "How do you fucking explain that, nurse?"

"I can't!" Leigh burst into tears.

"Leave her be!" Grant yelled. "God damn it, you fucker, leave her!"

James rounded on him. "You want a piece of me, huh?"

"Fuck yes," Grant said quietly. "Untie me, you psycho, let's go."

"Grant, no, please," Leigh said.

Clay became ever more desperate to be freed. He willed his son to stop antagonising James further.

James began pacing, swinging a shotgun dangerously from side to side, his face a mask of shadows in the firelight from the loungeroom hearth. Simon's pistol was jammed into the back of his jeans. "Paul says the lights sucked out his blood and then slithered away, out through the kitchen. All the blood is gone from there too, and the dining room. Every bit of spilled blood, gone like some ghost maid came and mopped up!"

Paul and Deanna stood close together by the dining room door, watching. They looked almost resigned, like they had seen these storms before and hoped this one would pass like maybe the others had. But what blew them over? Would James only calm down with an act of violence? He seemed the type, Clay thought, to pressure up and blow, repeatedly.

"How can that happen?" James yelled, rounding on Deanna and Paul at last.

"Bro, I told you what happened. I wasn't dreaming!" Paul wrung his hands together, like he was trying to wash blood from them. "I woke up. The stuff, the red stuff, it emptied him out and scurried away. It had these tendrils, these waving things like something from underwater, that ran it along somehow."

"It?"

"Them! All of them, loads of the stuff."

"What stuff?"

"I don't know! I don't know what it was. He woke up, you know? As it happened, he looked up and begged me to help him, but there was nothing I could do."

James tipped his head back and spat an incoherent shout into the rafters. When his eyes came back to stare at Clay and then Grant, they were frighteningly calm. "This makes no sense," he said in a low growl. "But I guess we don't have Rick to worry about any more. Maybe that makes things simpler, yeah? You people know more than you're telling me, and I will have answers. Who do I need to hurt first."

Leigh's sobs had become short, sharp gasps and the strength was back in her voice. "We can't tell you anything, James. We don't know. Let's wait until morning. Until it's light."

Clay wasn't sure what difference light would make now. The lights in the dining room were bright. But it was perhaps distraction enough.

"Really, James," Grant said, his voice cold. "We don't know what happened to your friend. Maybe you should all just go, before it happens to you."

James looked at Grant, his eyes narrowed. "That likely?"

Grant smiled, shrugged as much as his bonds would allow. "No idea. Really, I have no clue. But you want to risk it?"

Without another word, James returned to the couch where had been sitting before the mayhem, watching them manically. Clay had hoped the man would fall asleep, but the mania that drove the murderous lunatic kept him alert and focussed. Scarily focussed. James sat there, perched on the edge of the cushions, the shotgun across his knees, and he stared. Clay had to look away. Those eyes were themselves an abyss he had no desire to gaze into for any longer than he had to.

"I'm not going back in there," Paul said.

"Then sleep here." James didn't move when he spoke, like a snake coiled, ready to strike.

The lounge sank into tense silence once more, but for the crackle of the fire. The orange light of it flickered, shadows writhed. Deanna turned out the dining room lights, then came and picked a couch to lie on. Clay watched the silhouette of a stuffed stag's head shift uncannily on the wall in the firelight. Paul chose a couch too. James remained perched. Slowly, dark silence settled.

Clay wasn't sure if he slept, fear and pain kept him from any real rest. Maybe he dozed. Before too long, the russet smudge of dawn began to lighten the windows.

Get going, Roo, Clay thought to himself. *Get to Laura and Bob. Get the police up here.*

RUEBEN

RUEBEN ran through the trees, lit silver by the light of a full moon that hung gravid and heavy, too low in the sky. He felt that if he could just reach out far enough he would be able to grab it, climb aboard and be swept to safety. But his arms were too short, as were his legs to outrun the slavering beast that hunted him.

Leaves crunched, as dry and dead as the thin branches that whipped and snatched at him, the roots that tried to trip him. His breath rasped, tore at his throat as it tried to escape his tightened chest all at once. Tears squeezed from his eyes, blurred his vision, spikes of pain punched behind his forehead. He would never make it, never escape the beast, and its giant jaws would close, its myriad teeth, sharp as diamonds, would tear and crush his flesh, crunch his bones, rend him into memories.

Something huge loomed from the bush to his left, tall and red and muscular. A kangaroo with burning crimson eyes and a forest of sharp teeth in its overstretched maw. Rueben cried out, swerved away through the trees, but the bigger, older, meaner thing was still behind him.

A hard, scarred root curled up from the desiccated leaf litter, arching like a snake and grabbed his foot, sent him sprawling into the hard ground. The last of his breath shot out and he wheezed, whined in pain and panic, coloured lights danced behind his eyes. He scrabbled at the ground, managed to roll over onto his back. He was surrounded by demonic kangaroos and wombats, all red-eyed and slavering, they circled him, growling. Then the bigger thing caught up. Bright moonlight between the tall, skeletal trees became obscured with a stain of black, like ink spreading through the sky. It loomed, grew larger and lower, a behemoth, inconceivable in size, swooping low through the forest, uncountable teeth glittering as a fetid gale of breath stole the last of Rueben's will. Two bright red eyes, each the size of a car, slashed through the middle with a vertical pupil that contained galaxies, sprang open, piercing, and pinned him to the ground like a bug. Rueben screamed.

He found himself swaddled in something clinging and hot that rustled and scratched, and he thrashed against it. But it was natural, not the cold, terrible beast of his dreams. He fought his way out from the crinkling space blanket and the damp blankets beyond, and sat up in his quiet, cold treehouse. For several seconds he simply waited, taking quick, sharp breaths, trying to shake off the terror of the dream. It had been so real, more than any other nightmare of his life. He still smelled the dry leaves and the beast's foul exhalation. He swallowed a sob, watched his breath mist in the wan light.

It was amazing he had fallen asleep at all, convinced as he was that fear would keep him awake all night. He had lain huddled in his tentative protection for hours, terrified, just waiting for day, but obviously exhaustion had been more powerful than fright. Grief sat heavy in his gut as memories of Uncle Simon flooded back. And with those memories, the faces of the gang with their guns, his parents frightened eyes, Grandpa Clay's stoic, furious acceptance. And Rueben's sure knowledge that only he could help, only he could do anything about it.

He realised the day outside was bright. Bad enough that he had fallen asleep, he had also stayed asleep well past dawn. He scrambled on his knees to the window and looked out at the cold, gloomy woods, the trees scratching at the pale grey overcast sky. He looked at his watch. After half past eight.

He had intended to run all the way to Laura and Bob Hickman's place at first light, to get there as early as possible. He was already well over an hour later than that, maybe more. But no matter. The plan remained the same. He had to get there, explain, call the police. Then everything would be okay.

He trembled, with more than simply cold. He had never felt so alone in his life. Movement made him turn and he saw Grandma Molly standing just inside the door of the treehouse, smiling at him. "Not real, and not crazy," he muttered, but stared at her all the same. He remembered the horrible situation on the driveway the day before, of Uncle Simon flying backwards from the ear-splitting blast of a shotgun, then Grandpa Clay looking up at something and nodding. And Rueben had seen Grandma Molly.

"Are you really there?" he asked, desperate for her to be real, or even not real but still there nonetheless, just so he wasn't so alone any more.

Molly's face blossomed in joy. "Yes, child!" she said, and moved nearer to crouch in front of him. "You hear me now?"

Incredibly, he did. "Is it really you?"

"Yes, it's really me. Oh, Rueben, I'm so pleased you've finally accepted your gift. You have the sight, as I did, as your grandpa does. Your daddy doesn't have it, it skipped him, but his sister, your Aunt Cindy has it. Though she's never accepted it. Perhaps one day you can talk with her about it. But none of that matters right now. What matters is that you embrace it, can you do that?"

"My gift?"

"You have the sight, child. You see the dead if they choose to reveal themselves to you. I always thought we could see them whether they willed it or not, but I was wrong about that. Sometimes the dead linger, and you can talk with them. So can Clay. Which means I can talk with you both and you'll all get through this."

Rueben swallowed, mouth dry, mind spinning. Surely this was all a madness, born of his desperation not to be alone. Maybe he was still asleep and this was some new twisted aspect of his dream. "How can that be real? How can *you* be real?" Could grief-induced hallucinations be this clear?

Molly favoured him with a soft, indulgent expression. "Let's just consider for now that maybe it's real, maybe it's not. Perhaps it's your mind, filling in gaps, presenting me to give you something to hold onto. Someone to talk to. Maybe I'm a coping mechanism. Is that so bad? Or maybe I'm really your Grandma. Does it matter?"

He stared for long moments, considering. All he wanted was to no longer be alone. "I guess not."

"No. What matters is that if you can hear me, I can help you. But for now, you already know what to do, don't you?"

Rueben nodded. "I need to get to Laura and Bob's place. Tell them what's happening. To call the police."

"Exactly. And it'll take you a few hours to get down there, so you better get moving. But eat first. Take care of yourself, yes?"

Rueben nodded again, tried to lick dry lips. He was so thirsty. "Okay." He punched the straw into a juice box and sucked it dry, then immediately drank another. He tore open a muesli bar, ate it in three furious bites. His strength seemed to harden with the sustenance.

He grabbed a few more muesli bars and stuffed them into his coat pocket. "Tell Grandpa I'm leaving now. I'll get help! I'll eat more on the way." He pocketed another juice box too.

Molly reached out, as if she wanted to lay her hand against his cheek as she had done so many times before, but stopped short and smiled. Then she stood and left, fading as she went through the door. Rueben stared for several seconds at where she'd been. Was it possible that all this time she had been there for him to talk to and he'd kept denying her? She was real and he was crazy, after all.

Well, so be it. He would take any help he could get. Anything to give him courage, and he realised that's what she had done. A ravening hunger tore at his stomach. He grabbed two muesli bars from the box and tore them open, wolfed them down in quick succession, desperate to ease the dizziness he felt. It was exhaustion, he knew, despite the hours of broken, nightmare-filled sleep. He may have been unconscious, but it was far from a good rest. And it was fear too, stealing his equilibrium. But as the food hit his insides he felt a little better.

He scrambled from his tree house via the branches, not willing to leave his ladder down for someone else to find. It seemed irrational, but anything to protect his bolt hole, however tenuous, gave him a sensation of control, albeit largely false.

Okay, he could do this. Grandma Molly would tell Clay he was on his way, and Clay would reassure his mum and dad, and Uncle Marcus. Would they even believe Clay? They'd have to. What choice did they have? And they would stay brave and quiet, they would do whatever the bad people asked of them until help arrived. Rueben imagined a huge team of police, armed and armoured, storming the place and taking away the evil shit who had shot Uncle Simon. And the bastard's evil friends. It would all be okay, he only had to get to the road, and then it was simply a matter of time. He took a deep breath and set off at a jog through the trees.

CLAY

I JAMES finally moved, standing from the couch like a snake uncoiling. His eyes were no less wild, and tension seemed to vibrate from him, like he might literally burst if stuck with something. And how Clay would dearly love to stick him with something, and absolutely would the first chance he got, even if it meant his certain death.

"Paul, Deanna, get up!"

His accomplices rose bleary-eyed from their couches and moved to stand beside him.

"We need breakfast." James pointed to Leigh. "Deanna, get her up. Bathroom break then get her cooking. She knows where everything is. Paul, you take each of the others, one at a time to the bathroom, then tie them back here."

"What about..?" Paul gestured with his head to the dining room.

James scowled. "I'll move him." He stalked off, limbs tight with barely contained fury. They heard him grunt with effort in the next room, then his footsteps stomped away through the kitchen.

Paul and Deanna complied with his orders without comment, too tired, too frightened, Clay thought, to say a word.

"I'll need things from the trailers," Leigh said. "Then I can feed us all."

"Deanna, she's your responsibility," Paul said. "I'll deal with these three."

Deanna nodded, untying Leigh. "Just be good, okay? No funny business."

"Sure."

Paul took Grant first, Clay's son looking left and right, as if searching for something. Was he looking for a weapon? An opportunity? Now wasn't the time. Clay gently shook his head when Grant caught his eye and Grant nodded. He returned from the bathroom and meekly allowed himself to be retied. Paul didn't ask Marcus anything, just untied him and hauled him up. As they headed into the dining room, Marcus stumbling stiffly, robotically along, Paul said, "You gotta piss, maybe shit, whatever. Just do it and I'll sit you back down."

They were gone for about five minutes and Clay began to worry. He heard Leigh and Deanna talking in low tones in the kitchen, the sounds of pans and crockery. He wondered if his daughter-in-law might be making bonds with Deanna, building an alliance against James. Leigh was smart enough, cunning enough. He hoped she didn't blow it.

Then Marcus and Paul returned and all seemed normal, within the circumstances.

"Get me up slow!" Clay barked as Paul took the ropes away from his wrists. "I got a bum hip and it's agony right now. I might fall down."

"It's okay." Paul put an arm around Clay's back, almost tenderly, and lifted him. "I'm real sorry about all this."

"Are you kidding me, son?" Clay staggered, winced at electric jolts hammering through his hip and thigh, down into his knee and back. He gasped, then stood still, breathing the pain down, slowly letting his aging legs get used to his weight again. His hands buzzed and burned as blood came back into them, his shoulders afire. "You're as responsible for all this as either of them."

"He's right," Grant said, staring daggers at Paul from where he sat on the floor. "You make a choice, son. End this now. That's within your power."

"James might not think so."

"Fuck James!" Grant spat. Clay saw the fire in his son's eyes. It frightened him a little. "Untie me and I'll finish James with my bare hands, you think I won't? You think I can't?"

Clay understood that urge, and he thought perhaps Grant did have it in him. Assuming he could avoid being shot first. Assuming Paul and Deanna let him. Both those things seemed unlikely.

"James is my brother," Paul said, as if that explained everything. Maybe for Paul it did.

Grant sneered at the kid.

"Don't think you'll get any sympathy from me," Clay said. "You want to show you're sorry? You shoot James in the bloody face and then you and Deanna leave us all the hell alone." Clay's rage surprised him, maybe spurred on by Grant, but finally given vent to his frustrations, it seemed at least cathartic to berate this idiot boy.

"He's my brother," Paul said again, weakly.

"Yeah? And Simon was my nephew. He was Marcus's husband. How do you think that feels?"

Paul's face crumpled up and for a second Clay was convinced the young man was going to cry. Then he rallied and turned to help Clay along. "Come on, you gotta go piss. Then I have to tie you up again."

"Sure. You gotta obey your psycho brother."

"He'll get you killed!" Grant yelled.

Paul tried to lead him away and Clay let out an involuntary yelp of pain.

"Wait a second. I'm an old man, dammit." Cursing his aches and pains, the years that had flown by like dry leaves in a gale, Clay leaned into his bad hip a couple of times, hanging most of his weight on Paul. He worked his shoulders, curving his chest as pain lightninged around his body. After a moment, though short of breath, he nodded. "Okay, let's go. Slow."

Freer movement began to return as they limped through the dining room, heading for the bathrooms in the back. Clay looked into the hearth as they passed. Logs stacked on the grate burned merrily, deep red underneath, the flames licking at the brickwork up into the chimney. It all appeared entirely normal. The connection wasn't there, he thought. Not now. That was just another symptom. Of what? It was beyond, somewhere. But he couldn't help thinking it was coming inexorably closer. Clay tore his gaze away, looking back towards the bathrooms. And there was Molly, smiling widely.

Paul led him past the stairs that went up to the Moore family residence, to the doors marked M and F side by side in the back wall of the dining room. As they drew near, Molly said, "He sees me. He finally spoke to me!" At Clay's raised eyebrow, she added, "Rueben! He has the sight and finally accepted me."

Clay gave an imperceptible nod as Paul led him past the spectre of his wife, through the door on the right marked M. The bathrooms were a good size, each with six stalls, and a big double sink at the end nearest the door. Narrow windows of frosted glass about eight inches deep ran along the back wall just below the ceiling.

"I gotta take a crap," Clay said.

Paul nodded, gestured inside. He remained standing by the doors, leaning against the sinks.

"You can't wait outside?" Clay asked. He pointed to the long narrow windows. "No way I'm getting out of here except through the door we came in. You really want to stand there and listen to an old man shit?"

Paul grimaced. "I guess not. Just don't be too long. I'll be right outside that door." He stepped out.

Clay went into the first stall and stood to piss. "Molly?" he asked quietly.

"Finish your business first."

He smiled, the sensation of relieving himself almost euphoric. Then he turned and saw her standing outside the stall door.

"I lied about needing a crap to buy us a couple of minutes."

"I guessed that."

"What's the betting I'll really need to go about five minutes after I go back out there?"

"Then you can just blame your age." She lifted a hand, like she wanted to lay her palm against his cheek, and the pain in her eyes was awful to behold.

"So Rueben talked to you?" Clay said, keen to distract the moment.

Molly dropped her hand, nodded. "He's accepted his gift. We can communicate now."

"And what good will that do?"

"I don't know, but there's a link between him and his family. That's good for him to know, at least."

"I can hardly tell Grant and Leigh, they won't believe me. Or understand."

"I know. But at least you know he's safe. He's scared out of his skin, but he's a brave young man. Even now, he's heading back through the bush. He's going to the Hickman's for help."

"Good boy." Clay allowed himself a smile. Maybe this would be over soon. Rueben, their secret weapon, silently being deployed. "Good boy," he said again, quietly. Then he looked up. "You know what happened last night?"

Molly's face hardened. "I heard you all talking about it, and those others."

"So what was it?"

"I don't know."

Clay frowned. "Even now, you can't tell? You can't... I don't know, go and see?"

"It doesn't work like that, my sweet sharp sword. I'm tied to you, and Rueben, others of my blood. And to this place. I can't roam too freely. I can't explore. But I feel... something. Out there."

"I was hoping you might be able to tell us what it is. And maybe what we can do."

Molly looked at the floor, shook her head. Then she looked up again. "I think maybe whatever psychosis got hold of Michael Ellery, perhaps there *was* some other trigger, after all. And it's still here."

"Yeah. But what? And what can we do about it?"

"Maybe nothing. Perhaps simply leaving is the best option."

"I tried that, after you died. Grant and Leigh put it down to grief. They want to stay, remember? At least, Grant does. I think Leigh is on the fence. She wants a more normal life for Roo."

"Maybe after all this he'll change his mind."

Clay nodded, realizing that was quite likely. Assuming there was an *after this* for any of them.

"Rueben will get help," Molly said. "Hopefully before tonight. Let's focus on that. Anything else can wait."

"You didn't tell him about that Rick guy? What happened?"

"Of course not! I told him to hurry to the Hickman's and get help. Nothing more. That's all he needs to do."

"How the fuck long does it take you to dump, old man?" Paul's voice was tense, but wavering as he pushed in through the door.

Clay stepped out of the cubicle and headed for the sinks. "I'm coming right now. Be patient, will ya."

LEIGH

I

LEIGH was a great believer in the power of food. Beyond its obvious nutritional value, she held food and the feeding of her family to be a way of showing love, of encouraging solidarity, of calming tensions. She'd learned long ago, from her mother and her grandmother, that while so many gender roles were bullshit, it seemed that women understood the power of food more intrinsically than men. She had every intention of being an agent of change on that front. Marcus was a great asset, one of the few men she'd met who embraced food on every level.

His family, his grandmother in particular, had encouraged that in him. He was passionate about food, and his passion was infectious. She remembered the offer of the spring rolls recipe to Rueben in the car and swallowed down emotion. Hold onto that thought, she told herself. They would make that happen. All this would be over soon, and one day Marcus would teach Rueben how to make Grandma Cheng's spring rolls.

Leigh herself had taught Rueben a lot of cooking tricks. When he was a toddler, he had loved to stand on the little wooden step beside the kitchen counter so he could reach to help when she was baking. He loved stirring the bowl, he studiously added ingredients, his little round face a mask of concentration. By the time he was ten he probably knew more about food and cooking than most grown men. Positive change in the world was slow, but it was inexorable.

And now Leigh tried to apply the same principles to the nightmare situation in which her family found itself. "Grab some butter from the fridge?" she asked Deanna.

The other woman nodded, retrieved the butter and handed it over. Leigh added a generous lump to a pan, then nodded to the big pile of mushrooms on the wooden board. "They need cutting. Into quarters." She crushed garlic while Deanna chopped. If only they'd let her touch a knife, it would all go more smoothly. Ironically, Deanna had put her shotgun down on the bench under the window in order to help with the preparation, and Leigh mentally calculated how easily she might make a lunge for it. But every time she moved even slightly away from the cooker, Deanna shifted herself to be between Leigh and the weapon.

Leigh tested the theory again, stepping back quickly. Almost on auto-pilot, Deanna moved, glanced up. Consciously or sub-consciously, she protected that weapon. And Leigh knew she would lose out in a physical struggle with the woman. Deanna's arms were corded with thin but strong muscles. Leigh was fit, but Deanna was mean. Where Leigh might be able to lash out in anger, Deanna carried the quiet confidence of someone who had already fought for her safety, maybe her life, on more than one occasion. She was still here.

Leigh took dried oregano from the shelf beside the cooker and added it to the butter melted in the pan. "Throw the mushrooms in."

Deanna stepped over and scraped them from the chopping board into the butter, garlic and oregano, where they sizzled and the smell instantly mixed with the strong aroma of bacon in the oven. Leigh mixed eggs and stirred them into another pot. "You want to get some bread in the toaster? Two pieces for each of us? The toaster takes eight at a time." The advantage of a kitchen designed to feed a hotel full of guests. While they hired staff to help clean the rooms and service the hotel when it was open, the kitchen remained the domain or her and Marcus. Leigh remembered all the times she and Marcus had moved around each other in here, a chaotic though graceful dance of cooking. She loved those times, loved Marcus's smiling, contented face. He was in his element in a kitchen. He called it his natural habitat. And they had learned so much from each other.

"You don't have to go to so much effort," Deanna said, loading slices into the chromed slots.

"It's no effort."

"Really? Honestly, you could just spread peanut butter on bread or something."

Leigh shrugged. "That would be enough to keep you alive, sure. To block the hunger. But it wouldn't satisfy the soul. Food should be more than survival."

"I don't think anyone ever cooked like this for me before," Deanna said, almost wistfully.

Leigh looked down to cover her smile. *Exactly as I'd hoped*, she thought to herself. "Cooking itself is an act of love," she said. "Eating together is a manifestation of family."

Deanna looked at her, licked her lips once, then shook her head. "Your privilege is showing. Ideas like that, *words* like that, don't exist in my world."

"I get it. Really, I do. But it doesn't have to be that way. Even if all you can afford is peanut butter on the cheapest white bread, you can still prepare it together with people you love. Sit together and eat it. Be with each other." She gestured at the various ingredients on the cooktop. "If you can afford all this, that's special, sure. But the simplest things or the most complex, it doesn't matter. It's the act involved that counts."

Deanna stared a moment longer, then shrugged, turned back to the big toaster.

"James never cooks for you? Or you for him?" Leigh asked.

Deanna barked a laugh. "James never cooks for anyone. Anyway, we aren't together if that's what you're thinking. We run together, a crew, but we're not *together* together."

"Even so, you're friends. You love and care for each other." Leigh stirred the mushrooms as they shrank and fried, then opened the oven and turned over the bacon. "You shouldn't stay with friends who don't show they care."

"By making a fancy-arse fucking breakfast? You don't get us at all, lady."

"No, I don't think I do. But I do know respect when I see it. And there's not much respect coming from James, is there? For anyone."

Deanna turned, put her hands on her hips. "See, you *don't* get it. It's not about choices, it's about survival. The world I live in, you stay with a pack or you get eaten by one. James respects me in ways you wouldn't understand, that's why we run together. That's how we survive. I don't need fancy breakfasts or some candlelit dinner or any other shit. There's no room for that where I come from. That's *your* world, and honestly, it makes me sick. It's all so superficial, so much play-acting bullshit. What we have, what we *do*, that's real. You have the time for playing. We don't."

Leigh hurt a little inside for the woman, because she knew every word was true. The way Deanna described her reality was absolutely honest. It was all she knew. But still Leigh had to try to convince her otherwise. Even for Deanna's truth, this situation had gone beyond normal. "You say it's not about choices," she said quietly. "And I understand that's true. Normally. But it is choices now. Look at this situation you're in, following James in this madness. That's not normal, not for anyone. Even you. Right? You can choose to change that. You and Paul together can make different choices."

"I see what you're doing, and it won't work. I'm not stupid. Don't think you can trick me."

"I'm not trying to. I don't think you're stupid. Honestly, you're clearly one of the smartest and strongest women I've ever met. You're really something. That's why I'm trying to show you that you *do* have choices."

Deanna stared again, the skin around her eyes crinkled in something like discomfort. Leigh turned back to the cooker and began serving up the bacon, eggs, fried mushrooms, and allowed herself a small smile. She wouldn't push any more. Sowing tiny seeds of doubt would be enough. James she wanted to see dead. She'd pull the trigger herself in an instant if the chance arose. But she tried to hold onto the thought that Deanna and Paul were more victims than perpetrators. She had to hold onto that, because it meant she might get through to them. She believed in kindness, trusted in compassion. She'd push a little more the next chance she got. Slowly, hopefully, she would bring this woman around.

RUEBEN

IN THE bush was thick, the undergrowth snarled and deep even in its winter somnolence. In truth, even this high up, Australian bush never really went into hibernation like the European forests Rueben had read about. But this was what he'd always known. In summer, in the heat and dry, he was always extra paranoid about snakes and bugs. Spiders the size of his hand that he knew were largely harmless, but freaked him out nonetheless. It was the smaller ones a person needed to worry about. Snakes of all sizes, and some of the world's most venomous, were a bigger concern. But for some reason they freaked him out less. One advantage of the colder months was most of the dangerous critters were resting even if the bush itself wasn't really.

Regardless, Reuben stayed in the densest areas, slowly making his way back towards the side of the large lawns behind the hotel. If he went too far, it was easy to get lost. The bush and the wide open deserts of Australia swallowed up a tourist or two every year. Many were lucky enough to be found and rescued, starving and haggard, but not all. Rueben had had it drilled into him from a young age that it was too easy to get turned around in the bush. Without a landmark or a guide, a tiny miscalculation could put a person off-course by hundreds of metres and that could turn into kilometres in no time. That's mainly why he hadn't simply run to the Hickmans the night before. That and abject terror. He was still scared, but daylight felt safer. Find the lawns, keep them and the hotel just in sight to make sure he was going the right way, but stay as deep in the bush as he could. Find the long driveway out to the road. Once he was on the road, it would be plain sailing.

He pushed aside some branches, brushing bits of leaf and lichen from his arm, and saw a brighter patch of sky. He smiled. Rather than follow the old wombat trail from his treehouse to the back of the lawns, he'd gone obliquely, trusting his sense of direction this far, and it paid off. That open sky marked the wide expanse of grass and garden beds, and the big veggie patches on the other side that Marcus tended so well all summer. Planting out the veggies one of the first jobs of spring.

Gonna need a lot for those spring rolls you're going to teach me to make, Rueben thought, and pushed away the thought that he might never actually eat a spring roll again, from Marcus or anyone else.

He moved deeper into the trees. Now he knew he was lined up to the hotel, he just needed to get past the lawns, the main building and then the garages and cottage. Once he was past that by a couple of hundred metres he could come closer to the driveway and move more quickly.

With a smile, heart racing, he pushed forward. As he came alongside the front edge of the lawn, the angular shape of the hotel just visible through the branches, someone came barrelling through the bush at him. Branches snapped, undergrowth crunched, as whoever it was powered ahead.

Rueben let out a cry of fear he couldn't suppress, pictures of James and his shotgun filling his mind. He saw Uncle Simon's gaping chest. His mind spun, his legs turned to jelly, his stomach to water. The sudden, desperate need to piss flooded his system.

Then the person burst through the nearest branches and it was a grey kangaroo. A big one, nearly as tall as Rueben himself, and just as scared. When it saw him, it braked its forward momentum, rearing back on its strong hind legs and tail.

Don't kick me! Rueben thought.

Everyone knew the stories of how a kangaroo could lean back on its tail and eviscerate someone with a mighty kick from that vicious central back claw. But the animal twisted sideways and bounded away, crashing harder through the trees.

Rueben's heart thumped in his throat, his legs shook like saplings in a gale. He started to let out a strangled laugh of relief when a gruff voice yelled, "Yeah, fucken run, ya bouncy bastard!"

That *was* James.

Rueben's legs gave out and he sat down in a tangled patch of bracken, the long, fractal branches of ever-reducing triangular leaves brushing and scratching at his face and neck.

"Shoulda fucking shot ya," James said, amusement in his voice, but something else too. Something vacant.

Rueben heard the man, but couldn't see him. He sat frozen, indecisive. If he stayed here, would James stumble right onto him? If he tried to move, would James hear or see him and *boom!* The end of Rueben?

chest wide open glistening organs

There was more muttering, now too low for Rueben to make out the words, and then some crunching of undergrowth. His whole body vibrating in fear, Rueben risked rising up just a little, to peer over the bracken. He looked in the direction the roo had come from, then to his left. Nothing. As his eyes scanned right, his heart slammed and he barely managed to suppress a gasp at the sight of James only five or six metres away. The man was a little ahead of Rueben, in exactly the direction he needed to go. He was busily focussed on something.

Despite his fear, Rueben shifted slightly to his right to see better, willing the dry bush to stay quiet. James had a pocket knife in hand and was carving at the bark of a snow gum, eyes narrowed in concentration, the tip of his tongue gripped between his front teeth. The shape he carved into the trunk of the tree was unpleasant to look at for reasons Rueben couldn't quite understand.

But James was busy, so this was a chance. On hands and knees, moving painstakingly slowly, Rueben crawled through the bracken. He watched everywhere he put his hands and knees, desperate to not accidentally lean his weight on a stick that would snap. He'd seen enough movies to know a sudden *crack* in the air would be what gave him away. But if he was careful, slow, he could make space. He had to, in case James came deeper into the bush.

Rueben wished he had a weapon and could surge up out of the undergrowth with it and finish the bastard. Imagine the hero Rueben would be then. But he was smaller, younger, weaker. He had no weapon and James had guns and knives. While a part of Rueben wanted to be a hero, another part recognised the ridiculousness of the thought. No way he could beat a grown man, especially a psycho like that guy. At least, not in a fight. He could beat James by getting away and getting help. That's how he'd be the hero.

He crawled on, deeper and deeper into the bush. When he was sure he was far enough away, he cautiously stood. James was entirely obscured by the bush between them, which meant Rueben was obscured from James too.

Swallowing his hammering heart, taking a deep breath, Rueben pushed forward. A dead branch cracked under his heel and he stumbled.

"You back for more, Skippy, ya bastard?"

Crashing from behind as James suddenly pushed through the branches.

Stifling a sob of terror, Rueben ran.

"I'll shoot ya dead this time, Skip!" James yelled.

A gunshot rang out and Rueben threw himself forward, hitting the ground with enough force to push most of the air from his lungs. Gasping, he drove himself up and ran on. Staggering and stumbling, branches whipping and scratching at his face, his cheeks awash with tears, he simply ran. James hooted and hollered, seeming to get nearer, and Rueben ran harder. He ducked left and right, gasping breaths into a chest tight with exertion.

"Next time, ya fucker!" came James's distant voice.

It took Rueben a moment to register that James had given up the chase. The man had assumed all along it was that roo, or another like it. Rueben slowed to a fast walk, then eventually came to a complete stop. He stood still, listening hard. Nothing but the wintered sounds of the high bush. No James, no chasing footsteps crashing through. He'd got away.

But where the hell was he now?

PAUL

I JAMES was unstable at the best of times. No one knew that better than his little brother. So often, Paul had been bashed and beaten simply for saying or doing the wrong thing at the wrong time, even though there had been no way to know it would annoy James. Something fine one day would be a mortal sin the next. It had always been that way. Paul, like others around James, had learned to walk cautiously. But the thing about James was that he got things done. He had big plans, big ideas, and while he might be a little crazy around the edges, he came through. This idea, the rural bank robbery, was perhaps the biggest idea James had ever had. The long drive from Sydney's suburbs all the way to Enden had seemed like a stroke of genius.

James had arranged other crimes, they'd robbed service stations and bottle shops, they ran drugs sometimes, even moved some guns once. Like James said, when you got dealt a hand in life like they had, you made your own rules and your own way. Every time, if he'd been allowed along, Paul had been terrified, but he'd trusted his big brother. *You stick with me, and you'll learn to take on the world*, James had said once, and Paul believed him. They lived in a shithole, but were beholden to no one, owed nothing. That was all thanks to James. So a cool bank heist idea didn't seem like such a leap. In truth, to Paul it had seemed like a natural progression, and one that should have set them up. Off with their score and happy for years.

Except the instability always evident in James's life had become something more. Deanna saw it, Paul could tell. It was in her eyes. And if he was honest with himself, he'd noticed it before they even left the city, and she had too. But they'd both ignored it. And here they were. They should have tried to put the job off, perhaps. But who ever questioned James?

Paul thought about Imogen, with her wry smile and long brown hair. She had her crazy ways too, but the calming influence she had on James was undeniable. For a long time it had been good. Then her exasperation, her patience running out.

And so, of course, Paul also thought about little Cooper. Ever since he was born, James had called his son Cooper, but Imogen had always used the kid's middle name. She'd call out Louis, and the kid would come running. He accepted that his mum called him one thing and his dad another. That was normal for them all, since Cooper could walk. *We couldn't agree on a name*, Imogen told everyone. *So we use both.* Of course, Cooper came first on the birth certificate and the kid had his father's surname. Cooper Louis Glenn. That disagreement on a name was an obvious warning sign in hindsight.

James doted on his kid, but Imogen grew ever more distant. Paul thought perhaps James treated her badly. He certainly spoke to her with venom, would undermine her at every turn. Paul thought maybe, in the privacy of their own spaces, James hit her too. He should have challenged his brother about that, but what good would it have done? No doubt James would simply deny everything, or more likely hit Paul too, for bringing it up. For daring to question the reign of King James. It was inevitable what would happen with Imogen, he supposed. She would only put up with James's shit for so long. Maybe she thought she could change him, or that fatherhood would change him, and it quickly became apparent that James was James and that was it. Paul never thought for a moment it would lead to this. Cooper had only just turned three when Imogen took him away. They should have put off the heist.

"You listening?"

Paul startled, stood up straight from where he'd been leaning against the dining room doorframe, staring into the lounge, seeing nothing. "Sorry, what?"

Deanna scowled at him. "I said to help carry these through."

She stood at the kitchen door, frequently glancing back at Leigh while the woman moved pots around. Several plates of toast with bacon, scrambled eggs, mushrooms stirred through spinach sat in front of her, a fork resting on each one.

Deanna picked up her shotgun and covered Leigh while Paul put his down on the bar in the lounge, well away from the tied family, and then ferried plates from the kitchen, two at a time. He put the first two in front of Clay and Marcus on the floor.

"How are we supposed to eat?" Clay demanded, gesturing with shrugs of his shoulders that made the old man wince, hands still tied back to either side of the wooden column.

"Just wait." Paul went back and retrieved two more plates.

Deanna and Leigh followed, carrying a plate of their own each. Paul put one plate in front of Grant and looked around. "Where's James?"

"No idea," Deanna said. "His breakfast is in the kitchen. Let's get these guys sorted out first. Loosen their ropes." She turned her attention to the others. "One hand free, eat, and no funny business. You sit there," she said to Leigh, who complied, sinking onto one end of a couch.

Paul untied the men and told them to eat. He picked up his shotgun from the bar and held it loosely, more to remind them not to try anything than to genuinely threaten them. He put his breakfast on the bar, sat on a stool and ate one-handed while he watched. Deanna did the same from across the room, shotgun resting against her thigh.

Clay winced and gently rolled his shoulders, looking from Paul to Deanna and back with undisguised loathing. "You really think this is going okay?" he asked. "Where do you see this going? What do you think?"

Paul noticed Leigh catch the old man's eye, and she gave a slight shake of the head. He wasn't sure how to interpret that.

"We're not going to discuss it with you, gramps." Deanna gestured with her fork. "Eat your eggs."

Clay managed to sarcastically fork up a mouthful, then looked to her again. "You think it can get any better than it is now? It can only get worse. You know that, right?"

Deanna shrugged. "Not for you to worry about."

Leigh sat forward and Deanna flinched, reached for the shotgun. "I haven't forgotten you're untied!"

Leigh raised a hand. "I'm not doing anything. I just wanted to say, Clay is right. It really can only get worse from here. Did James sleep at all last night? Even a few minutes?"

"I don't know."

"He's not thinking straight, you have to realise that."

Deanna stared, chewing slowly. Paul watched her closely. He agreed with the woman, and thought they should get the hell out. He and Deanna could maybe convince James to leave if they were united in it. Tension rose in the room, Grant and Clay watching closely. "Eat your fucking eggs," Deanna said, and stood, walked around the other side of Clay. She looked down at Marcus, who stared at the floor, his food untouched. "You gonna eat?"

He didn't respond, didn't move

"Last chance," Deanna said. "When these guys have finished, I'm clearing it up."

Still nothing.

"Marcus," Leigh said, her voice plaintiff. "Please, you have to eat."

Paul scanned the faces in the room, the despair in Leigh's expression, Clay's disdain, Grant's crestfallen impotence. Deanna caught his eye and he shrugged. Silence hung like a pall while they ate, disconsolate in their own ways.

"The others are finished," Deanna said, and picked up Marcus's untouched plate. Maybe she was girding herself with meanness. "Tie them back up," she told Paul. "Then we'll take them for a toilet break, one at a time." She pointed at Leigh. "You first. Come on."

A few minutes later they returned and Leigh sat back in her spot without being asked. Paul secured the ropes then spent a while taking each of the others to the bathroom. No one spoke, but the silence was loud with all kinds of accusations and entreaties. He did his best to ignore them.

Deanna slumped into an armchair and eventually Paul fell into a sofa. The family stared from their entrapment. Paul felt lethargy soaking through him. He was so very tired. And where was his brother? A couple of tense hours passed and Paul could finally take it no longer. He had to do something.

"I'm going to find James."

Deanna shrugged.

Paul knew James wasn't in the kitchen or dining room, so he left the large lounge area on the other side, going through the door beside the reception office into the guest wing. The temperature dropped immediately. Though the heating was on, throughout this side it was apparently down low, and no blazing hearths held back the chill. He passed the storage cupboard, feeling as though he were walking in a large refrigerator. The doors to the bedrooms were all open, the beds bare of linen, but everything neat and tidy. Most of the rooms were well-appointed, with polished hardwood furniture and rustic art prints on the walls. They all had curtains drawn, diffusing the early morning light into little more than a grey gloom. He smelled dust and wood, and an edge of something a little stale. The whole place needed airing out. But James was nowhere to be found. He went back and up the stairs opposite the closet, finding similar rooms along the top floor. There were six rooms on the ground level, but eight up here, each a little smaller, a little less luxurious. But none contained James.

Paul was heading back for the stairs when he paused, a thought occurring to him, and went into one of the rooms at the back of the hotel. He moved the curtain aside an inch and looked out over the wide lawn that led away from the back deck behind the lounge. James stood out there, motionless, staring into the tree line.

The lawns took up a good acre, maybe two, with a few ornamental trees and garden beds scattered around, a big vegetable garden off to one side. But to either side and along the back, the bush was thick and shadowed after the first few yards. Even from the second floor, Paul couldn't see over the trees to determine how far the forest reached, but he had the feeling it probably went on for close to forever. In the far distance the ground rose and the forest undulated in green waves, ever upwards. Hills and peaks in the distance showed more rugged country further out. He couldn't see a single other dwelling, no signs of human life at all. He sighed. It had been a good idea to detour here, if only the damned family hadn't come up early.

He looked back to James, stock still, exactly as he had been before, watching the trees. Paul went back downstairs, through the lounge, and out the back door beside the bar, ignoring the family who scowled at him as he passed. Deanna was slumped in an armchair, the shotgun resting on her leg. She raised an eyebrow at him, but Paul ignored her as well.

The back deck was big and stretched the width of the lounge room behind it. Wooden tables, chairs and loungers, all silvered with age, were stacked up against the back wall. They had been covered with tarps and most still were, but winds had loosed some corners revealing the piles beneath.

Paul walked softly across the dark wooden planks and down three cement steps to the damp grass of the lawn. It was slightly uncanny how still James stood. Without really understanding why, Paul moved as silently as possible over the grass. Somewhere in the back of his mind, he thought it might be foolish to sneak up on his brother, but something made him throw that caution to the wind.

As he got nearer, he heard James's voice, barely above a whisper.

"...as easy as all that. I don't know. What if they–" James spun around, piercing Paul with eyes like flint.

Paul danced an involuntary step back.

"What are you doing?" James demanded.

"Just coming to tell you there's food inside. Leigh. She made breakfast. Yours will be getting cold."

James stared, his eyes laced with bright red veins, dark underneath like bruises. His mouth hung slightly open and something whirled in his over-wide pupils, almost as though tiny tornadoes twisted in their obsidian depths.

"James... are you okay?"

James jerked and Paul cried out, stepped back again. "I'm fine, little brother. Why, you worried about me?"

"I am actually. Did you sleep?"

"Don't need to."

"You do, James. You should sleep. And eat."

James surged forward and collected a handful of Paul's jacket. It stretched tight across his shoulders as James hauled him forward. "You think to tell me what to do?" James's face was barely an inch from Paul's, his breath foul and acrid. Paul had a sudden flash of memory, his mother when he was small, using a white plastic bottle, tipping it up onto a tissue and cleaning away chipped and ragged nail polish. Before she had died, leaving them with their father and all that entailed. James's breath smelled like the stuff in that plastic bottle.

"No, bro! I'm just worried about you, that's all."

James's face split in vulpine grin. "You don't have to worry about me, little brother. I'm the one to do the worrying. I'm here to look after everyone else, yeah?"

"Okay. Yeah, sure."

"What the fuck happened to Rick, Paul? Huh? Can you tell me that?"

Paul swallowed hard, tapped at his brother's hand. James let go of the jacket and Paul staggered back, his mind awash with images from the night before. Those dark tendrils, glistening tentacles of night. The glowing red, skittering about the floor, then gathering together, moving like small creatures across the rugs and boards. Rick's head tipped back, eyes wide, terrified, pain-wracked, as his skin undulated. His grey hand, lifting and flopping back toward Paul.

Heeelllpp meeeee...

Paul gasped in a breath. "I told you what happened."

James's face shot forward, mouth stretched in fury. "That's not possible!"

Anger came up to dance with Paul's fear. "Well, maybe not, but it's what fucking happened! Why would I make it up?"

"You were dreaming, idiot! You imagined it all."

"Then what the fuck happened to Rick?" Paul yelled. "You saw him! What was left of him!"

He flinched, expecting a blow from James, but it didn't come. "I'll tell *you* what happened, little brother. He died. That's all. He died like we knew he would."

"Where did all the blood go?"

"He died. Okay? Nothing else."

Paul swallowed, staring hard into his brother's eyes. He saw the conflict there, knew James was saying these things as much to convince himself as anything else. "I saw what I saw, James. I promise you. I wasn't dreaming. I don't know what it was, but I saw what I saw."

His brother stared a moment longer, still straining forward as if held by an invisible leash, then the tension drained from his body and he stood back. "That old fucker knows more than he's letting on."

Without another glance, James walked past Paul heading back for the hotel. He hopped up the steps to the deck like he was in a frivolous mood, almost dancing as he went. Paul stared, thinking that kind of change in energy couldn't mean anything good, and quickly followed.

James pulled the pistol from the back of his jeans as Paul ran in and closed the door behind himself.

"Tell me everything you know!" James yelled at Clay.

"About what?" Clay asked.

James swung a booted foot into the old man's thigh, making Clay howl. Blood drained from his face and his eyes rolled up. For a second he was tense as if frozen, then gasped rapid, almost sobbing breaths, head lolling in semi-consciousness.

"Hey, don't hurt him!" Grant shouted, twisting against his ropes. "You want to hurt someone, try me, fucker!"

"Grant, no!" Leigh said.

James turned and strode across the gap, trailing his arm behind him like a sail, then pistol-whipped Grant so hard his head rocked to the side and he phased out of consciousness for a moment, head hanging limp. Leigh yelled for James to calm down as he turned back to Clay. Grant's eyes swam and he looked up groggily, blood running from a gash above his eye, over his cheek to soak into the neck of his shirt.

Leigh said, more quietly, "Calm down, please. Everyone calm down."

Deanna sat rigid in her armchair, watching closely.

James crouched in front of Clay, the pistol hanging between his knees. "Something fucking weird happened to my buddy Rick last night. Right?"

Clay gasped, tried to still his breathing enough to talk. His eyes were wet with tears. He nodded rapidly as he gathered himself, clearly trying to show James he would talk. Paul remembered the old man complaining about his hip and wondered just how much damage James might have done with that kick. Tears streaked Clay's cheeks as he gasped again, his face still bone white, and said, "I don't know. Don't know what it is. I can tell you what I do know."

James fell back from his crouch to sit cross-legged like a child at story time. "Go on."

"A minute." Clay sucked in a deep breath, then another. Paul was impressed with the old man's steel. "When Molly and I bought this place, nearly fifty years ago," Clay said finally, "it wasn't quite finished. The family who had been building it were all killed by their oldest son. He went psycho. Then killed himself. It's a horrible story. But we bought the place anyway. When we moved in we realised something of the killer still remained."

"What, a ghost?" James demanded. "You expect me to believe this?"

"What you believe is up to you. I can only tell you what I know. What happened."

"Dad, you never told me this before."

Clay looked to his right, raised an eyebrow at his son. "You never asked." He looked back to James. "But we fixed it. Well, Molly did. Right by that hearth in the dining room. It was where the killer chopped up and stacked his mother, incidentally."

"Jesus, Dad, really?"

"Clay, are you serious?" Leigh asked.

James looked around the room, grinning like this was the best joke ever. "You've all been living and working in a charnel house and youse had no idea? Oh, that's priceless. But do go on, old man. What about that hearth?"

Paul shivered. He knew the tone of James's voice. His brother sounded happy and interested like this right before he snapped. Something volcanic was rising.

Clay shook his head, looking at the ground. "I don't claim to understand it. It's not that hearth, specifically. Not really. It's this place, something about it. We sent Michael Ellery's ghost away in the hearth, and Molly sealed everything up. That's it, that's all there is. It's been peaceful here ever since. We thought it was done." He looked up again, found James's eyes. "But from what Paul says he saw, maybe it was more than the ghost of Michael Ellery back then. Maybe something else drove that boy. And maybe it's woken up again."

"Remember the weird fire?" Deanna said quietly.

James turned to look at her. "Weird fire?"

"When Leigh threw Rick's blood-soaked shirt into the fire, it flamed up. And for a moment it was cold."

"You threw his blood in there?" Clay asked. He frowned. "Maybe that's it?" he mused quietly, almost to himself. "Enough blood finally to wake something up…"

James bounced to his feet, agitated. "So what if we did?"

Clay looked up at him. "Maybe you broke Molly's seal. I don't even know if that's possible, or relevant, but it might be."

"This is bullshit!" James roared. "This is all bullshit! How can any of what you're saying be real? This is the real world, man. Shit like that doesn't happen."

"But it did happen," Paul said. "It's *something* to do with blood. All Rick's was taken, all the blood off the floor and in the kitchen, all gone like it was cleaned up. I saw it rise up, glowing red, and scurry away. I *saw* that, James. Those black writhing things, bright red inside…"

James turned on the spot, trying to see them all at once. His lips worked, his cheeks flinched as he ground his teeth. Suddenly he dropped to a crouch in front of Clay again and the old man jerked back, wincing against another imminent strike.

"Can you fix it?"

"Fix what?" Clay asked.

"Whatever the fuck is happening. Whoever the fuck Molly is and what she did. Assuming all this absolute crap isn't just a far-fetched fairy tale, can you do it again?"

Paul saw desperation in James's eyes, like his brother was trying to resist something intangible. It wasn't like him at all.

"Seal the hearth?" Clay licked his lips, frowning. "Yeah, maybe. I could try. I could do again what Molly did all those years ago. But I can't guarantee it'll fix anything. That was to get rid of the ghost of the Ellery boy. This... whatever this is, I think it's different."

"Or maybe you could just go," Grant said quietly. "Why risk it, huh? Leave us here and get out, before it gets dark again."

James leaned in past Clay and tore at the ropes. He undid the knots, retied them to hold Marcus in place, then hauled Clay to his feet. The old man yelped in pain, staggering to keep upright. Paul hurried over and put Clay's arm around his shoulder, took all the weight he could. Clay trembled, sucked in breath after breath.

"Maybe a last chance," James said, like he was talking to himself instead of them. "Before I can't... before I should..." He snapped his head up, as if suddenly realising they were all listening. "Let's go!"

Movement caught Paul's eye and he glanced back, noticed Marcus look up at them. The man's catatonic state had become so normal that the sudden perusal was profoundly disturbing.

"Bring him out here," James said.

Paul saw Grant's head tip forward, the man still groggy from the blow of James's pistol butt. Blood from the cut over his eye dripped onto the floor between his legs. Marcus turned away to stare at the ground again. Paul helped Clay follow James through to the dining room. Deanna stood and came along behind. James pointed at the crackling hearth.

"Well?"

Clay stared for a moment, shook his head. "I'll need some stuff," he said. "Rock salt, sage oil, some other things. It's all in the kitchen. And we have to put out the fire."

James pressed his lips into a line, clenched his fists. "Okay, come on then. We'll find the stuff you need first."

As James strode into the kitchen, Deanna put herself under Clay's other arm. She and Paul helped the old man walk. Paul was thankful for it, but saw Clay's face, how he hated needing the help. Getting old must suck.

As they made it across the large dining room, Clay began to take more of his own weight. He winced, let out involuntary whimpers of pain, but as they entered the kitchen, he said, "Let me stand. I'm okay."

"You're tough," Paul said. "I respect that."

Clay shot him a derisive glare.

James gestured at the kitchen cupboards. "So where's the stuff you need."

As Clay opened his mouth to respond car tyres crunched on the gravel driveway outside.

CLAY

THE pain in Clay's bad hip was white hot, tendrils of fire radiating from his lower back to his knee. He refused to be carried any more by these bastards, and despite the discomfort, and the fear he might collapse any moment, he stood on his own. He knew repeating Molly's actions in the hearth would do nothing at all. They were well beyond that. But he'd agreed because it got him away from his bonds. Anything that let him up from the ropes and the column was a good start. Plus, James had looked scared of something, and Clay thought maybe playing that up would help. It was dangerous to keep someone so unstable off-centre, but any distraction might be worthwhile. Then maybe he'd be able to find a weapon, take some chance, anything. He needed to do something. If only he could get past the pain that smeared his thoughts to jelly. Then the sound of tyres on the gravel outside made him briefly forget all his physical concerns.

"Who the fuck is this?" James started for the door.

Deanna and Paul, still either side of Clay, shared a look past him, fear evident in their eyes. They knew as well as Clay did that this would be a real problem.

"Go," Clay said. "I can barely stand, I'm not running anywhere."

They bolted for the door right as James pushed through it and followed him out. Clay limped after them, pulled the door wide and stood in its frame in time to see Bob and Laura Hickman, faces shocked through the windshield of their old Holden ute, skid to halt as James stood in a wide stance on the driveway and levelled Simon's pistol at them.

"DRIVE!" Clay yelled. "Go! Now! Call the police!" His outburst might get him shot, but if it got the message out, that was good enough.

Bob Hickman, behind the ute's wheel, glanced briefly at Clay, then back to James. The lunatic stood right in front of him and the three other cars were still half blocking the driveway. But if Bob just drove, even right over James, he would get away.

"You move one muscle and you'll be dead before you can draw a breath," James said, the pistol steady in his hand. His voice was loud but even, belying the madness Clay knew swirled inside the crazy bastard. *Just go*, Clay begged in his mind. *Run him down!* But all the other cars and trailers… Bob had driven into a kind of trap.

Bob and Laura both had their windows down a few inches, clearly able to hear well enough.

"What's happening here?" Bob called out.

The scene was faintly ridiculous. Both Grant's and Marcus's cars stood with their trailers opened up to the weather. The invaders' no doubt stolen car had all its doors wide open, then James, with Deanna and Paul right beside him, all staring at the battered red ute with the Hickmans inside.

"Drive, Bob!" Clay yelled again.

Deanna ran back to Clay and there was murder in her eyes. "Shut the fuck up, old man. You'll make this worse."

"How much worse can it get? You think them staying here will help anything?"

"Get out slowly with your hands up," James said.

Clay watched in dismay as Laura and Bob slowly opened their doors, and his heart sank. They were the best chance any of them had of ending this nightmare. If they didn't get away, he saw no other escape for his family. He should have found a weapon in the kitchen while he had a moment's grace, maybe he could have rushed James with a knife and ended him. Though he knew that was a fantasy. James would have dropped him with a single shot from the pistol and then still had Bob and Laura under his control.

"Move around in front of the vehicle," James demanded.

They complied and Clay shook his head. There it was, the Moore family's last chance flying away like a cheap shopping bag in the wind.

"Who are you two? Why are you here?"

Despite staring down the barrel of a gun, Bob Hickman was indignant. "I was about to ask you the same thing, son. I don't take kindly to guns."

James shot him.

The report was sudden and like a punch in the face. Clay staggered, as if struck, crying out, "No!" but was restrained by Deanna clamping her hand around his arm. Her vice-like grip and clenched teeth belied her shock at the sudden assault. He wanted to hit the woman and run over there, to tackle James to the ground and beat him senseless. Twenty years ago he would have done exactly that, and maybe even won the fight, but now he'd most likely break his hand on Deanna's face and fall flat on his own within the first two steps of an attempted sprint.

Bob Hickman hit the gravel gasping as blood flowered across his flannel shirt right above where it stretched over his rotund belly. He hitched breaths that were each small cries of pain and shock. Laura screamed, her whole body clenching as she simultaneously wanted to drop to help her husband but was also too scared to move. Bob writhed on the ground, groaning. His blood began to drip on the stones.

"They're our neighbours!" Clay yelled. "They help out, keep an eye on the place when we're not here."

"We didn't know you were back," Laura said, her voice high and barely below another scream. Then she turned to her husband, reaching down toward him. "Bob!" She looked up at James. "I need to call him an ambulance!"

"Who else knows you're here?" James demanded.

"No one!" Laura said. "We thought we'd pop up and check on things as we haven't been for a couple of weeks. Clay, you didn't tell us you were back."

"Only yesterday. Leigh was supposed to ring you. I guess she forgot." Clay's mind spun as he tried to figure out a way to diffuse the situation, to calm things down. Bob had curled into a ball and was making deep, huffing noises of pain and fear. Paul's face was pale as he looked from the suffering man to his brother and back again. James's face was calm. Too calm, impassive.

"Where else were you planning to go today?" James asked Laura.

She looked at him with a creased brow, and Clay's heart thudded. *If she says nowhere, she's dead*, he thought. *Please, Laura. Please tell him you're expected somewhere, even if you're not.*

"Just back to our property," she said in a soft, confused tone. "We have work at home."

A smile spread across James's face and Laura's frown deepened right before Simon's gun barked again and a red hole burst between the woman's eyes. Her face managed to momentarily register shock before she collapsed like her strings had been cut.

"Fuck!" Clay barked.

Deanna's grip on his arm tightened painfully, though he doubted she was aware of it as she stared at his fallen neighbour. Paul turned to his brother, shaking his head, eyes and mouth wide.

"James, no more killing!" Paul said, almost a whisper. "Please! No more!"

James spun to face him. "No more? Really?"

Still staring at his brother, James took three long strides over to the fallen, grunting form of Bob Hickman. "No more?" James asked, pressing the pistol to the side of Bob's head. The large man squirmed, tried to shift away, yelping in pain as he did. "*No more?*" James yelled and fired, then again. Bob's whole body twitched and jerked up off the gravel like a beached fish as the ground beneath his head became awash with scarlet.

Paul shook his head, staring. "Fuck fuck fuck..."

"Get him inside!" James yelled, and Deanna spat something under her breath and dragged Clay back through the door.

As they went he heard James yell his brother's name, and a high smack, no doubt a palm on a cheek. "Get it together! Drag these two into the garage with the other one. Now!"

Clay's whole body shook, his mouth dry as paper. He had to do something, anything, to shift the balance of what was happening. With the Hickmans gone, what other options remained? Where would Rueben go? Was the poor child already on his way down to their house? A tiny ray of light lanced through the black fog of his thoughts. If Rueben was on his way to the Hickmans place, he would be safe from all this. And once he got there and found they were out, maybe he would wait for a little while, then what? He'd know the situation was dire. He'd surely only wait a short while before he broke a window and went inside to use their phone to call the police. The kid was smart, he wouldn't quit. They probably didn't even lock the door, he could just walk in. Or maybe he would carry on, further down the road. It was a long way from Eagle Hotel to the Hickmans, but then it was less than half that far again to the collection of farms and properties nearer the main road. Rueben would find help one way or another, whether he could talk to the Hickmans or not. And now he certainly couldn't. Maybe all wasn't lost. Except Bob and Laura were dead. Clay's hatred for James burned so hot he thought he might pass out.

He flinched with pangs of grief. He'd known Bob Hickman the man's whole life, some forty-something years. Bob's father, Dutch, was the first friend Clay had made when they bought the hotel. The man and his wife, Clara, knew the history, were sympathetic and impressed with Molly and Clay taking it on, so young and full of dreams. Dutch and Clara, and then Bob and Laura, were nothing but good neighbours.

And now Bob and Laura were gone.

Clay's trembling wouldn't stop, anger and grief and impotence raging inside him. Clay realised Deanna was standing with him beside the sinks, presumably at a loss for what to do next. James strode back into the kitchen.

"Tie him up!" James said through clenched teeth, pointing at Clay. The whole thing with the hearth apparently forgotten.

Deanna swallowed, looked from James to Clay and back again.

"Can you cope with that?" James asked, leaning close to her. "Can you cope with one half-crippled old man?"

"Sure."

James nodded once and stalked away.

"So what now?" Clay asked her as James kept walking, disappearing into the dining room.

"Shut the fuck up." She dragged him along, less sympathetic now to his aches and pains. "I don't want any conversation."

RUEBEN

IN the shadows behind the cottage, Reuben's breath came in rapid, shallow pants, muffled in the sleeve of his jacket as he watched, tears pouring over his cheeks.

After the close call in the bush with James, he'd spent a couple of hours lost, trying to retrace his steps without running into James again. Through luck as much as judgement, swallowing panic as he made his way through the trees, climbing some to try to see further, he had eventually spotted the roof of the hotel again. Almost dizzy with relief, he reoriented himself and pushed forward, aiming to find his way to the driveway. As he moved, Grandma Molly appeared again. "Rueben, child! You must go!"

He startled, looked up at her, haloed by the crowns of the trees. "I got lost!"

"Something evil lurks in these woods, Rueben. In all our years here, I never felt it, but something has woken it up. Again. Something old and bad is stirring. Quickly, go."

He put his back to the hotel, striking deeper into the trees, his sense of direction true once more to guide him to the long dirt driveway and then to the road leading to the Hickman's place. Nothing else could distract him, he had to get to Laura and Bob.

It had taken a while to fight through the bush, the undergrowth thick and tangled. Several times he'd had to double back, find a different way, but he had pressed on and determination made him barely notice any fatigue. After all, he had a long way to go yet and couldn't afford the time to rest. And then he'd seen a band of light, the pale wintry sky showing through more clearly. Cautiously, he approached it and smiled, recognizing the unsealed drive that led from the mountain road right up to the gravel surrounding Eagle Hotel. He wasn't sure how far along the drive he was, he couldn't see the hotel for the trees, but the whole thing was only a couple of kilometres or so long. It couldn't be far to the road and then it was all downhill to the Hickman's.

Just in case one of the invaders decided to jump in a car and head out, he stayed away from the drive, but kept it in sight as he pushed on. He was sure he couldn't be far from the road when he heard an engine. Freezing, indecision curdling his gut, he stood and watched. Then the Hickman's battered red Holden ute bumped along the drive, heading for the hotel.

Rueben swallowed hard, denials swarming through his mind. Without thought for personal safety he pushed out of the trees and sprinted back up the drive, desperate to yell but not having the breath or the nerve to do so. He waved his arms at the disappearing car, but it moved too fast for him to catch up. It didn't stop, so they must not have seen him. He ran after it.

As he neared the hotel, some sense of self-preservation steered him back into the bush and he pushed through behind the cottage where it backed up almost into the woods. As he came around the side, peering from the shadows, he saw James take a stance in front of the ute and level a gun. Uncle Simon's gun, he noticed with surreal clarity.

There was shouting. Grandpa Clay in the doorway.

And James fired. Bob collapsed to the ground.

More shouting and James fired again, and the back of Laura's head opened up like a flower blooming. An instant spread, not there then suddenly a blood-filled crater of bone standing out through her hair and she collapsed out of sight behind the ute.

Tears blurred Rueben's vision and his breath became staccato, sharp and shallow. His head swam, dizziness rising up like a shark from deep waters, to swallow him whole. He pressed his face into his jacket to muffle his breaths, his entire body wracked with shivers, his face and hands so cold, and he stared.

They were supposed to help. Bob and Laura Hickman were the ones to fix this, to call the right people, to save the day. They weren't supposed to arrive here and die. Die like Uncle Simon. That glistening round thing that fell with a slap to the drive. Paul's boot tip trying to nudge it back in. Laura's head opening in an instant. Bob's grunts and wails of pain and fear, silenced with two sharp reports.

Rueben's heart slammed in his throat, pushing the breath ever shallower, the dizziness higher. What now? Oh for the love of everything, what now? How could he save his family without the help of the Hickmans? He was no hero.

His brain floundered, the dizziness rose. He wanted to lay down right where he crouched and close his eyes, just go to sleep and blot everything out. He wanted to run deep into the woods and never stop running. He wanted to barrel screaming into the driveway and bullets wouldn't touch him and he'd lay about himself with fists and break faces, knock teeth out, destroy these invaders who killed the people he loved. He wanted to be back in the city and never see trees again.

But he did none of it. He crouched, frozen, crying, gasping, sure any moment his heart would burst from beating so hard, so fast.

Grandma Molly stepped in front of him, tried to block his view of the carnage. But the image was burned in his mind. He squeezed his eyes shut and saw it over and over again, Bob dropping, Laura's head opening, James walking over yelling, "No more? *No more?*" The sharp, hard reports of the gun. Uncle Simon flying backwards, his chest opened to claw at the sky. That shining organ slapping the ground.

Grandma Molly moved again, eyes wide as she implored him. He saw her mouth working but heard nothing past the roar of his blood in his ears, like a tornado tearing every thought away with it. Movement beyond his grandmother caught his eye and he watched Paul dragging Bob Hickman by one arm. The man's large body shifted in starts and jerks as Paul took a step, hauled, took a step, hauled. Bob must weigh in excess of 100 kilos and Paul struggled to shift his dead weight. Dead. Bob Hickman dead. Laura

Hickman dead. Uncle Simon, dead and blood-soaked, his insides glistening in the light. Rueben wanted to scream.

Paul dragged Bob through the doors into the garage, no doubt to lay him alongside Uncle Simon. Uncle Simon who would be cold and stiff and blue by now. Would he be starting to decompose? Stink? How long did that take?

The pulse pounded in Rueben's ears as disparate, unhinged thoughts tumbled over each other in his mind. Then Paul re-emerged and headed for Laura, much smaller than her husband. He picked her up easily, cradled in his arms, and as he headed for the garage again her head lolled back, stared upside down at Rueben with wide, imploring eyes, and a stream of blood poured from the back of her head and spattered the gravel.

Suppressing a scream, Rueben bit the sleeve of his coat, squeezed his eyes shut, but saw it all again in perfect clarity, in mental replay.

Then Paul emerged again, and stood looking at the four cars lined up on the drive. After a moment, he moved to each one, closed all the doors, pocketing the keys each time. He stared into the car he'd arrived in for a long time before he locked it up, shaking his head slightly like he couldn't believe what he saw there. "Where is it?" he said aloud, incredulous. He leaned in, patted around in the back seat a moment, then stood quickly again. He looked back to the garage, then into the car. After a moment more, Rueben realised the young man was crying, his shoulders trembling. Then he shook himself and went back inside the hotel.

At last alone, breath constricted in his throat, Rueben pushed up, ignoring the howl of pain in his legs from crouching in the cold for so long, and ran. He smashed back through the trees, back alongside the lawns. Repeatedly Grandma Molly appeared in front of him, saying something as he ran by. Then she would step out again further along, and again and again. But he ignored her, ignored everything and ran, tears streaming, running chilled under his ears and down the sides of his neck. His breath came in gasping sobs and he let them out, far enough away now to give voice to his grief, to his fear and pain. He was no hero. He had failed.

He looped around the edge of the lawns and pushed deeper into the trees. He found the familiar path, saw his refuge high above the ground. The only place he could think of going. He wanted to switch everything off, hide, go dark. He kept running and leaped, grabbed the lowest branch and pulled himself up. He turned and climbed, sidestepped along the heavy bough, jumped to the treehouse veranda with a crash. He ran inside and slammed the door behind him and scrambled onto the mattress, pulled all the blankets over himself, wrapped up as tightly as possible, and shook, howling sobs of absolute loss. He refused to hear Molly's cries or the slick whispering in the hollows of his mind.

LEIGH

I LEIGH wondered what Clay was up to when he talked about doing that crazy stuff with the hearth. Was it really possible, everything he'd said about the original owners? Then the shouting, the gunshots, and her gut turned to ice water. When Deanna dragged Clay back into the lounge, Leigh watched. There was a long mirror behind the bar and if she turned her head far enough she could just about make out the other side of the big room, could see where Grant and Clay were tied. The old man gritted his teeth against pain as he staggered with Deanna. She dragged him none too gently. But he held his tongue as Leigh assailed him with questions, as Grant kept saying, "Who got shot? Dad! Who got shot?"

Deanna sat Clay roughly against the column and reworked the ropes to bind him up with Marcus, and Clay finally spoke.

"They're dead." His voice was thick with grief.

"Who is?" Grant said.

"Who was it?" Leigh heard weakness in her voice, the seeds of despair. She had told herself again and again to stay strong, but it was getting harder. Her neck strained as she twisted to see Clay in the mirror.

He shook his head, staring at the autumn tones of the rug between his feet. "Bob and Laura Hickman." He ignored Grant's shocked questions and Leigh's gasps as he silently gave in, at least for a moment, to tears. Deanna finished securing his ropes and went back into the dining room.

"Clay," Leigh said, then had nothing more. "Oh, Clay," she managed.

Clay's tears dried up after a short while, but she knew the pain of grief lingered, identical to the hard rock in her chest. Clay had known Bob since he was born, Grant and Bob were childhood friends. Even she considered the Hickmans as good as family. Leigh cried, too. As her tears fell she watched Grant in the mirror. He sat stony-faced, staring hard at the wall opposite him. His lips were pressed into a thin line, his cheeks pale, eyes red-rimmed. She remembered the cut above his eye from James's pistol butt. When she had been moved before, she'd seen it had swollen to an angry red, but the blood had congealed, stopped dripping. His face, shirt collar, shoulder, and the rug beside him were stained dark with it. It was on the opposite side, she couldn't see it now in the mirror, but the undamaged side of his face was visible, and twisted with rage.

Leigh recognised the fury of impotence in her husband. The man was supposed to be the provider and the protector for his family, that's the way he thought. Yet there he sat, tied up and useless, while more people died. While his own son was out in the cold. Leigh knew that's how Grant felt because she shared the sentiments. And it was all bullshit, of course, that Grant would think it was all on him. Leigh was as much responsible for protecting her family as he was, and she sat there just as trapped, just as restricted. But it would prey harder on Grant because men took these things on. They carried the weight of those responsibilities whether it was all theirs or not, whether the women in their lives wanted them to or not.

She heard Paul and Deanna arguing, their voices muffled and indistinct by distance. They must be in the kitchen. She craned her neck to see around, wondering where James had gone. The man was becoming ever more unhinged, and now these two additional murders would only make him worse. Surely Paul and Deanna saw that, recognised the hopeless mess of their situation. Were they arguing about standing up to James at last? Maybe Deanna wanted to, Leigh knew she'd got through to the woman, at least a little. But perhaps Paul refused, determined to ally with his brother, loyal.

Deanna was certainly the stronger of the pair. Leigh thought maybe Paul had spent his whole life following in his brother's shadow and had no way of knowing now how to step out of it. But Deanna was smart, she was tough. Surely she wouldn't let this continue. Perhaps if they had a chance to talk to them while James was AWOL she could force that wedge deeper, provide a bigger gap to allow Deanna to take control. Deanna and Paul were both free and armed. If they stood up to James together, what chance would he have?

"We need a plan."

Leigh twisted to see her husband, but he still stared dead ahead. They'd shared glances in the mirror several times, tried to reassure each other with eyes and mouthed platitudes, but he wasn't looking now. "What do you mean?" she asked.

"We need a plan," Grant said again. "This has gone on long enough. We have to do something."

"Like what?" Leigh asked. "If we make too much fuss, they'll hurt us."

"They won't. James will. We need to convince them to kill the bastard."

Clay sighed, shook his head. Grant, it seemed, had been thinking along similar lines as Leigh, but with a harder, more darkly malevolent outcome. More final. "We don't need them to kill him," Clay said. "We just need them to disarm him, to hold him accountable. Or at least hold him, and end this."

"I want them all dead."

"I get that," Clay said. "Me too, if I'm honest. But more important than them dying is you living. You and Leigh and Marcus and especially Rueben."

"Not you?"

Leigh couldn't see Clay as well in the mirror, but she saw as he turned to stare across at his son. Saw the haunted desperation in his eyes. "Not if it means you guys survive."

Grant shook his head. "No, Dad. No way. You're not sacrificing yourself for us. How would you, anyway?"

"Let's try to find a way where we all live," Leigh said. "No more dying!"

"You think I'm afraid to die?" Clay asked. "Maybe I was once, but not any more. I'm tired, can you understand that? I'm tired and everything hurts."

"Dad, no..."

"Clay, what are you talking about?" Leigh asked.

"I don't want to die," Clay said. "I don't seek oblivion, but I'm past the point of fearing it. And if it can save you guys, why not?" Before they could protest again, he said, "You know the funny thing about age? It's only in your body. Not your head. I don't feel any different now than I did at twenty-five. But when you're young, you're immortal. The entire world is yours. There's you and a bunch of other young people, and then there's everyone else in the world, all older than you, all one step closer to death. All those squares, they have no idea, and you're young and cool and better than everyone. You remember that? Sure, I'm wiser now, I guess. I know more stuff. But the thing inside, the part that's *me*, that makes me who I am, it still feels the same. Think about yourselves. You feel any different now than you did twenty years ago? Add another thirty years to that and it won't be any different."

"If anything that's a reason to live, Clay," Leigh said. "You're still you, still vibrant and valuable to us, and to yourself."

Clay let out a soft, humourless laugh. "I remember being young. I'd look around and everyone was older. *Everyone* was *old*. They didn't have a clue, the world was mine. Then I made it into my twenties and realised, yeah, okay, adults have some clue. But I was one of them then, a young adult, full of life, full of potential. My future stretched endlessly ahead. We bought this place, Molly and I, in our early twenties. Can you believe that? And we fought what we fought here and we won. At least we thought we did."

"Dad..?"

"But I kept aging. It's relentless. I hit my thirties and I'd look around and there'd be a bunch of young idiots who knew nothing behind me, but most people were still older than me. Age wasn't something I even thought about in relation to myself then.

"And there's a sweet spot, you know? Around your late thirties, there's this time where you're more than a youngster, you're a grown adult, responsible and respected, but not past it. It's a golden age. But it's as fleeting as every part of life.

"Then I got through my forties, into my fifties, and I suddenly saw I was one of the older ones. Out of nowhere, how did it happen? Not old yet, but there were a lot of people younger. Maybe more younger than older for the first time in my life. I'd see adult professionals, people at the top of their game, and I'd realise they were younger than me by ten or fifteen or twenty years. They were having that moment in the golden age. That's when time started to really slip for me. What was happening? I still felt the same. I still had so many dreams and goals."

"Clay," Leigh said quietly. "What are you–"

"But I still wasn't old yet," he said, ignoring her. "I'd see real old folk and think, well, I have a lot of time before I'm there. Then the aches and pains increased. Time began to have a physical effect instead of just a philosophical one. One day I looked around and was shocked to see that I *was* one of the old ones. Just like that. Old. You see everyone else in the world has it better except you and a handful of other old farts with one foot already in the grave and you think, what the hell happened? Where did it all go? Pretty much everyone else is younger than me, their lives ahead of them, and here I am, slow and decrepit. Seems like only five minutes ago I was in my twenties looking at everyone older than me and now? Now I'm in that narrow wedge of people lucky enough to reach old age. Growing old is a privilege, right? Lucky? From this angle, it doesn't feel so fortunate. This aging carcass, these discomforts, the long, insomniac nights that are the last hours of life leaching away in the darkness. What the hell happened? How did I get so old? And why? What's the damn point of it all?"

"Dad, I don't understand. Why are you talking like this? We still need you. Rueben needs you especially. You and him, you have something special."

Clay carried on as though Grant hadn't spoken either. "I still feel the same. Inside, I still *am* the same. I can't believe I'm an old man. That it really happened to me. More than that, I can't believe it happened so damned fast." He looked up, caught Grant's eye at last. "But I'm tired, son. I've been around a long time, and I'm not afraid to die."

"So what are you planning to do?" Leigh asked. "For all that nihilism, what can you do that won't only make things worse for all of us?"

Clay shook his head slowly. "Honestly, I don't know. But Grant's right. We need a plan. We need to do something and I can't help thinking that anything we do will mean someone gets hurt, to give the others a chance. So that someone should be me, that's all. I'm already close to the end."

"Rueben is still out there," Leigh said. "He's running for Bob and Laura's place even now, right? We have to believe that. He could be there already, or nearly there. And even if he finds them not home, he'll break in and use the phone. Or carry on to another property. It'll take longer, but he'll get help. We have to believe that, don't we?"

"What if he isn't?" Grant said. "What if help isn't coming? We have to do something."

"I've been working on Deanna," Leigh said. "I told you guys that. I still think I might be able to talk her around. She's scared and uncertain. Let's tread carefully, walk softly instead of stamping around in steel-toed boots, getting ourselves killed." Leigh swallowed, wondering how to get time alone with Deanna again. She knew she could get through to the woman with time. Just a little more time.

"They're all in the frame for multiple murders," Clay said. "I can't see any of them backing out now."

"Then what will they do?" Leigh demanded, anger making her voice rise.

"Dad, what did you mean when you said you and Mum fought something here and you thought you'd won?"

Clay sighed, nodded. He needed them to understand that. "There's more happening here than just these bastards holding us hostage, you know that. There's an evil here, that was here when Molly and I moved in. We thought we dealt with it, but I think maybe we only treated a symptom. The cause is something else. And these idiots have… let it out again somehow."

"Come on, Clay, you can't be serious." Leigh said the words, but in her heart she knew he was serious. Something broken was happening. *Had* happened to Rick.

"Leigh, what happened to their friend?" Clay said, echoing her thoughts. "Paul said he saw that guy drained to a husk. Black tendrils glowing red coming up through the blood on the floor or something. You think he made that up? It's nigh on fifty years ago now, but I've seen something of what he's talking about. I don't know what it is, and for half a century we've been lucky here, but our luck ran out. I think it ran out when those bastards started spilling so much blood. It's all true, Leigh. I'm scared about the night coming, it's stronger then. Molly always said so. We're strong in the light, but at night? That's when bad things take over. Even little kids know that. Bad things to make James and his cronies the least of our concerns. We have to do something, and soon."

"Clay," Leigh said, then ran out of words. What could they do?

"What is it?" Clay said suddenly. Leigh twisted, saw him looking away from them, away from Grant, into nowhere.

"Who are you talking to, Dad?"

"What's happened?" Clay asked the empty air. He listened more, then said, "No! He has to go for help! Even without Bob and Laura he can use their phone. He *has* to go for help!"

"Dad, what is happening?" Grant shouted.

"Clay?" Leigh's voice wavered, weak with concern that Clay had lost his mind.

"Go," Clay said. "Stay with him, talk to him, bring him around. He's scared but he loves you. Trusts you. Be there for him and convince him to run for help."

He was silent again a moment, Leigh chewed her lip. Then Clay said, "Getting to him how?" Then, "Go to him. Talk to him. You have to convince him to get away from here and get help. Or at the very least, just get away. You can do it, my love."

Clay stared at the spot for a moment longer, then twisted back to look at his son. "Your mother and I have the sight, son. You've heard us talk about it before."

Leigh frowned, but held her tongue. Grant had told her about this once or twice, about how his parents always said they could see dead people, communicate with them. Grant always brushed it off, but Clay just then had seemed entirely sane while he spoke to no one she could see.

"And it drove Cindy away," Grant spat. "You're still going with this stuff? Even now?"

"Now more than ever, Grant. Your sister has the sight too, but she doesn't like it. To say the least. She holds it against us. You don't have it, so I know it's hard to understand, but you have to believe me. Your mother, she talks to me sometimes. She was here just then. She's been watching over Rueben. And she told me Roo saw everything, with Bob and Laura. And he's hiding in his treehouse, terrified. He's not going for help."

Leigh let out a sob and Grant stared.

"You have to believe me, son. Molly is going back to be with Rueben, to try to talk him around. But meanwhile, no help is coming. He panicked and ran back to his treehouse. He's only a kid, for god's sake, this is too much for him."

"Dad, seriously?"

"Yes, seriously. And Molly told me something else, that I've suspected and was just telling you. She thinks something old and evil has been woken up. And she doesn't think it's the ghost of Michael Ellery but rather whatever drove him to do the things he did."

"Clay," Leigh said. "What made him do those terrible things?"

"We don't know. We never even suspected there was something else until now. Maybe, when we sent Michael Ellery on his way, we managed to cut it off from here, for all those years. But now it's back. And Molly says she thinks it's getting to Rueben. And Rueben isn't running for help. We have to do something ourselves."

"You murdering fucking scum!" Marcus yelled, his voice hard and raw.

Leigh jumped, turning to see him. "What are you doing? Marcus, calm down."

"You deadbeat, murderous pieces of shit!" Marcus yelled at the top of his voice.

"No, Marcus," Leigh said. "Not like this!"

The man's face was twisted in rage, his black fringe hanging over his eyes as he leaned forward in his bonds. Then he tipped his head back again. "You fuckers, come and get me!" he screamed.

Paul and Deanna's footsteps sounded, coming through the dining room. Leigh clamped her mouth shut, heart rate rising. This wasn't right. This wasn't the way to deal with anything. *Why now, Marcus?*

As Paul and Deanna appeared in the lounge room doorway, the back door beside the bar opened and James strode in, brows furrowed in a frown, his eyes glittering darkly.

"What the fuck is happening in here now?" he asked, and his grin was feral.

PAUL

I JAMES'S face had become more frightening than ever. It seemed to be coated with a sheen of sweat but also one of madness. In previous situations where James's rage had enveloped him like this, it took a while for the pressure cooker to pop, but eventually it did, and then James equalized again. Settled back into a cold, hard, but fundamentally balanced individual.

This time though? Paul wasn't so sure. After the bank, surely that intensity, that adrenaline, had been enough to bring James back down. And maybe it would have if they'd arrived here and found the hotel empty like they'd expected. Finding the family here had ramped his brother up again, created a new build-up to account for. A new volcano to erupt. And it had done so, swiftly, with the murder of Simon. But that fool had been creeping up on them with a gun. He deserved what he got, the idiot. But still James hadn't come back down.

Then the horrible thing with Rick, and now that couple from down the mountain showing up unannounced, leading to more shooting, more death. Had James somehow punched through his rise and fall nature to some undiscovered country on the other side where he would be forever raging? Never coming down? Looking at his crazed eyes now as he stared at Marcus, Paul wondered if maybe he had. And, if so, what the hell were they going to do about it? And did he tell James what he'd seen in the garage? Simon's body sucked empty like Rick's had been. And all the blood from their car where

Rick had lain gone like it had never been there. Had James already seen those things? The blood on the driveway where Simon had been shot was gone too.

Deanna kept talking about standing up to James, insisting they leave or something. In the kitchen, before Marcus had yelled for them, she'd even suggested just the two of them, Paul and Deanna, slip out to one of the cars and bolt. Leave James and everyone else here. Paul was too scared to consider that. If his brother was snapping this easily with strangers, surely it wouldn't take much more for him to snap with his own kin, and his friends. What if he caught them leaving? Paul had put all the car keys in a pile on the kitchen bench, but now he wondered if maybe he should pocket some. Just one set, as insurance. But he couldn't leave his brother. And what might James do if he caught Paul with a set of keys?

Deanna had asked Paul where he saw this whole thing going and he'd answered with the only reply he had. The only one he ever had. "I don't know. It's up to James."

It always had been up to James and always would be. That's how life worked. His brother looked after him. Their father had been brutal and mean, and some of that was in James, but James had protected Paul from their father too. Despite anything else that went down, James always came through and he carried Paul with him. Paul held onto that, like a life preserver in a stormy ocean. Be patient, he told Deanna, see it through, and James would carry them to the other side.

"I need a bathroom break," Marcus said, his voice hard between gritted teeth.

"Seriously?" James said, tapping the barrel of Simon's pistol thoughtfully against his chin. Paul wondered where his brother's shotgun was. "That's what all the hollering was about?"

"*You* take me." Marcus fixed James with a steely glare.

"Me?"

"You. Just you. Or are you scared of me?"

James barked a laugh.

"Don't do this," Leigh said, looking across. "Just chill out, please."

"She's right," Grant said. "Let's all just settle down, yeah?"

James strode around to Grant's side of the column and swung a short but heavy kick into the man's ribs. Grant grunted and scrunched up, but his bonds prevented him from curling into the ball he clearly wanted to. "Settle down?" James shouted at him. He slapped the man, opening the cut above his eye to drip blood again. "This is the first thing the fucker has said since we got here, don't you think it's even a little exciting?"

He left Grant gasping for breath and went to crouch in front of Marcus. "You want a shot at me? Is that it?"

"Untie me and take me for a bathroom break, you worthless chickenshit piece of crap," Marcus said, his voice a low growl.

James rocked back on his heels, grinning. "Woooo-ee! You have found some fire, man. You were a zombie and now you're an avenging angel, that it?"

"You too scared to untie me, fuckface?"

"What's to stop me just popping you right here? Right now?" James pressed the barrel of the pistol into Marcus's forehead.

Marcus drove forward as far as the ropes would allow, pressed his head hard into the gun making James stumble back slightly. "Fucking do it if you want! You think I care?"

"Marcus, please!" Leigh's voice was thick with tears that hadn't fallen, but were clearly imminent.

"Why are you holding us all?" Marcus said, loud and angry now. "What for? Huh? What's your plan, genius?"

"This isn't helping," Clay said, but the old man's head hung as he stared at the floor. He seemed deflated, beaten.

Paul's entire body shook in anticipation of the almost certain violence to come. He wanted this all to be over.

James lowered the gun, let it hang between his legs as he rested his elbows on his knees and stared at Marcus. Marcus stared back, unflinching. James tipped his head to one side, like an inquisitive bird wondering if it dared to snatch a morsel near someone's boot. The moment dragged on, the two men perusing each other. A smile slowly spread over James's face.

"Maybe I *should* untie you and let you take a swing, huh?" James said. "You want that?"

"James..." Deanna's voice was pitched low, wary.

"How about it?" Marcus said. "You and me, no weapons, no nothing. Right here. You untie me and let's go, you worthless fucker."

"You really think you can beat me?"

"I know I can. I bet you're too chickenshit to let me prove it."

They stared hard at each other, silent again. Paul's mouth was dry as he watched. He remembered something James had told him a long time ago. A fight, James had said, is usually finished before it starts. Some fights just erupt out of nowhere and that's different, but if two guys are warming up to scrap, sticking chests out, strutting around, the actual blows are largely irrelevant. All the posturing decides the fight. Paul had doubted that was always true, but a couple of times James had proven his theory when guys they knew got aggressive and James would always predict which one would win before they came to blows, and he'd always been right. But they knew those guys, it was easy to guess. This was different. Unknown quantities. Marcus was fit, lean, his shoulders rounded with muscle. He was almost as tall as James, maybe only an inch shorter. Who knew what experience or training he might have? And he was furious, driven by a powerful grief, that surely had an empowering effect. Paul believed the man when he said he didn't care if he died. A man with nothing to lose was a dangerous opponent.

James licked his lips, smiling again. He reached up one open palm and slapped Marcus hard across the face. Marcus's head whipped to one side and he growled, straining forward suddenly against his bonds, desperate for release.

"Chickenshit motherfucker!"

"You're not getting a shot at me." James stood and turned away, heading for the back door again. Paul knew his brother had considered the odds and decided maybe Marcus could beat him. Paul lost a little respect for James then and it burned him inside.

"I still need the bathroom," Marcus said, resignation in his tone.

James stopped, looked back. "Really?"

"Really."

James walked over to Paul and took his shotgun, then tossed the pistol through the air as he turned away. Paul was caught off-guard, nearly tripped over his feet as he juggled the small weapon once, twice, then managed to hold on. He looked at James in surprise. What did his brother want him to do?

"You take him," James said. "Watch him like a hawk and tie him up again afterwards. That gun is reloaded, I found a box of ammo in the cottage over there."

Paul looked at Deanna and she shrugged. "Okay," he said to James. Was his brother really this unconcerned?

"You just keep your distance and you shoot him at the slightest wrong move, okay? He doesn't get to have a go at any of us. He hasn't earned it."

"Okay," Paul said.

James nodded and went behind the bar at the back of the lounge. He started rummaging through the bottles of spirits on the back shelves. Paul frowned. If his brother started drinking, things might get worse. Alcohol mellowed James at first, but the man had no internal limiter and always kept drinking until his mellow buzz became an angry simmer. And that only meant another kind of pressure cooker. Paul shook his head. Too much to worry about now, too many things going on. But perhaps Deanna was at least partly right. She had said they needed to talk to James, try to come up with a plan. If they couldn't, she had suggested they turn against his brother, and Paul couldn't countenance that. But maybe they could talk, find a way through this. And perhaps if James had only a little buzz going from booze, he might be more receptive. If they timed it right, Paul and Deanna may talk him down a little. James had a bottle of Jack Daniels in one hand and stared from behind the bar, one eyebrow raised.

"What are you thinking about, little brother?"

Paul forced a smile, a single shake of the head. "Nothing. Sorry. Just... tired. I think we all need a good night's sleep." Where the hell had that come from? He was exhausted, sure, but that was no excuse to ramble.

"Just take that guy to the damned toilet," James said, and headed out the back door, carrying the whiskey with him.

Deanna returned to her armchair, shotgun resting across her knees, as Paul crouched to untie Marcus. He glanced into the man's brown eyes, but saw none of the fire from moments before. Had he retreated into catatonia again?

"Come on. On your feet."

Marcus stood and stumbled slightly, shook himself and shifted from foot to foot a couple of times to exercise out the stiffness of extended sitting. Then he turned to look at Paul. Paul lifted the pistol, levelled it at Marcus's ribs. "After you."

Marcus stared at him for a moment and the man's gaze was disquieting. Paul felt as though he were being measured somehow. Then Marcus headed for the dining room, Paul staying close behind, the gun trained on his back.

"Marcus," Leigh called. "Be cool, yeah?"

The man didn't answer her, just walked. Paul glanced back, saw Leigh straining fruitlessly to see around the column. Grant and Clay both faced them as they left, Grant watching stony-faced, Clay staring at the ground between his knees.

Grant and Paul locked gazes for a moment and Paul sensed the man really wanted to say something, like it writhed inside him, but he couldn't force it out. Paul raised an eyebrow and Grant's lips parted, but still no words.

"Paul!" Deanna snapped.

He startled and looked around. Marcus was almost through the doors into the dining room.

"Focus," Deanna said.

"We need to talk to James," he said quietly as he passed.

She nodded once.

Marcus walked past the table where Rick had been. Paul couldn't help looking, all that blood gone like it had never been there. He knew what he'd seen. Rick's heavy body withered and emptied, sucked dry. And when he'd taken those two neighbours into the garage before, dropped them down beside the corpse of Simon, he'd seen that man's body equally desiccated, drained just like Rick. And James must have seen that when he dropped Rick's body next to it, Paul realised now, but his brother had said nothing.

Paul was sure those two, the Hickmans, would be emptied the same way come nightfall. Why? What happened to the blood? Where was it going? All of a sudden he couldn't wait to team up with Deanna and talk to James. Maybe they could convince him to leave before night. Paul didn't want to be here after dark again. Fuck the Moore family, they could leave them tied to the columns for all he cared. He wanted out.

Marcus headed past the stairs leading to the upstairs private living area and in through the door marked M. Paul caught the door as it started to swing closed and followed him in. They passed the big double sinks and Paul slowed, his pistol still aimed at Marcus's back as the man turned to look at the stalls. Why he didn't just go into the first one, Paul didn't know, but he went towards the second one, looked at the third, then turned slightly and looked back at the first stall door. Paul sighed, opened his mouth to tell him to just get on with it, and Marcus launched at him, lips peeling back from his teeth in a feral snarl.

Paul yelped in surprise and no small amount of fear as Marcus crashed into him. His stomach turned to water, his legs soft, but he pulled the trigger anyway. Marcus's eyes were filled with agony and fury, but he slammed Paul back against the closed bathroom door and pounded once, twice, into Paul's face with his elbow.

Pain blossomed like an explosion across Paul's left cheek and eye socket and his ears whined with a sound like electronic static. His vision crossed and his legs went further to jelly, but he refused to fall. Marcus had his wrist in a vice-like grip, forcing the gun away from them both, and drew his free hand back to punch again. Paul used the moment and the fractional space he had to put his free palm against Marcus's chest and shove, desperate to make room. Paul wasn't a big guy, but he was almost the same size as Marcus, and strong enough. The man staggered back and Paul saw blood on his shirt, on his left side above the hip. The shot had at least winged him.

Paul yelled, an incoherent shout of fear and desperation, and tried to wrench his gun hand free, but Marcus refused to relinquish his grip. As he staggered back, Marcus used his momentum to haul Paul with him, slinging him sideways as they went. Paul stumbled, pulled off-balance, and tried to right himself before he fell, but Marcus reached over the gun arm and grabbed the back of his neck, wrenched his gun hand up and back, and slammed Paul's face down and forward. It all happened so fast, so relentlessly. The shining white porcelain of the large sinks rushed up to meet him and he heard the strangely distant *tink* of his forehead bouncing off the rock hard ceramic, then a whine as his vision blackened and swirled.

A tooth cracked painfully from his jaw and stabbed back into his tongue and he realised it was because he had faceplanted into the cold tiles of the floor. Blackness receded briefly from his vision and he twisted to look up in time to see Marcus back-pedalling with the pistol held in both hands pointing directly down at Paul's face, the barrel an endless black hole. Paul screamed and the black hole exploded with fire and noise.

DEANNA

"WE need to talk to James."

With that single sentence, Deanna felt a large portion of the tension of the last couple of days drain away. If Paul had finally come around to her way of thinking, maybe there was a chance yet to extricate themselves from this mess. Either convince James to leave, all three of them together, or convince Paul to leave with her once it became obvious there was no chance to change James's course. And then what? Who knew. But maybe keep moving, cross the border into Victoria, keep going, anything to get far away from this. And James had grabbed that bottle of Jack. If they could catch him when he was a little buzzed they had the best chance of getting him to listen. It was the first moment of possible hope she had allowed herself.

Then the hollering.

The crashing.

The gunshot.

Then the shout and the scream.

Then another gunshot.

Deanna was up and running after the first shout, Leigh's cry of, "No no no!" fading behind her, before she realised she'd stood up. Her entire body operated on lizard brain, the shotgun pressed across her chest and she sprinted through the large dining room. She heard a crash and yelled out, "Paul!"

As she slammed into the door of the men's toilet she had a moment to think that barging in there blindly might be a foolish approach, but she'd already hit the door and it was swinging inwards. Then it stopped abruptly and she bounced back off it. In the gap before the door swung closed again she saw a body on the floor, the back of the head a red mess. But the clothes were easily recognizable and she knew without a doubt it was Paul lying there. Dead. She barked a sob and then another gunshot split the air. The door splintered with a ragged hole right in the centre and Deanna leapt back frantically looking down at herself. But the bullet had passed through the wood and missed her. It must have buzzed within an inch of where she stood and she figured maybe that was all her luck used up.

She jumped to the side as another bullet tore through, pressed her back to the wall beside the door. Taking a deep, steadying breath, she twisted around and jabbed the door open with the hard barrels of the shotgun. It bounced once more against Paul's hip, the same way it had stopped the first time and probably saved her life, and she fired her shotgun blindly through the gap she'd made as another pistol shot took out a chunk of doorframe right above her weapon. Surely the blast radius of her shot would be enough to at least wing Marcus?

She heard a yelp of pain and, as the door swung closed again, she caught sight of him stumbling back into the third cubicle along. She crouched low and tentatively pushed the door open again with her foot, clearly revealing Paul lying in a rapidly spreading pool of blood, obscenely scarlet against the white tiles. The door opened about halfway before it fetched up against his hip as he lay on his right side, one arm crooked behind him. Deanna panned the shotgun, waiting, wondering if she could fire through the stall door from this angle.

Then she heard a wail that curdled her blood, part scream, part roar, and James barrelled past her, knocking her sideways.

"He's got the gun!" she yelled, but James jumped his brother's corpse and slammed his palm against the first stall door. It banged back against the wall, and Deanna shouted, "Number three!" as the door to that stall opened and Marcus stepped out, the pistol held up in front of him.

Deanna had a moment to notice his shirt was red with blood, his face as pale as the tiled floor, before James's momentum kept him moving and he blocked her view. The pistol fired again and James zigged his head and his left ear burst with blood, then he was swinging his right arm upwards.

Deanna realised he wasn't carrying Paul's shotgun, or his own, but still holding the bottle of Jack Daniels. It connected with something, a glassy *thunk*, and Marcus fell back into the stall with his eyes rolled up to the whites. James wheeled and followed him in, the whiskey bottle somehow unbroken, arcing over for another hit. As James vanished into the stall, Deanna heard the bottle connect with Marcus's head. Surely only a combination of heavy glass and human skull could make that noise. Then again, and this time the crash of glass shattering. Over the stink of blood rose a sharp tang of alcohol. James's incoherent screams became ragged as Deanna heard a wet *thwack*, then again.

She made it to the stall door, shotgun gripped level in front, as James staggered back out, jamming the pistol into the back of his jeans. Marcus lay twisted back over the toilet bowl, his face swollen and blackened, teeth missing from his bloody mouth, one eyebrow a ragged mess, more blood on his shirt. The broken neck of the bottle stuck up from the front of his throat. The place stank of blood and whiskey.

As she stared in horror, her mind spinning its wheels in the slick mess of her incoherent, tumbling thoughts, James pushed back past her and fell to his knees by his brother. The left side of James's face was awash with blood as he gathered Paul up, crushing the smaller man to his chest, saying, "Pauly, Pauly, Pauly" over and over. Deanna saw Paul's brains.

Her hands shook so hard she could barely hold onto the shotgun. She stared down at James cradling his brother and finally one thought pushed through the maelstrom of her howling mind.

This is it. They're all dead.

For a moment the thought of shooting James surfaced. She could end this now, finish him, cut the family free, and then run, take her chances. Almost of its own accord, her shotgun began to tilt towards James.

He looked slowly up from his brother's blank staring eyes, a stark red bullet hole right between them, and Deanna felt a chill ripple through her when he met her gaze. She froze. His teeth were clenched, lips pulled back in a snarl. Blood covered the left side of his face, down his neck, the top of his ear missing and an angry gouge along the side of his forehead, but it looked relatively superficial. He'd come so close to being shot right in the head. He breathed hard, chest rising, falling, rising, falling, as he stared.

"James..." Deanna finally managed through lips dry as sand. But no more words followed his name, just her empty breath.

Something slid over his eyes then, a shadow of sorts. His breathing slowed, became deeper, longer. Then he said, "Get them out of here."

"What? Who?"

James nodded at the cubicle. "Him. And Paul."

"Out? Where?"

"To the garage with the others."

"James, we have to–"

"Get them out of here!" He stood, stepping over Paul to open the bathroom door.

"James, this has to stop. No more, please. You and me, let's go. Just go. Take one of the cars, the clean ones, maybe that ute that couple arrived in. Take it and go, find somewhere to hide, somewhere to hole up..." Her voice petered out in the face of his furious glare.

"Finished?" he asked. He was holding the pistol again. She hadn't seen him draw it.

Deanna sucked in a gulp of air, tried desperately, and failed, to still the shaking in her hands. "Please. No more killing. No more."

"I'm not going to kill them. We need them." Despite the new shadow over his eyes, Deanna saw the pain of grief there too. The haunted howling wind of loss behind his gaze. And she saw madness, some line crossed, some land entered from which there was no return. And no reasoning. He winced, frowned like he was trying to work out a difficult math problem. "Enough blood..." His voice whispered out, then he shook his head. "For now. We need them. For now."

"Okay," she said quietly, confused. Was he talking to her or someone else? "Okay. I'll take them outside."

James nodded once and his lips flickered, somewhere between the crazed snarl of moments before and a manic grin. He snatched the shotgun from her unresisting hands and then he turned and swept out of the door. Instead of turning towards the lounge, Deanna caught a glimpse of him stalking off to the right, towards the kitchen, then the bathroom door swung closed.

CLAY

I DESPITE knowing it was going to go down, Clay's body trembled. A tectonic vibration in his bones. He hadn't needed to watch Marcus walk past, knowing from the tone of the man's voice that he was planning violence. He'd wanted a shot at James, and fair enough. That fucker had murdered his husband. Clay wanted a chance to take James down too. He was sure they all did. When that bid from Marcus had failed, Clay hoped the man would bide his time, but it wasn't to be. The poor bastard was in deep pain, grief chewing holes in him, and he needed to let that out. Clay knew also that despite the seeming catatonia, Marcus would be thinking of Rueben. He loved that boy as much as they all did. Rueben's uncles were some of the best things in the young lad's life. Once Molly had reported that Rueben was hiding, terrified, perhaps Marcus's course was set. Then the shooting. And the screaming.

Come on, Marcus, Clay thought to himself. *Kill all those fuckers and come cut us free.*

But he knew it wasn't to be. After the swift and brutal sounds of violence, James had come barrelling through. Then more violence. Then James's voice. Clay nodded to himself. Marcus was dead. Did he get any of the others first? And what might that mean for them now?

Everything remained still. Clay expected James any moment, but he didn't come. Then he heard sounds of effort, grunting and laboured breathing, and realised that was coming from Deanna. Doors bumped against walls and something was being dragged. But he didn't hear Paul.

"Is he dead?" Leigh asked in a weak voice.

Clay had the best vantage point, could see part of the dining room from where he was tied, but not enough. And he couldn't see the kitchen at all. "I think maybe Marcus got Paul," he said quietly. "But I think he died for it."

A sob burst up from Leigh like a bubble through thick mud and Grant kept repeating "Fuck fuck fuck," over and over again.

They fell into silence for a while, left alone by their attackers, and leaving each other alone with their thoughts. Leigh cried quietly but Clay heard her pull herself together, a kind of steel rising through the upset. She let the grief out, then girded herself once more, ready for any opportunity, he suspected. She wasn't the type to quit. Leigh was strong. He chanced a sidelong glance at Grant. His son, on the other hand, wasn't so tough.

Grant was a great dad, and a good husband, but he had a tendency to let things get on top of him. To blow things out of proportion and give in to ranting and raving instead of calmly seeking solutions. When it came to things like repairs at the hotel or problems with suppliers, that tendency was simply irritating. And Leigh's calmness always brought him around. Together they made a great team. But in a situation like this, things falling apart like they were and Grant tied up and impotent to help? That spelled a different kind of disaster for Grant's mental health. Sure enough, from the corner of his eye, Clay saw Grant grinding his teeth, his lips rippling in furious conversation with himself. Blood soaked his face and neck from the cut above his eye, that still leaked a little from Grant's frowns and grimaces. The man's wrists were bleeding where he'd struggled incessantly against his bonds, trying to pull free, or slip out of the tight loops. But these bastards knew how to truss up a person and there was no escaping the tight knots. Clay hoped Molly could talk Rueben around, get the kid to go for help still, but the day was wearing along once more and night came early.

Noises in the dining room distracted all of them, their attention suddenly focused on it. Someone passed through and then the familiar squeak of the women's bathroom door. How often had he and Grant said they'd straighten up and oil that crooked hinge, Clay wondered idly.

A moment later, Deanna strode into the room, her face a dark cloud, eyebrows cinched together creating a deep line in her forehead. She was a little out of breath and headed for her armchair again without a glance at the three captives, shotgun hanging alongside her leg. Clay noticed it wasn't the one she'd carried out there. Was it Paul's? He'd been trying to keep track of the weapons, but it wasn't easy. Three shotguns, similar but not identical, and the pistol, kept changing hands.

"What's happen–" Clay started, but she spun and shouted at the three of them.

"Paul's dead, okay? Marcus killed him. And James killed Marcus. Now shut the fuck up." She slumped down into the chair, shotgun across her knees.

Clay saw her hands were shaking.

"This has to end, Deanna." Leigh's voice was level, steady. And kind. "You see that, surely."

Deanna's jaw worked as she clenched her teeth.

Clay couldn't see Leigh, but he heard her scuffing against the carpet, no doubt trying to twist against her bonds to see Deanna. He saw movement in the mirror over the bar and realised Leigh was using it to see their side of the room. He caught her eye there, raised an eyebrow. Leigh licked her lips, shook her head.

"James isn't going to get any better," she said. "You know that's true. Now his little brother is dead he's only going to get more crazy."

"Shut the fuck up," Deanna said.

"No, Deanna," Clay said, firm where Leigh had been kind. "You have to listen. Leigh is right. James is way off the deep end. What happens now?" How many times did he have to ask that question?

Deanna sprang up out of the chair and Clay flinched, sure she was going to kick him, or strike him with the butt of the shotgun, but she just paced one way across the room and then back. "I don't fucking know!"

"He'll kill us," Grant said.

Clay looked over and saw Grant turning to catch Deanna's eye.

"He'll kill us all," Grant said. "You too, I expect. Because what other choice does he have now, huh?"

"He said he's not going to kill you. Said he needs you." Deanna's eyebrows creased again as she spoke, the frown betraying her doubt of that claim.

"For what, exactly?" Clay asked. "He's had you destroy all the communications we've got. No one knows you're here. There are cars outside full of petrol, and an open road through the kind of country where you can drive for an hour and not see another soul. You can go in any direction you want and just keep going. You don't need us. *He* doesn't need us."

Deanna kept pacing, tapping the shotgun along her thigh as she moved. "I think he's trying to figure out where to go. Where to… I don't know, hide or whatever."

"There's no hiding from what he's done," Grant said and Clay shot him a glare.

"Where is he now?" Leigh asked.

Deanna shook her head. "No idea. He keeps disappearing. Not sure if he's elsewhere in here, or in the cottage across there, or out in the fucking bush. He keeps talking about blood."

Clay shuddered at those last words. "He's mad," he said. "Mad with all kinds of pain. He's not thinking clearly and his only recourse is violence. That will include you eventually."

She stopped marching to look at him.

Clay barked a short laugh. "Oh, you think it won't? Grant's right. You think you're on his side and he'll always be good to you? Look how easily he quit on your buddy Rick and let him die to come up here rather than get him to a hospital. I heard you guys talking. He will protect himself at all costs." Clay drew a breath, warming to his ideas. "Way I see it, he'll decide we're ultimately fucking pointless in this situation. Right now, we're all baggage, that's all. So before long, we'll be stacked up in the garage out there with all the others. That's where you just took Marcus and Paul, isn't it? Quite a collection building up out there, huh? Piled up like firewood, are they? And then he'll hole up here for a little while, just you and him, let the heat die down a bit. But people know about this place. As the season comes around, in a couple of weeks, more folks'll start wandering through. You've only got a short window. So he'll give it, what? Maybe a week? The food will start to run out, the bodies in the garage will start to stink, and he'll decide it's time to bug out. Take his chances on slipping away. And his best chance of never being caught is no witnesses. No baggage." Clay fixed her with a stare. "Not even you. Huh? What are your chances then, do you think?"

She looked back, matched his gaze for several seconds and he saw wheels and cogs turning. Leigh and Grant were thankfully silent, letting the tension build. Clay was in no doubt James would eventually decide everyone had to die. His only uncertainty was whether that really would include Deanna or not. She finally shook her head.

"No. You know what? You're probably right about the three of you. You'll die, sure. But he'll take me with him. We go back a long way, James and me."

"And that's okay with you, is it?" Clay asked. "Three more murders on your conscience?"

Deanna laughed, but her eyes were pained. "At this point, who fucking cares? This thing has gone so far down the shitter, what else is there? I'm going to live with the crushing guilt of all this anyway, so three more won't make a difference."

"It will," Leigh said. "You know it will. If you think in your heart you could have done something about it."

"Like what?"

"Like letting us go. Or convincing James to go and leave us here."

Deanna drew a deep breath and blew it slowly out again. "No," she said eventually. "The old man has it right. The only way we have a chance is with no witnesses. You know, Paul and I had decided to try talking James into leaving, before Marcus did that hero bullshit. Now? There's no chance now." Clay saw something harden in her then. "I'm sorry. Really I am. You people don't deserve any of this. But it is what it is. In my world, it's survival first and other people second. I'll survive."

Clay saw the conflict in her statement, but saw her resolve too. It was a terrible combination, but it could only bode ill for the family.

"We only know your first names," Leigh said. "What if we promise to never tell anyone even that?"

"As if we'd believe you! James especially."

Clay had anticipated this, but he had one more line of attack. "Okay," he said, catching Deanna's attention again. "Let's say you're right and James comes around to the idea of killing us, but not you, and holing up here a little while until the heat's off, before making a run for it. That's probably a good plan, all things considered. Right? Given your limited options, it's the best course. But the staying here bit? Are you sure? What about the thing that happened to your buddy, Rick? You forget about that? You think you can survive here with it, night after night?"

Deanna stared, licked her lips. Clay popped one eyebrow at her. In truth, he was terrified of night falling, and what the darkness might bring with it. If he could pass that fear on and convince Deanna to convince James to leave now, well, that might give them a chance to survive. And if not them, at least Rueben. He didn't want to die, despite the unburdening speech he'd delivered earlier. He certainly didn't want Grant or Leigh to die. But if James killed all three of them and bugged out with Deanna, at least Rueben would survive. The poor child would live his life with a shocking weight of trauma, but he'd live.

"It happened to Simon too," Deanna said quietly.

Clay frowned. "What did?"

"The way Rick got all dried out and deflated like that. When I took those two out there just now, I saw Simon's body the same way, all dried out, the skin stretched across his bones."

"Seriously?" Clay asked. "Then you know it's true. Something evil is happening here."

"Those two idiot neighbours of yours are there, still just… dead. And now Paul and Marcus next to them." She looked up, her eyes haunted. "You think they'll get… drained tonight too?"

"I think of course they fucking will," Clay said, fear making him angry. "Given what little we know, it's a certainty, don't you think? And we have no way of knowing how or what for. We just need to get the hell out of here! Whatever you've woken up, it's not going to sleep again any time soon. Not while living, bleeding people are around."

"Please, let us go!" Leigh said, her voice weak with fear.

Clay glanced across at Grant and saw the impotent rage vibrating through his son, the man's face drawn and pale and on the edge of insanity. Blood stained his face and wrists as they twisted, twisted.

Deanna spat a low, "Fuck!" almost under her breath and turned. In three strides she was out of the room, leaving Clay, Grant, and Leigh in a thick, heavy silence.

RUEBEN

RUEBEN had no idea how long he'd been crying, deep sobs wracking his body in convulsive waves. It must have been hours, but he finally ran dry. He lay wrapped up in the dark warmth of his blankets, shutting out the whole world. The world where Uncle Simon was dead. Where he watched friendly neighbours he'd known his whole life gunned down. In the close dark of his hiding spot, images assaulted his mind's eye, playing on endless repeat as he cried. His body shook as if he were cold to the bone, never to warm through again. Tremors rippled up from his bones, his heart stuttered, pulse slowing and speeding up seemingly at random. He felt hollowed out, skinned alive, every nerve raw with electric sensation that somehow combined both pain and numbness. Over it all was the crushing weight of failure. He slipped in and out of consciousness and wondered if at some point he might go dark and never wake again.

When his grief and shock had whittled him away to a husk, a restless sleep finally stole over him. He wanted everything to go away. He would give anything to be back in the city, in their winter apartment, to never return to Eagle Hotel. He didn't care if he never saw the place again. But mostly he simply wanted to switch off. Sleep was the next best thing and he let himself fall into it willingly.

Hunger dragged him back to the pain-filled land of consciousness. Without throwing off the blankets, he felt around the rough wooden floor outside, the air cool on his hand. His fingers found the box of muesli bars and he dragged it into his cocoon and methodically chewed his way through one, then two, then a third. He would be glad to never see or taste a muesli bar again too. Slowly he felt some strength return to his muscles, though he was still ravenous. He hadn't eaten nearly enough for his fast metabolism and he thought perhaps his stomach was starting to digest itself. But the chewy snack held it at bay a little.

He refused to witness the thoughts tumbling through his mind. Refused to pay attention to the mental images assaulting him. Shining innards, opening skulls, horrified eyes, so much blood.

As he swallowed hard to drag the last of the third snack down his dry throat he realised he was desperately thirsty. He reached out again, found a juice box and slurped it down.

He couldn't stay wrapped in blankets forever. His meager supply of muesli bars and juice would run out soon. He needed to do something. But what? He had never felt so useless in his life. Whatever he did meant leaving the safety of his blankets. It meant returning to the outside world. The real world. Where death lived in numerous hideous forms.

A soft voice pushed through his muffled hearing. "Rueben, sweetheart? Please talk to me."

Grandma Molly.

"I know you hear me, child. Please listen to me."

Rueben exploded from the blankets, grief giving way to fury. "And what if I do? You're dead too! What has listening to you got me so far?"

Molly's face blanched as she took a shocked step backwards, then immediately moved closer, her hands reaching out, eyes haunted. "Oh, child! I'm so, so sorry."

"What good is it?" Rueben demanded. "The Hickmans are dead now. Everyone is dying!"

"But they're not all dead yet. Not everyone. You can save them."

Reuben gulped down another sob before it escaped. "Why me?" he demanded. He knew it sounded petty, childish, but he meant it. Why him?

He couldn't handle this, couldn't cope against these deranged adults. He wasn't grown, he shouldn't have this responsibility.

"I can't answer that," Molly said quietly. "It's not fair, and life sometimes isn't. There's no way on this earth you should have to be responsible for the lives of your family. You should be looked after by them. I hear you, I believe you."

Rueben frowned. He hadn't said that aloud, so how could she hear him? Or perhaps simply *Why me?* spoke all that was necessary.

"But sometimes, child, this world is topsy-turvy. Sometimes it throws shit in our face and we have to wipe it off and keep going because there isn't any other choice."

Rueben's eyes widened. He had never heard his Grandma curse in life. "They're dead!" was all he managed to say. "Who is there to tell?"

"You don't need them. You just need to call the police. You can do it yourself from Laura and Bob's place. Smash a window and use their phone. Hell, the door is probably unlocked, you know how it is up here."

Rueben stared, horrified. It was so obvious, why hadn't he realised that? When he saw Laura and Bob gunned down, he had been convinced the bottom had fallen out of the world. That it was all over. All done and dusted, his dad would say. But he should have run the other way, kept going to their house whether they were there or not. What an idiot he was, how could he have been so stupid?

"It's okay, child," Grandma Molly said, patting the air with her hands. "You're scared and you're lost and that's okay. It's normal, you aren't ready for this. No one could be ready for this. Grief and shock do terrible things to a rational mind. But you can still do it. You have to get help."

"Why is this happening?" Rueben said.

Molly opened her mouth to reply when a breeze seemed to push through the closeness of the treehouse. An oily voice carried with it.

Answers…

Rueben flinched, looked around. "Did you hear—"

"You get away from him!" Molly screamed, her face drawn with desperation. She turned to Rueben. "Don't listen, child! Don't you listen to that evil. You listen to me, you hear? You have to go, now. Run all the way to a telephone and get the police up here."

Answers... Such things to show you.

A zephyr stirred Rueben's hair, lightly whispered across the sensitive skin at the back of his neck, raising gooseflesh.

"I hear a voice," Rueben said. The sound of it filled him with fear, but also wonder. It seemed a balm to his ragged nerves, a soft stilling of his tumbling mind. He stepped around Molly and opened the door of the treehouse, looked out into the gloom between the trees. How long had he stayed wrapped in his blankets, crying and sleeping? The light was low, already well into the afternoon. Almost dark again.

The whispers swirled around him, a snaking breeze that brushed across his face and neck, raised more gooseflesh on his arms. Not exactly words, but promises all the same. It promised him answers and knowledge. It promised him things no one else would ever be able to supply. It was slick and oily, simultaneously repulsive and compelling. But above all those sensations was need. He *needed* it.

"Rueben!" Molly said, right by his shoulder. She wafted her hands at him, around his body, trying desperately to push him, drag him, but she was as insubstantial as mist. "It's using you! Your confusion. That's what it does! Be strong, Rueben."

The trembling stilled throughout Rueben's body and he turned around, slid over the edge of the treehouse veranda and hung from it, then dropped to the loamy ground below. He bent at the knee, sank into a deep squat to absorb the impact, placed one hand on the cold, damp leafy ground. But maybe not so cold as he would have expected. Perhaps a distant warmth rose up, along with a kind of pulse. Not like a heartbeat, but like long, endless breaths of something far away, transmitted here. He stood and turned in a slow circle.

The cajoling zephyr wafted around him again, circled him and nudged him along. He let it push and guide him, registering distantly that he was moving away from the hotel. *This* was the way he was supposed to go. This way there would be answers and a way out. A way to finish this. Yes! An end to it. Not some long trek, but a solution.

"Rueben!" Grandma Molly yelled, but though he sensed she was right behind him, her voice seemed to come from miles away, like she was at the bottom of a deep well, howling to be heard. It was easier to simply ignore her and let this dark gossamer touch guide him gently along.

Think of the power I can give you, the not-voice seemed to suggest. It was a slippery sensation, like grease in his mind, but intimate and exciting.

What power? he wondered, and let it nudge him further, deeper into the bush.

Oh, such strength!

He followed the urging. Or did it push him? He wasn't sure any more and it didn't matter. He vaguely registered that he was heading directly west of the hotel, into the deep forest he'd been forbidden to enter since he was a child. Where he'd always been told it was dangerous.

He paused and turned slowly around. Right behind him was his grandmother, her face drawn in desperate pain. Her mouth moved as she harangued him, trying to tell him something, but he couldn't hear what. He frowned. Molly's voice swelled in a muffled, undulating way and words almost formed, then a breeze wrapped itself around him like a hundred loving arms.

Such wonders to show you… Such things to reveal…

That not-voice, that awareness, it was honey and spice, it was oil and water, it was hot and cold. It clawed into his skin and wriggled along his veins, both painful and pleasant, but ultimately irresistible. He distantly registered Grandma Molly's dismay as he turned back to the west and let the soft wind guide him again. Sure enough, the ground began to slope downwards.

He noticed a mark on a tree and went to it. A strange, disconcerting shape, freshly carved into the bark. He lifted hand and touched the tip of his index finger to the pale wood, revealed where the bark had been taken away. It was soft, aqueous to his touch. It felt strangely like touching an eyeball, even had a little give if he pressed. And it was warm. A soft laugh bubbled from him as he ran his finger around the shape and back again, revelling in the weird, soft smoothness of it.

Such wonders...

He turned and moved on again. He stepped over the low wire fence that he'd always been told was his boundary, everyone's boundary. Even the hotel guests were told not to pass it as the ground there dipped sharply, became loose and dangerous. He kept moving.

He stumbled on shifting rocks and put his hands down to catch himself. The stone his palms landed on was as warm as the shape in the tree, and seemed to pulse and flex. He remained on hands and knees, felt the entire ground gently lift and fall as if it breathed.

Come along, come on, comeoncomeon...

Rueben let laughter bubble up again. What else might he find? He stood, engorged with a kind of power, a sense of invulnerability. He moved on, noticed the trees around him were shorter, twisted and constrained, their bark blackened. The leaf litter under his feet was black too, and a musty, fungal aroma rose from it. The smell should have been disgusting, some deep part of him recognised that, and yet he couldn't find it in himself to be appalled. The same sensation that forced a person to try something they were told would taste foul encouraged him to breath deep of the fetid air. And as he did so it snaked into his lungs and filled him with itself, writhing into his blood. He laughed again, buoyed by it, engorged further. It was intoxicating.

The slope he moved down steepened, the ground both warmer and looser than it had been before. He slipped and slid, but didn't care. The voice swirled around him on the wind, its need obvious, its joy at his presence palpable. He sensed the thing building itself through his body, somehow taking him over, and the thought disturbed him, but thrilled him too. It was okay, wasn't it? To give himself to this ancient power?

"RUEBEN!"

The shout startled him. He stopped, looked around, both annoyed and intrigued by the intrusion. It wasn't Grandma Molly. A male voice.

Night had fallen fully. How long had he been here?

Noooooooooo!

Tendrils of darkness snaked up from the ground, pushed the blackened leaf litter aside and writhed like questing snakes. They glowed a deep scarlet inside. Shocked, Rueben turned in a circle, horrified at the black worms stretching up, extending as far his as his knees, then higher still.

"RUEBEN!"

And something else caught his eye. Far away, high on the edge of the deep slope he'd travelled down, two people stood. He realised he'd descended into a deep hollow in the landscape, a bowl with ever-steepening sides that had to be half a mile across, maybe more, stippled with stunted black trees and loose, broken ground. The whole place heaved with some strange breath.

His laughter of moments before sickened into sobs, confusion flooding in. That whispering voice cajoled him once more, desperate now, anger beneath the need. A red rage soaked through it. And then that other voice again, so strong.

"RUEBEN, PLEASE!"

He looked up the slope and saw the two figures once more, almost silhouetted by distance. One was his Grandma Molly, her iron grey hair a pale cloud against the night. But next to her was a man, taller, strong-shouldered, a headful of loose sandy curls.

"Uncle Simon?" Rueben ventured, unable to trust his eyes. Love and grief flooded him.

Simon pushed forward, like he was trying to walk against a gale. "Yes, Rueben! It's me. Please, come back to us." He pushed on, his form starting to tatter and tear. "We can't go down there and you shouldn't. You have to come back. Please!"

Fear flooded through him. He stagger-ran back up the broken, slippery incline, the oily voice howling its displeasure.

Noooooo!

Those black tendrils snaked and whipped at him, grabbing for his feet and ankles. With a sob of horror, he danced left and right, lifted his knees high and fought against the loose ground, against gravity, against the clinging tendrils, and drove himself up, up, up, out of the dark and desperate crater in the forest. He had nearly gone so far that he would have given himself over to that thing altogether. Would have simply given himself away. The thought horrified him.

Molly and Simon both leaned into the hollow, arms outstretched, reaching for him, willing him onwards. The dark and slipping voice dragged at his back, made him promises and threatened him with terrors, but he focused only on Uncle Simon, refusing to think of anything but reaching the man who had died so violently. So needlessly. He knew, deep inside, he couldn't ignore the truth that Simon was still dead. Like Grandma Molly was dead. The man he saw up there was a shade, a ghost of his beloved uncle. But it didn't matter. He had started talking to Molly before, and he wasn't crazy. It had been real enough. Simon would be equally real. Uncle Simon had come back for him. If the voice tearing at his back, and the horrible, impossible landscape he staggered through were real—and they palpably, physically were—then the shades of his family who loved him were real too.

He fell and hauled himself up, ignored the abrasions on his palms and knees. The ground pulsed, sent him stumbling to one side, red-centred tendrils of black snagged at his foot and sent him sprawling, pain whining up from his elbow where it struck a rock as he landed, but he rolled over and dragged himself to his feet again. Those reaching black tentacles tried to hold onto him, but he ripped himself free, felt them breaking and snickering back to the loamy ground. They weren't strong, but soft like the rippling arms of an anemone. They quested but couldn't hold. He fought and fell, fought and fell, for what seemed like hours. Exhaustion tore at him, dizziness threatened him, but he pushed on. All the time Grandma Molly and Uncle Simon called to him, encouraged him.

He realised he could barely see, darkness more than the shadows between the trees surrounded him. How long had he been wandering? How long had he spent trying to escape this foul depression in the forest? The night was deep.

He finally made the edge and stumbled into the darkness between the trunks of tall, healthy trees, the air ice cold and fresh again. His grandmother stood to one side, his uncle to the other. They both reached and clutched at him. He felt nothing as their insubstantial forms passed right through. But their voices were clear.

"Well done, Rueben!"

"I knew you were strong, child! I thought I'd lost you. Couldn't bring you back on my own, but your uncle is here now. And you're strong, you never forget that!"

"Keep running, Roo," Simon said, jogging alongside. "You have to get away from here."

The raging, whispering voice howled for him, but Rueben gritted his teeth against it. "What is this place?" he asked, his voice tremulous and ragged. He was spent, like he'd run a hundred kilometres.

"I don't know, champ" Simon said, face creased in concern, in confusion. "But whatever it is, you need to stay away. There's something out there. Something ancient and evil and deadly."

"I need to get help for my family!" Reuben stumbled as he spoke, his legs weak with fatigue, voice slurred.

"Not now," Simon said. "You're wiped out. You can barely stand. You have to rest. And it's dark. The night is dangerous."

"Not the treehouse," Molly said. "You need to stay away from this place. At the very least, *you* have to survive."

What did she mean by that? Rueben looked left and right at them as he stumbled on through the night black woods. The only light came from a sliver of moon, barely enough to see by, but he saw the ghosts and they guided him. "Where then? I should make for the road."

"Not now," Simon said again. "Not in this state. Imagine collapsing halfway there and dying in the cold. It's not worth the risk."

"But Mum and Dad, Grandpa Clay and Uncle Marcus."

"They'll just have to make it through one more night," Simon said. "Go to the cottage. Sneak in, hide upstairs, I'll show you where. It's warm, and there's food, water."

Rueben staggered, fatigue clawing at him. "The others," he said. "The ones holding my family. They're not in the cottage?"

"One of them was," Molly said.

"It's okay," Simon said. "I can show you where to hide. You just have to get in unnoticed."

"Are you really here?" Rueben asked.

Simon smiled, but it was tinged with hurt and sadness. "Does it really matter?"

"They killed you. I saw..."

"I know, champ. I know."

Tears poured over Rueben's cheeks. It hurt to look at his uncle, but he couldn't tear his gaze away. And all the time, that furious, desperate voice from the hollow at his back.

They ran on in silence, the cajoling of whatever had tempted Rueben down into the darkness slowly growing weaker with distance. Before long they came alongside the lawns of the hotel. Lights burned inside, but there was no sign of anyone on the grass. Staying in the trees, moving slowly now, they crept past, around behind the garages. They moved alongside the cottage, heading for the back door Simon assured them was unlocked.

Rueben reached for the door handle with a shaking hand. They were masked from the hotel by the cottage itself and Rueben stepped into the darkened kitchen, and closed the door quietly behind him. The warmth inside was like a hug.

"There," Simon said, pointing.

A loaf of bread and a box with a few tins and packets sat on the kitchen counter.

"They might have noticed this stuff," Simon said. "So be frugal. Take a few slices from the loaf, then close it up again. Grab a tin of fruit in syrup and maybe a packet of cookies from the box and leave the rest there.

Rueben did as he was told, cold dread soaking his heart at the thought of the front door opening any second, James with a gun levelled at his face. But his hunger was furious.

"In that cupboard," Simon said. "Take one of the bottles and fill it with water. Quickly now."

Rueben did as he was told, paused to gulp some water down, like nectar pouring over his parched throat. Then he filled the bottle again. Clutching it and his food, shakes rippling through his whole body, he turned to his uncle.

"This way," Simon said.

He led the way up the stairs to the landing between the cottage's two small bedrooms. Another door ahead led to the bathroom.

"Stand on the banister there," Simon said. "And open the hatch into the attic."

Rueben looked up and sure enough there was a small, square access hatch above him. He put down his food and water and clambered up, one hand steadying himself against the wall, the other stretching up, up. "Come on," he hissed to himself, his bones creaking, pushing precariously onto his tiptoes on the thin bar of white-painted wood.

"You're tall enough now," Simon said, though his voice was tinged with hope rather than certainty.

As he felt sure he would overstretch and fall, headlong back down the stairs, Rueben's fingers found the edge of the hatch and he pressed up with the last millimetres he had left. The hatch clicked open and swung down, nearly knocking him back off the banister and he wobbled, staggered a step and switched sides, quickly saved himself against the opposite wall.

"Just as well this landing is so small!" he said with a nervous laugh of triumph. Whatever had happened out there in that crater, it had sucked all the energy from him, he shook with fatigue.

"Hang in there," Simon said. "Get the ladder and get yourself inside and safe, then you can sleep."

Where the hatch had opened, a short rope with a knot in the end hung down. Rueben pulled on it and a step ladder hinged out of the hole in the ceiling. He unfolded it once, then again, then gathered his food and bottle and hurried up into the cold attic space, terrified the front door would open any second.

"Not as warm as the house," Simon said apologetically. "But warmer than the treehouse. And much safer."

Rueben nodded. He put his stuff down and pulled the ladder back up behind him and then pulled the hatch closed. He sat back, shaking with relief and exhaustion. It was almost pitch dark inside, just a little weak moonlight through the one small skylight window, but he felt secure and contained. If he was silent, no one would find him here. He moved back a safe distance from the closed hatch, then settled himself and attacked the food and water.

"Well done, Rueben," Uncle Simon said from somewhere in the darkness. "Be sure to save some for the morning, don't make yourself sick. Rest and get your strength back. Then go for help."

Rueben tried to relax, to accept what his uncle said as true. But another part of him couldn't help remembering the voice out in the bush and the promises it made.

CLAY

PAIN had transcended discomfort and become a kind of physical white noise. Clay's hip burned like he had magma in his bones, his knee on that side ached like a ball-pein hammer had shattered his patella, and his foot was mostly numb. His shoulders burned too, but that was almost an itch compared to the leg. Though his hands, tied low and back to either side of the column, fizzed with pins and needles on their way to numbness too.

And it was dark.

Molly had come by, told him what had occurred with Rueben. They'd come so close to losing him, but thankfully Simon had arrived. Whatever lay back there, slowly awakening, was becoming stronger and harder to resist. The boy was shattered, she said, but would be okay. Safe for now.

Clay was terrified of what the night may bring. Would any of them make it to morning? As long as Rueben got away, it would be enough. Clay had resigned himself to that, though he hadn't said as much to Grant and Leigh.

Deanna had gone looking for James, he assumed, but they'd seen neither her nor James since. They might be gone, he thought. Maybe they left. Or they might be back any moment. Time seemed to flex and warp. They were hungry. Clay had pissed his pants, unable to hold it any more. The indignity of aging.

He'd shared Molly's news with Leigh and Grant, but wasn't sure how much they believed. Leigh seemed to accept things on face value, though Grant persisted with his scepticism. Was it because he didn't want to believe or simply couldn't comprehend? It didn't matter, Clay thought, the net result was the same.

Now Grant hung loosely in his bonds, chin on his chest as he dozed fitfully. Clay could just see Leigh in the mirror. She was still, head down like Grant, but in the heavy stillness of the hotel he heard her breathing and she sounded awake. He turned to look out the large windows above the reception office again. The tops of trees had been visible as shadows, blackened silhouettes scratching at the slate-grey sky. But the hint of dirty peach to the west had gone and the windows were black mirrors of night. Had been for some time. The sense of impending doom grew.

A sound caught Clay's attention and he looked back towards the dining room to see Deanna come striding through and into the lounge. She said nothing, went to stand in front of the fireplace, rubbing her hands together for warmth. Grant grunted and came awake, looked to her, then Clay. Clay shrugged.

Deanna took logs from the large pile beside the big stone hearth and added them to the dying blaze, crouching there to watch the flames leap and dance again, licking up the blackened bricks of the chimney.

"Where is he?" Clay asked.

Deanna didn't react. Grant looked to his father, then back to Deanna, seeming to suddenly catch on.

"Yeah, Deanna," Grant said. "Where's James? What's happening?"

Deanna sighed, her shoulders rounded like she carried an almost unbearable weight. "I don't know."

"You've been looking for him all this time?" Clay asked. "Haven't you."

"Not all this time, no. I've been thinking too."

"And? Any answers present themselves?"

She still didn't turn to face them, but her voice hardened. "Don't talk to me, okay? Don't try to reason with me or convince me of anything. I'm not listening."

"Neither is James, by the sound of things," Clay said. "Seems to me maybe no one is listening to you."

Finally she spun around. Her face tight with anger, but hurt overrode the fury in her eyes. "I told you not to talk to me!"

"What the hell else do I have to do?" Clay shouted.

"I'm going to take each of you for a bathroom break. At gunpoint. I want no conversation there or back. Then I'm going to make something for us all to eat." She paused, swallowed. "Maybe James will show up for dinner."

"Dinner?" Clay said. "Bit late for that, isn't it? We could be gone by now, all of us. Maybe James has gone, eh? Or he's dead in the bush? Either way, we could all leave. Cut us free, then you can take a car and run."

Deanna turned to him again. "Maybe I'll leave you there and take a car and run."

"If you were going to do that, you already would have," Grant said. "You're waiting for James, aren't you? Even after all this, you can't leave him. You think you can change him? Bring him around? You're too weak to go it alone?"

Clay felt his son's seething anger, didn't know if it would help or hinder.

Deanna stared hard for a moment, then straightened. "I told you what's going to happen."

Grant shook his head, disgusted.

"Let me help you," Leigh said. "With the food, I mean."

"I don't need any help. And I don't need any more of your fucking counselling. Who's first for the bathroom?"

Clay took a deep breath His pants had mostly dried again, and he didn't want a repeat. "You better take me. But I warn you, this position has ruined my leg, you may have to pretty much carry me."

Deanna nodded and came around the column to loosen Clay's bonds. Despite the pain, he was grateful that he managed to walk to the toilet on his own, albeit leaning heavily on Deanna to do so. As they moved through the dining room, he headed towards the men's, but Deanna guided him left.

"Ladies," she said.

"What?"

She looked at him, one eyebrow raised. "It's full of blood in there."

Clay's gaze lingered on the door to the men's bathroom as he wondered what that might mean.

Then Deanna tugged at him. "Come on, willya!"

He moved with her, then she paused.

"Why are you so concerned about it?" she asked.

Clay took a deep breath, shook his head. "You need to clean up in there. Clean up all the blood."

"Fuck that, I'm not a maid."

"If you want to get through tonight, you should clean it." Before she could ask more, he staggered on towards the women's bathroom, forcing Deanna to help him along. Maybe if she didn't clean up, whatever took Rick's blood would come back for it. But if there was none, maybe nothing would come. Then he remembered his son sitting there with blood all over his face and shoulder, soaked into the rug beside him and between his legs. His red raw wrists. "And we need to clean up Grant too."

She ignored him, shoved him towards a stall, so he went in and took care of business.

Before long, all three had been ferried to the toilets and back, and tied up against the thick, dark wooden columns once more.

"I'm going to make food," Deanna said, and left for the kitchen without a backward glance.

Clay stared at the darkness through the high windows above the office, fears he didn't want to acknowledge squirmed in his guts. After about twenty minutes, Deanna returned. She'd heated beans and vegetables in canned tomatoes, and carried a stack of buttered bread. She put a plate on each of their laps, slopped on food, added bread, then freed one hand each and handed them forks.

"As soon as you're finished, I'm tying you back up. Make the most of it."

She sat in her usual armchair, shotgun resting against her knees as she ate her own serve, the whole time watching the three of them intently. Clay ate automatically, barely tasting but knowing he needed to keep what little strength remained to him. They all three tried to ask Deanna questions, engage her in conversation, but she ignored them.

Not long after they started eating, a bang and a gust of cold wind from the back of the room announced the return of James. Clay sighed. Another chance gone.

Deanna stopped eating, put her plate aside and stood. James walked into the room, looked around. He swayed a little, his eyes ruddy and slightly unfocussed. His face was a mask, a plastic simulacrum of the man he had once been. A large band aid covered the left side of his face, from halfway down his cheek to just above his ear covering the lobe completely, making a strange lump of that side of his head. Several band aids, Clay realised on closer inspection, overlaying each other. The dressing was clean, but blood had dried a dirty brown on his collar. He grinned loosely and approached Deanna.

"Feeding 'em. Good. You make some for me?"

"Of course. There's plenty more in the pan. You want me to fix you some?"

"I think I can cope with that. You keep an eye in here."

He strode from the room, slightly uncertain on his feet. Deanna watched him go then slowly returned to her chair, began mechanically shovelling food into her mouth again.

Clay finished up, put his plate aside. "Pretty drunk, isn't he?" He phrased it like a question.

Denna looked at him for a moment, eyes narrowed. "Yeah, maybe."

"Maybe?"

She scowled, tipped her head to one side. "Almost certainly."

"He must have found more booze since what happened in the bathroom. There's plenty in the cottage."

"So what?"

"What do you think?" Clay asked. "Does being wasted make him easier or harder to deal with? More reasonable or more violent?"

Deanna looked back through the dining room, staring over her shoulder for so long, Clay thought she wasn't going to answer. Then she sighed and turned back. "You can never know for sure," she said. "Shut up now."

She finished her food, then went and collected the plates, re-securing each of them as she did so. Clay said nothing as she looped and tied his ropes again, then she picked up the stack of plates and forks and left the room. Before she went, she took a deep breath, nodded to herself.

"She's going to try to talk to him," Clay said. "The bonds of love and friendship are strong and strange indeed."

A few moments later he heard her speaking with James, the low mumble of their voices. He couldn't make out the words, but the conversation sounded calm and even. That, at least, was something. For now. He sighed, tipped his head back against the column trying to ignore the furnace of pain roaring in his leg bones again, the sciatic bolts of agony that seemed to ebb and flow like a tide.

"You think he's okay?" Leigh asked quietly.

"Rueben?" Clay said.

"Yeah."

"He's fine, I'm sure. He's safe for now."

"How do we know that?" Grant asked.

Clay sighed. He was too sore and too tired to buy into his son's scepticism. "You'll just have to take my word for it."

"That's not what I mean." Grant twisted in his bonds to look at his father. "I mean, how do we know James won't find him in there? We know he found Simon's ammunition in the cottage, he said as much. And he seems to have found their booze."

Clay licked his lips, unsure of the answer to that.

"How do we know where he's going?" Grant persisted. "He could have been sitting in that cottage, drinking and stewing, all afternoon. One slip from Rueben, one inadvertent noise. He's trapped up there."

"I don't think so," Leigh said. "Remember Deanna told us she'd been looking for James and couldn't find him anywhere. She'd have checked the cottage, for sure. I think he's been going into the bush."

"What for?" Grant asked.

"Quiet," Clay whispered quickly, catching movement across the dining room.

They fell silent as James wandered in and looked around. He grinned, chewing lazily at a slice of bread. "Don't let me interrupt your conversation. What were youse chatting about?"

Deanna came in and sidled around James, took up her spot once more. Her expression was guarded, eyes a little wild. She watched James the way someone might watch a lion loose on the savannah.

"No, really," James said. "What was the topic of conversation."

"We were wondering what might happen tonight," Clay said. "After all, it's full night outside. What is it now, nearly ten o'clock? Eleven?"

James smiled crookedly. "Something like that. You scared?"

Clay drew in a breath, then nodded. "You know what? Yes, I am. After what happened to your friend, you're damn right I'm scared. And you should be too. We should all get the hell out of here."

"And if we don't?" James asked. "What happens then?"

Clay let out a short laugh. "I don't know. That's why I'm scared."

James moved over to a deep sofa and slumped down into it. He had the pistol again, Simon's pistol, and lazily turned it over and around in his hands. Clay hoped to hell the fool had the safety on. His display was clearly meant to discomfort them, but it was idiotic to play around with guns in any circumstance. Then again, maybe the prick would accidentally shoot himself. Though that was likely more luck than they could hope for. Clay wondered again where the shotgun was. Only Deanna's was visible, so there were two more somewhere around, unguarded. He knew trying to keep track was pointless, but he drew some comfort from it. Maybe one moment, one bathroom break, there'd be a shotgun left carelessly within reach… He shook the thought away. As if!

"Let me tell youse a story," James said. "When I was about nineteen, and in charge given my mum was dead and my dad was a deadbeat loser we'd left well behind, we had a situation in the neighbourhood. I had to look out for Paul, that's always been my job."

He stopped, his throat bobbing a couple of times as he forced himself to swallow. Clay wanted to say something, needle at the bastard about how now his brother was dead and what was he going to do about that, but held his tongue. If James was talkative, perhaps there might be a chance to talk him around.

James made a noise, a suppressed grunt, almost a sob, then his eyes hardened over and that wolfish grin returned. "I had to protect my little corner of the neighbourhood, see, because this arsehole had decided to set up on our turf. This one guy, Omar, he looked after things around us. He controlled the dealing and the general order of activities. It was okay, as long as you stayed good with Omar. And I was good with him, always had been. Then this arsehole, name of Craig Benson, shows up. Big guy, holy fuck, he was like Arnold goddamn Schwartzenegger. And maybe a foot taller than me too, and I'm no dwarf. He brought a small crew with him and just stabbed Omar one day, right in the street. Said he was taking over." James barked a short laugh. "Look at your fucking faces. You have no idea what it's like to grow up like we did, do ya? Deanna, you believe these fuckers?"

She shook her head, mouth pressed into a flat line. James narrowed his eyes at her momentarily, then turned back, directing his story mainly to Clay.

"So Craig Benson takes over and he's not good to the people like Omar was. He's a dictator, wants to be a big man over everybody. So people started talking about taking him down. But no one had the balls. Big arsehole like that and all his people? No one dared." James leaned forward, teeth clenched and bared. "But I fucking dared."

Clay thought back to Marcus's challenge and James staring his challenger in the eye and flinching away. He wondered how much of this story might be true and how much was personal delusion on James's part. But it didn't really matter. Let him keep talking for now, for all the good it would do any of them.

"I made nice with Benson," James went on. "I got in close, made myself useful. Then I waited for my opportunity. Took a long time and I had to eat a lot of shit while I waited, but I was patient. Stuck to the plan. Eventually I found myself alone with him one night, his crew all elsewhere for various reasons, and I shot him. Waited until he was relaxed, said, 'Hey, can I check out that new pistol you got?' He was proud of it, pulls it out and hands it over. And I emptied it into his chest. Then I left. No one knew it was me. Word got around he'd been taken out, and his little empire fell apart. Only Pauly and Deanna here knew it was me that did it. It was done, that's what mattered.

"After a while, things settled back to normal. New power dynamics, of course, but no one like that prick took over again. People would ask if it was me who killed him and I'd just shrug and smile. They could think what they liked. But I'd returned order to our little corner of this shithole world. You should have seen his face as those bullets slammed into him, drove him back in that chair." James nodded to himself, eyes lost in the memory as he slowly sat back in the deep sofa, breathing long and deep.

Silence hung in the room for a while. Deanna remained tense, James lost in his thoughts.

"What the fuck does that have to do with anything?" Grant asked eventually.

James shot forward in his seat again, startling them all. Clay winced as pain flared in his hip as he flinched.

"It means I'm not scared of anything! Not like you!" He pointed at the weirdly dressed ear on his left side. "Lots of people have taken shots at me. No one finished me yet."

Clay laughed. "You think you can shoot this? You think you can loaf around until you get some chance to sneak attack it?"

"I don't know, mate. You tell me! What the fuck is it?"

"Not natural. We shouldn't be here. That's all I know!"

James shook his head and laughed. "My story should have helped you understand I'm the kind of guy who sniffs the wind and figures which way it's blowing." He stood, gave Clay an enigmatic look, and went over to the bar again. He looked through the bottles and came back with another Jack Daniels. As he slumped back onto the couch, Leigh spoke up.

"James, this whole thing is going too far, you know that, right?"

"Shut the fuck up."

"No, listen. You can go, get away. You need to stay ahead of what you've done. Hell, leave us here to rot if that makes you feel better, but the longer you stay the worse it gets."

James leaned sideways to see her better. "Now why would you suggest I just leave you here? You mean don't even untie you? Why not? You think someone might happen along and save you? Are you *expecting* someone?"

Clay clenched his teeth, desperately hoping Leigh didn't say anything stupid. If she gave away that there was any hope for them out there in the trees, Rueben's life was at risk.

Leigh sighed. "Frankly, I don't care if someone comes or not. Local staff help out here, they'll be up in a couple of weeks. I'll take my chances. I just don't like being held prisoner by you. I wish you'd just go."

"A couple of weeks!" James barked a laugh.

"Just fuck off!" Grant barked. "We'll take our fucking chances. Maybe someone will come to the hotel and find us and we'll still be alive, or maybe we'll all be dead hanging in these ropes, but we'll take that chance, you shit. Why don't you just fuck off!"

Clay grimaced, willing his son to shut up. James surged up from the sofa, stepped over Clay's legs, and swung a wide heavy punch at Grant. Unable to duck away, tied as he was, James knuckles slammed into the side of Grant's head with a fleshy crack. Grant yelped and sagged, blood dribbling from his mouth, the cut above his eye opened yet again, letting a thin stream of blood pool between his legs.

"You really got to learn to shut the fuck up, man," James said, and strolled back to the sofa.

Clay stared at the new blood in dismay.

Grant sucked in a few breaths, forced his head up to stare daggers at James. His tongue played around his cheek, no doubt torn up inside from the punch grinding it against his teeth. He flicked his head, tried to get the blood running from his brow out of his eye.

James laughed and leaned back into the sofa, then turned to put his legs up and lay back against one arm. "Now all of you shut the fuck up. Time to wait and see."

"Wait and see what?" Clay said.

"I told you, I'm the kind of bloke who waits to see which way the wind's blowing."

Clay tried to breathe deeply, still his fears. "You're not going to worry about what might happen tonight?"

James turned his head, staring, then pulled the cork from the whiskey bottle with his teeth and spat it at Clay. It missed. He took a long slug of liquor then grinned and said, "Dee, get the lights."

"You're gonna sleep?" she asked, hope in her voice.

"We're all gonna sleep," James said, drinking again. "Sleep and wait."

Clay's guts churned. Wait for what? Did James know something? Expect something? Had he made some kind of deal?

Deanna got up and moved through the dining room and lounge turning out all the lights. The place sank into a dim orange glow from the fire in the giant hearth, similar orange flickering in the dining room. Clay watched the flames dance and the shadows writhe. Slowly the room settled into a thick silence but for the occasional *glug* from James's bottle. Then he fell quiet. Deanna remained in her chair, shotgun across her knees. Her eyes were glassy in the gloom for a long time, staring into nowhere, then Clay noticed her lids had finally closed. She seemed to be sleeping. Grant's head sunk into his chest again and Leigh's breathing eventually became deep and even. Clay stared on into the flames, sleep as elusive as freedom.

Yet he must have dozed, as something dragged him from thoughts too deep to be anything but a dream, that flittered away from memory the moment he opened his eyes. He swallowed, looked around. What had woken him? The others slept on, breathing deep, James snoring softly. Then he heard it again, a distant tapping. Or perhaps more a slapping. Turning his head, willing his old ears to focus in, Clay nodded. It came from the other room, the dining room. And seemed to emanate from the far corner past the hearth, where the bathrooms were. As his ears tuned in, Clay couldn't avoid mentally picturing a hundred tiny naked baby feet pattering against the cold tiles.

The sound grew louder as several somethings battered into a wooden door. Clay licked his lips, waiting. Then again, *thwack thwack thwack*, distant but distinct. A soft red glow pushed through the orangey darkness of the dining room.

"Hey," Clay said, and his voice was dry and cracked, lost in the dark. He cleared his throat. "Hey!" Louder this time. "Wake up, everyone!"

Various grunts and incoherent words came from around the room.

"What is it?" Grant asked, his voice thick as much from his swollen cheek as from sleep.

"Listen." Clay nodded towards the doors into the dining room, just as the sounds came again.

"The fuck?" Deanna said.

James snored on.

"I can't see," Leigh said. "What's happening?"

Tied to the other side of the column, she was the only one facing away from the dining room. Clay wondered if that might be better in the long run. "Nothing to see," he said. "Just listen."

"What's the red light?" Grant asked.

The wet, sticky pattering became more insistent. Deanna stood, moved to the doors and looked through.

"I wouldn't," Clay said.

She looked back at him, one eyebrow raised. He shrugged, shaking uncontrollably.

Deanna looked back into the dining room, then skipped backwards. "Shit!"

James startled awake, sat up and looked groggily around. "It's happening?"

"I warned you," Clay said. "Too late now."

James stood, staggering drunkenly and went to Deanna. "What is it?" he demanded.

"What the fuck is that?" Deanna asked, voice high and scared. "Those things, all across the floor!"

Without waiting for an answer, she swung her shotgun up and fired, the report deafening. She fired again, backing into the lounge. James stood beside her open-mouthed, just staring. Was he smiling?

"Is it doing anything?" Deanna shouted. "We blow them apart and the parts keep going!" Then she simply turned and ran, straight through the lounge and out the back door. A gust of cold air washed over them as she left the door wide open.

A hissing noise rolled out and James's turned back to face Clay.

"Untie us!" Clay yelled.

"For god's sake," Grant shouted, thrashing against his bonds. "Don't leave us here! *Cut us loose*!"

"What's happening?" Leigh's voice was high, close to panic. Clay heard her twisting around, trying to see or escape or both, didn't matter.

Then Grant started screaming. Red-tinged black tendrils whipped up through the floor all around him. They rose through the patches of blood, taking the blood with them.

"Cut us free!" he yelled again.

The russet whips of night writhed in the dim orange glow from the fire, questing around Grant's legs. He screamed again. "They're burning me! Cut me free, you bastard!" Grant bucked hard enough against the ropes that his head knocked into the wood behind him.

James barked a short laugh, then bolted from the room, out into the night.

Grant screamed, voiceless agony, as the tendrils wrapped all around him, seeming to dive into the fabric of his clothes wherever they were stained with blood. Clay wrestled uselessly against his bonds, Leigh shouted and cried, desperate to know what was happening.

Grant devolved into animal noises of rage, forcing his body up against the column, the ropes cutting into his arms and chest. He howled as the glowing tendrils wrapped around his face and drove into his mouth, into the wound above his eye. They burrowed into the flesh where his wrists bled.

"Grant, stop it!" Leigh shouted. "You're hurting me!"

Clay twisted to see, noticed the ropes Grant heaved against were pulling the knots tighter on Leigh's side too, grinding into her wrists. If she started to bleed... He looked back to his son and saw sheer madness in the man's eyes. And incredible pain. Grant's skin rippled and flexed as though things ran back and forth underneath it.

Clay yelled his son's name, but there was nothing he could do. Grant screamed as the dark whips wrapped all around him, coiling about his arms and chest, then up over his neck and face. Grant writhed and howled, then his skin began to shrink into his face, the hollows of his eyes deepening, his cheekbones seemed to carve upwards as his flesh drew taut. His entire body shuddered violently, stiffened and shrinking. Leigh wailed on the other side of the column.

Then the blackened tendrils were all inside, under his skin, and almost as quickly they re-emerged, swollen fat blobs of glistening black, glowing red inside, that seemed to shimmy and skitter across the rug. Tiny, tentacular limbs flickering in and out to carry them along with a wet pattering. Clay tensed, sure they would come for him next, but they swerved away, heading for the door. A swarm of glistening black and red surged out into the night and off across the lawns heading for the trees. Leigh screamed at the sight of them surging past her, then yelled, "What are they? Grant? Grant, answer me!"

Grant's arched body hit the floor, emptied and still. His skin grey and stretched tight over the bones, drained exactly like Paul had described Rick. Like that profane darkness had sucked every bit of blood, every bit of living moisture, out of him. Shining black scillae burst up through the rug everywhere blood had fallen, writhing frantically. They thickened and pushed out, absorbed the blood and fell as skittering, glowing blobs with some semblance of sentience, some driving force, and they scurried out into the night after the ones that had gone before. The last few seemed to quest around the floor and column, like sniffing dogs searching for the last morsels, mixing with the smaller ones. Every last patch of blood withered away, absorbed into the things.

"Grant," Clay managed, his entire body trembling. His son lay inert, his body looked as though it had been dead for centuries.

Silence fell but for the crackle of the fire. Clay sucked in hard fast gasps, tried to force down the panic in his chest. Was it over? For now, at least?

"Leigh?" he called. She didn't answer. "Leigh!" Louder, almost shouting.

He twisted in his bonds, shoulder and hips roaring in pain, and managed to see her in the mirror, her hair forward as she hung in her bonds. Had she passed out? Was she broken by grief, knowing what happened? Those things had all rushed right past her and out into the night.

“Fuck,” Clay said, sobs rising.

DEANNA

IT THERE was no denying the things Paul had said now. They'd both clearly seen those things taking away the blood, scurrying across the dining room floor after squeezing out under the bathroom door. Deanna had emptied shotgun shells into the thickest groups of them and watched those parts burst and splatter like ink, only to slither and writhe in smaller parts and keep going, some re-joining together, others continuing alone.

"What the fuck?" she yelled at James as they burst into the front door of the cottage, gasping for breath. She shook all over, could barely hold onto the shotgun.

James ignored her, went to the kitchen window and stared out. She looked over his shoulder to see swarms of glistening redblack surging off across the lawns and into the trees. James's teeth gleamed as he grinned. He wasn't scared, Deanna realised. He was exulting in this. He'd expected it.

"What the fuck is happening?" Deanna demanded.

He didn't answer. "Where's Paul's shotgun?" he asked instead, one hand absently touching the large band aid over his ear.

Deanna shook her head, mind spinning for a moment. "I… I don't remember… Oh, it's in the kitchen. In the hotel kitchen. And it's loaded."

"Well I'm most definitely not going back in there any time soon, but at least we know where it is. And where's mine?"

Deanna lifted her eyebrows, concerned. "I don't know."

"We can't leave guns laying around, Dee!"

"I know, I haven't. Mine's here and Paul's is in the kitchen. Where have you left yours?" She realised with dismay that the weapon she held was currently useless. She'd emptied it in the hotel and had no replacement ammo. That was in the hotel kitchen too. What she carried now was no better than a fancy club.

He stared at her for moment and she saw the lunacy in him. "What time is it?"

The question was quite the non-sequitur. "No idea." Deanna looked around, then pointed to the microwave. "3.49 am if that's right."

James looked over and nodded. "Seems about right. Close enough anyway. How long until dawn?"

"I don't know, James. I'm not a fucking weathergirl!"

His face twisted and he turned, grabbed her by the throat, his fingers like cold iron. "Don't you fucking diss me!"

"James, listen to me!" Deanna gasped for breath, forced her mind to calm, to drag back some control. "We have to go, simple as that. She's right, that Leigh. We could take one of the cars, take a bunch of supplies, and just get out of here. Leave them tied up in there. Hell, they're probably all dead anyway now." A mercenary thought occurred to her and she coldly embraced it, self-preservation the uppermost emotion in her mind. "Fuck it, James, even if they're not dead, shoot all three of them then just bug out, yeah? Let's fucking *go*! We can slip away unnoticed, no one will find their bodies any time soon!" Much as she hated to admit it, she would have a far greater chance of getting away clean with his help, his resourcefulness. For all his faults, James had taken care of them until now.

He let her go and went from the kitchen through to the cottage's small lounge and sat heavily into an armchair, sank his face into his hands. He massaged his forehead with fingertips, drawing long, deep, angry breaths. "No, there's more to do."

"What?"

He raised his eyes slowly to pierce her with a lunatic gaze. Then, unbelievably, he grinned. "I don't know yet. But, oh, there's so much more to see. Don't you realise? We're far beyond a bank robbery, Dee. So far!"

Deanna bit her lip, swallowing down any more words. A moment ago he had her by the throat. He still had the pistol. Who knew what he might do next. If her shotgun had still been loaded, she would have shot him then, and taken a car and gone. Would she? It was a moot point anyway.

She moved over to a short two-seater couch and lay on it, her back to James, legs hooked over the other arm. There she stayed, willing the trembling through her body to ease. Maybe she should run regardless of James's plans. He had the keys to the cars, stashed somewhere unknown, but she'd seen a battered old pick-up in the garage. Maybe the key to that stayed in it, right in the ignition, or tucked up under the visor like in Terminator. She chanced a glimpse back and James sat rock-still in the armchair, staring into some million-mile distance. Something else had hold of him now, something far worse than any rage or lunacy of his own. She'd never get by him unless he slept again and she had a feeling he wouldn't be closing his eyes any time soon. Resigned, she settled back and tried to breathe and relax. She was so damned tired.

James shook her out of a fitful doze moments later. At least, it seemed only moments, but the sky was bright outside, the night brushed away by greying whiteness.

"Get up."

She stood, stretched aching muscles. "What's happening."

"Don't know. We're going to see."

"Can I stay here?"

"Fuck no. Come on."

Deanna nodded and dutifully trudged behind James, out across the gravel driveway, the early chill biting into any exposed skin. Her breath clouded as she huffed, desperate to take a deeper breath, but her chest constricted with fear of what they might find in there. If all three of those poor bastards were dead, would it simplify things or not? She almost wished them dead to force his hand. But another part of her realised James was becoming tied to this place for other reasons. Perhaps he would never leave.

They cautiously entered by the back door, Deanna stretching up to look over James's shoulder as he stepped in. She first saw Leigh, tense and puffy-eyed, leaning back against the column. Then she saw Grant, drained and dead like Rick had been. Clay still sat tied in place, staring with pure hate in his eyes.

"That's it?" James demanded.

"You piece of shit," Clay said. "That's not enough? He's my SON!"

Deanna grabbed James's arm, pulled on him. "Let's go! Get out of here right now." The sight of Grant made her insides watery.

James shook her off. "It's day time, we're safe for now."

Leigh growled at them, inarticulate rage.

"All the blood then?" James asked.

"They… it, whatever, took everything, sucked up every last drop."

James crouched for a better look, nodded. "Yeah." He seemed elated. "Check her bonds," he said to Deanna, pointing back over his shoulder at Leigh.

Clay barked a short laugh. "She can't get out. Believe me, she tried."

"There's not enough slack," Deanna said.

James untied Grant's body and slid it away from the column. "Tighten her up anyway."

"James, we should go!"

He rounded on Deanna, face furious. "I said tighten her up!"

Deanna stared as James strode from the room, carrying Grant's body like it weighed nothing. She had no idea what he was thinking or planning. She began fixing Leigh's bonds. The woman stared at her with undisguised disdain. Deanna tried not to meet her eye.

"Are you hurt?" she asked as she tied.

"What do you care?" Leigh's voice was raw, husky from crying. Her husband and her brother were gone, after all. And her brother's husband.

"I care," Deanna said.

"Only because my health is tied directly to your survival somehow. Why do you trust James? Why stay with him?"

"No more questions. Are you hurt?"

"No."

Deanna finally let her eyes meet Leigh's. There was fear there, but such anger too. A blind fury. Deanna knew that if she loosened these bonds, Leigh would be on her like a starving tiger, would tear her to pieces. And she didn't blame the woman one bit.

"You have power here," Leigh said through clenched teeth. "You have a fucking gun. You *know* James is a psychopath. You know there's no reasoning with him."

Deanna stared, saying nothing.

"I think he's in league with it," Clay said. "Where does he go, huh?"

"Fucking shoot him," Leigh said. "Finish this, cut us free, take a car and go. You have the best chance to survive on your own, you know that. Why such allegiance to that fucking psycho?"

Deanna stared a moment longer. "Shut up," she said, and walked away.

RUEBEN

RUEBEN had managed to settle and fall asleep, but the sudden rapid shotgun blasts ripped him from slumber. He'd sat up, terrified, wondering why they were shooting and at what. Frozen with indecision, he'd still been listening hard when the shooting stopped and moments later someone crashed into the cottage. James and Deanna, it turned out, shouting at each other. He had no idea where the third one, Paul, was. Rueben had strained to hear the words, but they were muffled by distance and the walls and ceilings between them. Then everything had sunk into silence again. But those two were in the cottage.

Rueben didn't sleep properly any more. Terrified, he tried to stay alert in case James or Deanna ventured up to the attic. He had no reason to think they would and managed to remain relatively calm. But he also made sure not to make a sound. He sank into occasional fitful dozing, and the night passed interminably slowly.

He finally heard muffled voices again a little while after dawn, then the cottage door opened and closed. He moved slowly, silently to the skylight window and stretched up on tiptoes to look out. He watched James and Deanna go over to the back deck and presumably into the hotel through the back door by the bar. They seemed cautious, nervous. What had they been shooting at?

"I hope Mum and Dad, Grandpa Clay, and Uncle Marcus are still okay," he said softly, almost to himself.

"It's okay, child," Grandma Molly said from somewhere behind him. "It's light now. Go quickly while they're inside. Out to the road and away."

"Go on, champ," Uncle Simon said. "Please."

Rueben frowned, turning to see the gossamer presences in the gloomy attic behind him. Something in Uncle Simon's voice, some hitch, caught his attention.

"What's the matter? What's happened?"

"You just have to go," Molly said. "Quickly now!"

Rueben shook his head, stretching up to watch out the skylight again. "Not until I know they're staying in there. And where's the other one? Paul?"

"Paul's dead," Uncle Simon said.

"What?"

"It's true. Your Uncle Marcus got him."

Rueben turned, stunned. "Seriously? How? Is Uncle Marcus okay?"

A tear stood on Simon's cheek, just below his left eye, but he didn't look away from Rueben's searching gaze. His expression said it all.

"No," Rueben whispered, tears rising in his eyes too. "No no no."

"I'm sorry, child," Molly said. "But you have to go!"

Rueben turned back to the skylight and saw James come out of the kitchen door, carrying something long and thin, wrapped in clothes, his face like thunder. His lips moved in frantic speech, talking to himself. For a moment Rueben was distracted by a large band aid over the man's ear, then he realised what he carried was a body. And he saw it was his father's body, strangely reduced somehow. Thin and ruined. He slapped a hand over his mouth to hold in a scream, his gut turning to ice.

"I'm so sorry, child! So sorry. Don't look!"

But Rueben couldn't tear his gaze away. "What happened to him?" Tears poured over his cheeks, sobs muffled by his hand, wet and hitching.

"There's a powerful evil here," Simon said. "You have to go, Rueben."

James carried Rueben's father into the garage and then quickly came back out. He stopped on the gravel, equidistant between the hotel, the cottage and the garages, and looked around. The tendons in his neck were taut as shipping ropes, his eyes wide, too wide, the whites showing madly. He talked again, lips pulling back from clenched teeth. Then he turned in a full circle, shoulders bunched up. Rueben heard a bark of something, a noise more animal than human speech, and James strode off past the back deck and across the lawns. The angle of the cottage roof didn't allow him to see far and James quickly disappeared from view, heading out towards the trees.

Grief tore at Rueben, made his body shake, his mind spin.

I'm telling you as much to keep myself honest, Roo. I know I get busy and distracted. Not this year.

His father's last promise, before Rueben had run happily into the trees. Before hell came to Eagle Hotel.

"Where's the woman?" he said at last, under his breath.

"Maybe she'll stay inside and guard the family?" Molly said.

"They're okay? The rest of them?" Rueben asked. Then he stopped and devolved into deep wracking sobs. "Only Mum and Grandpa Clay are left!" he wailed.

He turned to see his grandmother and didn't miss the tightening of her face. Grief hung like an unbearable blackness in his gut that he pushed down, down, before it could froth up and drown him. Stifling another sob he turned back to the window to see Deanna emerge from the kitchen door and look left and right. Then she headed away from the hotel, off along the driveway, reloading her shotgun as she went. Where was she going? She turned suddenly, came back and looked into the cars parked on the driveway then turned and stared a moment at the garages. After a long time of seeming indecision, she spun and stalked off along the driveway again, away from the hotel.

Rueben watched as far as his limited view would allow, then nodded to himself. That accounted for them both, at least. Time to do something. He needed to save his Mum and Grandpa.

With a sob of anguish, he lifted the attic door and hurried down, and out of the cottage. He paused briefly at the front door, looking out for James or Deanna, but they were nowhere to be seen.

As he went to step forward, gravel crunched behind the cottage. A low voice, murmuring. Deanna. "Can't let him carry on," she said quietly. Then she muttered something else.

Rueben froze in a moment's indecision. What if she was heading back into the cottage? She'd find him there before he could get into the attic and pull the ladder back up. The garage door stood slightly open where James had left it. Without thinking too hard, Rueben ran across the driveway before Deanna emerged and ducked into the garage.

Light came in through gaps in the wooden siding, casting strange geometric panels of weak sunshine, creating deep shadows in the corners. He paused with a gasp at the growing pile of bodies. Uncle Simon was there, wrapped in the tarp, but next to him lay Bob and Laura Hickman. Beside them was Paul, and next to him Uncle Marcus, and beside him, Rueben's father. Six of them, dead forever. All were tight, drained husks, bare caricatures of their living selves, mostly recognisable by their clothes.

Rueben stared, sobs building somewhere deep in his chest. He knew if he let them go again he would devolve into jelly, so swallowed them down and ran through to the big, rusty black and red ute, and ducked in the deep shadows behind it.

He heard Deanna crunch past the garage, then pause. "James?" Her voice was uncertain. "Fuck!" Her footsteps moved further past, then back again. Hunkered down where he was, her direction was hard to determine, but she seemed to walking aimlessly, lost, frequently changing her mind.

Then the door moved and she came into the garage. Rueben held his breath, squeezed down into the shadows behind the ute. Deanna looked at the bodies, then came over to the ute, leaned into the open driver's window.

"Keys are there," she muttered. She looked up, lips pursed in thought, then nodded to herself like she'd made a decision, and walked quickly from the garage again.

Rueben was becoming dizzy from held breath, slowly took a soft gasp. He waited until he couldn't hear anything, then decided to wait a little longer, just in case. If he slipped out of the garages and around behind them, he could duck into the bush and hurry along the side of the driveway, but he didn't dare risk it until he knew both James and Deanna were nowhere near.

"Just head out," Simon said kindly, reaching uselessly towards Rueben. "Stick to the plan."

Rueben crept past him and crouched by the group of dead bodies. He didn't let himself look at his father, tried to pretend the drained corpse wasn't even there. But he knew it was, along with all the others. They were disturbing in their not-rightness, not only lacking life, but all humanity sucked out of them. These were people he knew. Loved. Living, breathing humans who cared about him and now they were still and wrong. Their skin sallow and drawn, the faces so familiar but so strangely different. Before he left, he would take anything that might be useful. He rummaged in Paul's pockets, the one person he was glad to see dead, but there was nothing of interest.

He moved around to the tarpaulin covering Uncle Simon and lifted it aside. Holding his breath, doing his best to still trembling hands, he began feeling around his uncle's pockets. The body was cold, and hard like stone, not the usual pliancy of flesh. Rueben whimpered, forced himself to carry on. He found Simon's mobile phone, still in his hip pocket, and quickly put it into his coat. Then he felt around the other side and found Simon's walkie talkie. The phone would have no reception here, and not for miles around, but their walkie talkie set was a good one. Essentially short range CB radios, with 80 channels, they could communicate with each other over about a kilometre or more of flat ground, especially if there were no buildings or hills in the way. It might prove useful, perhaps he'd hear a trucker or a farmer once he was far enough away to safely turn it on and surf the channels. Rueben and Simon always used channel 66.

One day we'll take a sweet car and cruise Route 66 together, yeah? Simon had said. *Just the two of us and an open highway, we'll drive all the way to California. But for now, channel 66 will have to do.*

Simon's shade stood silently over Rueben, tears running over his cheeks. They'd never make that journey now. Simon's walkie talkie was still on standby and Rueben's was in the kitchen of the hotel. He tried to think where he'd left it when he ran out to open up his treehouse. That seemed so long ago. He'd had to run the water and clean up the coffee pot when they arrived. He remembered taking his walkie talkie from his pocket and putting it on the shelf above the sink, next to the row of earthenware jars his mum kept up there. He put Simon's walkie in his other jacket pocket, then turned to look at the Hickmans.

"Just get going, Roo, please!" Grandma Molly said.

Rueben ignored her and searched through Bob and Laura's pockets. He found nothing except some loose change and a folding penknife with a bone handle and a three-inch blade. He pocketed that as well. Time to go. He crept back to the door and peeked out. His heart leapt into his throat at the sight of James striding along, heading directly for the garages.

Rueben scrambled away from the door and looked frantically around. James's voice came to him, muttering rapidly, but the words were indistinct. Rueben's legs were both jelly and frozen, weak, but immovable. Movement caught his eye and he saw Simon pointing at the space behind the ute again. A large, dirty canvas lay over a pile of firewood nearby. Breaking away with a force of pure will, Rueben dove forward and pushed himself into the space at the end of the stacked wood and dragged the edge of the canvas down. The garage door scraped open while Rueben was only half-covered and he froze. Despite the canvas only being over the top of him and not quite reaching the floor, it made a deep shadow that he hoped would be enough to conceal him in the gloomy garage. He could just peek beneath its leading edge.

James stepped inside, blinking as his eyes adjusted to the dimness. He scanned around and for a heart-stopping moment his eyes passed right over Rueben. James's face remained taut, like he was a rubber band primed to fly as soon as it was released. His gaze moved on and Reuben allowed himself a ragged, shallow breath.

James stepped further into the garage and crouched beside his dead brother, smoothing the young man's hair back with one dirty hand. "Pauly, it's all fucked up, bro. Everything so fucked up. But it's a new start, yeah?"

He sat cross-legged, one hand resting on his brother's sunken chest, and stared up into the darkness of the roof space.

"But they don't get it, do they? Huh? They can't *feel* it. I can. Oh, man, I feel it." He looked sharply down again, as if expecting Paul to answer. "But it's not that simple, you know? It's fucking complicated. It took one last night, but only one. Why only one? Taking its time, huh? Or only able to... to what? Not strong enough for more? Should have cut them, maybe. So it could find 'em. Doesn't matter, I gotta obey now. Then the benefits! Oh, Pauly, it'll be glorious." His voice changed, became hard-edged. "You know I don't bow down to no one. That fucking Benson learned that. But this thing, it could be different." He let out a short maniacal laugh. "I mean fuck, of *course* it's different! But it could mean something special. It scared the crap out of me last night, little bro. I'm sorry I didn't believe you at first. I mean, I kinda did, but I didn't want to, ya know? But it's been talking to me. Last night, it left no doubt! Fuck, I thought it might turn on me. But it didn't. It was pleased. It wants me to bleed 'em all. Gotta bleed 'em. But gotta wait for dark, power in the night. The sun hurts it."

He fell into silence and sat cross-legged, staring into nowhere. His eyes glazed, the band aid over his left ear grubby, hair dishevelled. He rocked ever so slightly, occasionally his lips would move in a ripple of muttering.

Rueben was trapped. He was glad of the distance between them, though it was only five or six metres. Hopefully it would be enough if he didn't move a muscle, kept his breathing slow and shallow. He felt as though James would hear his thudding heart, the blood rushing in his ears, but he talked himself down from those fears.

Just keep still, he exhorted himself. Over and over again. Was James going to sit there until it was dark, is that what he meant? That would mean Rueben was trapped here for the whole day.

Lack of sleep made him groggy in the dim, close confines, but he was terrified to let himself fall asleep. What if he inadvertently snored or farted? He remained tense, refusing to let his body give him away. His muscles tightened and threatened to cramp.

Rueben's mind began to wander in the dark. He thought about going fishing with his dad, out on the big river up the mountain a way. They'd gone often, one of the things he did with his dad, just the two of them.

"Father-son time, Roo. It's important. You get that, right?"

"Yeah, Dad. I like it. But we don't always have to fish, do we?"

"What do you want to do, son? What matters is that we hang out together. What we do is up to you. We can do anything you like."

"You know what, I actually kinda enjoy the fishing. But let's do other stuff too."

"Sure thing. You think of it and let me know."

I'm telling you as much to keep myself honest, Roo. I know I get busy and distracted. Not this year.

Rueben nodded, dozing with the memory and barely suppressed a sob as he started awake. *Dad!* They'd never do anything together again. Or go camping with Simon and Marcus. No driving lessons, no spring rolls recipe, no laughing and joking over the walkies. Tears poured silently over Rueben's cheeks as he thought of all the things these bastards had taken from him, from his family. They had taken his family!

And still James sat there, staring, muttering. Time stretched like toffee, became an inconceivable thing. It seemed as though hours passed. Rueben let more tears fall while holding back the sobs. Grief ripped him to shreds inside as he watched James sitting beside the piled corpses of his family and their closest friends.

He considered an attack. How quickly could he cover that distance, take James by surprise. Moving only his eyes he looked around for something he could use as a weapon. Something he could grab as he raced forward and bring down like a club onto the bastard's head. Maybe a weighty piece of the firewood beside him. Could he gently work a piece free without making any noise?

He had the bone-handled knife in his pocket from Bob Hickman's body. He could silently open the blade, then rush James and stab and slash at the bastard until he died.

Uncle Simon, bright but see-through in the dark garage, stood over him and shook his head. "Don't do it, buddy!" he said, eyes desperate. Rueben winced, even though he knew James wouldn't hear his uncle's words. "You'd never make it, Rueben. You're too far away. And James is big and strong and angry. You just have to get away. Don't take him on."

Rueben didn't reply, didn't even nod or shake his head, but he knew Uncle Simon was right. He was a kid, and a skinny, gangly kid at that. James seemed to be twice his size, was surely ten times his strength. Rueben couldn't risk hoping for a lucky rush now, it would almost certainly fail, and then how would he save his mum and grandpa? He had to save them at least. They had to survive. No more deaths.

Time stretched past. James sat motionless but for the soft rocking and near-silent muttering. Hours passed and Rueben's muscles cramped painfully. His body ached, his mind twisted with thoughts he couldn't ignore. All he'd lost, all he'd never do. All he wanted to do to the maniac sitting right there.

Rueben nearly cried out in surprise when James sucked in a breath and suddenly stood. He spun on the spot, eyes everywhere, and Rueben had to suppress a flinch at the unexpected physicality of it.

"Fucking talking to dead fuckers," James said, teeth clenched again, as if no time had passed. "Just gotta roll with this."

He turned and left the garage, his boots crunching over gravel, the sound fading as he marched away. After a moment, all was silence again.

Rueben sat still for several minutes in case James came back. When everything remained still, he finally let his fear out and sobbed. He shifted and stretched, muscles screaming, and let the tears come. Let his tensions drain out. Part of him wanted to simply quit, but he refused. He glanced at his father's body, then quickly away again. He hated that the enduring memory of the man would be that broken, desiccated thing. He moved to the door and looked out. The day had progressed, it had to be well after noon, but the light was wan and weak, high pale grey clouds covering the sky like a blanket.

"Go, child!" Molly said.

Simon stood beside her. "Roo, run!"

He heard gravel crunching again and ducked back with a soft curse. Deanna crossed the driveway. She cradled her shotgun at port arms, her face set. She looked to be on a mission.

As she headed for the kitchen door, Rueben saw James stalking across the grass, making his way up onto the back deck and the door by the bar further down the hotel. He heard Deanna yell out, "James! You in here?"

Something tickled the hair on the back of his neck, a charge in the air like an imminent storm. He couldn't help thinking something serious was about to go down.

"Rueben, they're both inside," Grandma Molly said. "Get away now. Get off along that driveway and out to the road."

"James!" Deanna yelled again, somewhere in the dining room maybe. "I need to talk to you!"

LEIGH

IN THE emptiness inside threatened to swallow her whole. Her brother and his husband were losses enough to hollow her out, but now her husband too? The man she had built an entire life with, had *created* a life with. The man she loved as much as life itself. She found it hard to believe Grant was gone, and in such a violent and terrifying way. But he was. And poor Clay. No man should outlive his children. No man should see his son murdered. No man should ever see what Clay must have seen in the firelit gloom of his own hotel last night.

Inside Leigh were two warring forces. The one was a dark absence, where all emotion had drained leaving her a husk with no desire at all. Except a desire for blackness to take her. What else was there?

But another force tried to drive itself up. An anger that burned with such furious incandescence it threatened to consume her as wholly as the black emptiness. Leigh knew if she let that anger rise, it would ignite every part of her and there would be no coming back from it. But to what end? Trapped here, what could she do?

Clay had cried and then become still, much as she had. She sensed the anger emanating from him even though she could barely see him. But what she could glimpse in the mirror showed he was alert, sat back up against the column. And her rage was as impotent as his while they were trapped here waiting to die. Something as common and simple as nylon ropes, that had hung in the garages for years, unnoticed, barely used, now dictated their entire lives. What little remained of those pointless, pain-filled things.

"James! I need to talk to you!"

Leigh startled and looked up as Deanna came striding through the dining room into the centre of the lounge. She stopped right between the two columns where Leigh and Clay were tied, looked around with dark eyes. Her face was twisted and, for a moment, Leigh thought Deanna was as angry as she was. Then she realised Deanna's expression was borne of fear. What had she seen? What had she done?

"Cut us free!" Leigh said, her voice strong again. "End this now, Deanna."

"Shut up. Where's James?"

"How should we know? Cut us free, Deanna. Let us go, and you and James can sort out whatever you want to do on your own. We'll just leave. You know it—"

"I said *shut up*!"

Footsteps banged across the back deck and the door beside the bar opened. James stepped in, still holding Simon's pistol. His face was drawn, bags under his eyes a deep purple edged in blue. His lips were peeled back, clenched teeth revealed. Dirt and grime coated his face and hands, bits of dead leaf caught in his hair.

"Hello, Dee." His voice was gravel and old smoke. His body seemed to tilt forward, a dog straining at its leash, a force about to whip and let go. Leigh tried to swallow and found her mouth dry.

"This has to end," Deanna said.

Leigh saw the woman's hands shaking as she tightened her grip on the shotgun held tightly across her chest. She backed up, past where Clay was tied, to stand near the couches at that end of the lounge. Leigh looked left and right, keenly aware that she and Clay were between Deanna and James, probably exactly as Deanna wanted it.

"End?" James said, like he didn't understand the word.

"It's enough. All more than enough." Tears stood out on Deanna's lower lashes, her face pale, but her cheeks flushed a rose red. "Let's just leave, yeah? This place, it's toxic. It's *fucked up*, James."

"You don't think things are just getting fun?"

"What?"

James's smile widened, his face an impossible parody of a grinning skull. "Oh, there's things afoot here, yes. There are all kinds of possibilities here."

Deanna looked around, eyes beseeching Clay, then Leigh. She was clearly lost, and scared. She was fighting against her abuser, Leigh realised. Finally pushing against something she'd used to support her all this time.

"Do it," Clay said quietly.

She glanced down at him. In the mirror, Leigh saw as he kept his face as neutral as possible and gave her one short nod, never breaking eye contact.

James took one large, deliberate step forward and Deanna's gaze jerked back to him. She took another step back.

"No? You don't think so?" James said.

"Then *I'm* going," Deanna said. "You can… do whatever you like here. But I'm out."

"Oh no, you don't get to leave. No one gets to leave."

"James!" The tears breached, as much frustration as fear or grief, Leigh thought. Even now, the woman was torn. Her feelings for James clearly ran deep.

He took another big step towards her, taking him past Leigh, the two of them only three metres or so apart now. "No one gets out alive!" He laughed, manic and high.

Deanna swung the shotgun around and up, levelled it James's chest. "I have to go, James! I'm going. And I'm going to cut these two free. Let them take their chances on foot, but let them go. And I go. And you… you do whatever the fuck you want."

"Gonna shoot me, little Dee?"

"Do it," Clay growled, more forceful than before, anger rising.

"I will! I'm scared, James. I've had enough. Let me go or I'll shoot you!"

James's grin widened further and he reached out, dropped his pistol onto an armchair as he took another step forward. "You can't shoot me, little Dee. Remember when I took care of your stepdad, hmm? You forgetting that?"

Deanna squeezed her eyes shut for a moment, swallowed hard. "Of course I remember. You can't hold that over me forever."

"Remember you and me at Garrie Beach? In the dunes under that bright full moon?" He took another step forward. Then he stopped and spread his arms wide, standing like a crucifixion. "I'll make it easy for you, little Dee. Can you really shoot me?"

Her shotgun shook but she didn't lower it. "James, don't make me. I will! Just let us go."

"Too late for that. Oh, far too late for any of that." He tipped his head to one side. "You can't shoot me, little Dee."

"*Stop calling me that!*" She moved one foot back, bracing herself, resetting her grip on the shotgun.

"Just do it!" Clay yelled at her.

Leigh sat stunned, holding her breath, terrified of any possible outcome to this standoff.

Deanna cried out, wordless frustration. James tipped his head back and laughed. Leigh saw it a moment before it happened, James's body tense, the air in the room crackling with hate, then he was barrelling straight for her. Deanna yelled again and James swung his hand out, batting the shotgun aside as she pulled the trigger. The weapon boomed thunder and fire and Clay yelped as the wood of the column beside him splintered and split.

Leigh watched in horror, James's right hand swinging back and in, back and in, the thick *chunk chunk chunk* of a large knife punching over and over into Deanna's ribs and abdomen. Where had he even drawn it from?

Deanna's eyes were wide, her breath escaping in a loud, sibilant hiss, as the blood drained from her face leaving her porcelain pale, a shocked, agonized doll. James stood over her as she slumped to the ground, blood pouring out of her, his free hand still clutching a wad of jacket to prevent her collapsing all the way. She hung there, legs folded up beneath, blood flooding from her side to soak her jacket, her jeans, the floor.

Her hissing breath began to wane, like a punctured tyre running out of air. It twisted into a soft word, "Jaaammmessss..." and then her head lolled back, eyes staring blind.

James let her go and she tipped back bonelessly, her head striking the floorboards with a hard *thock*. James was wound more tautly than a piano wire, his whole body vibrating, knuckles white on the hilt of the hunting knife he'd killed her with. He stared down, his chest pumping in rapid, shallow breaths.

"No one gets out alive," he said, laughing again, a thick, bubbling sound from somewhere deep in his throat.

Leigh stared, dumbfounded. That was it. Done and dusted. What a way to go, all taken out with such madness and violence. If nothing else, maybe she'd see her beloved Grant again. Maybe Clay would see Molly. Were Simon and Marcus together again now, or was all that just so much bullshit?

She selfishly hoped James would kill her now, and quickly, so she didn't have to suffer through Clay's death too. Or an end like Grant's. And she hoped it would be quick, but thought maybe James would make the most of it if he had the chance. Torture them first. Oh fuck, what else might he do to her before he murdered her?

As long as Rueben got away, that was all that mattered. It was already too late for her and Clay. Deanna had failed. Like Marcus had failed. But Rueben could survive. Get away. What trauma he would grow up with, what damage this might do notwithstanding, he would at least get to grow up.

"And now what about you two?" James said.

Leigh jumped, looked up to see James leering down at Clay, then moving around to look at her.

"You leave us the fuck alone!" Leigh said, and impressed herself with the power, the fury, in her tone. "You've done enough."

"Oh no," James said, almost singsong now. "Not nearly enough, especially not with you, pretty one."

Leigh sighed, nodded softly to herself. Of course. What else could she have expected?

"But I have to cut you this time. Yes. Bleeding. Before I bring others. Learn the right ways." James tipped his head again, studying them. "Both tonight, or one at a time? There's already little Dee, so maybe—"

"Hey, James, you useless piece of shit."

James stood ramrod straight, turning a full circle on the spot. Leigh's stomach turned to water, instantly recognizing that young voice.

"No no no," she said, the strength drained from her, replaced with despair. "No, no, my beautiful boy!"

"The fuck is that?" James said.

"You hear me, James, you murderous piece of shit?" Distant but clear enough, and kind of sibilant. Tinny.

"Who's there?" James turned and moved toward the doors into the dining room.

The sound came from that direction, but it was surreal, buzzy. Leigh knew why, and while desolation ate at her gut, she couldn't help being a little impressed too.

"You hear me, shitbag? You didn't know I was here, huh? Come and find me, motherfucker!"

James ran out through the dining room. Leigh heard him clatter into the kitchen, start smashing around in there. The voice sounded again, but she missed the words in the noise of James's furious searching. Then footsteps pounding back through the hotel and he burst into the lounge again, Rueben's walkie talkie clutched in his fist. "What the fuck is this?" he demanded. "Who the fuck is it?"

"Come and get me, shithead!" the walkie crowed.

James pressed the talk button, held the device so close his lips brushed over it. "I will tear you apart, whoever the fuck you are!"

"There you are, you prick! Come on then!"

With a wordless grunt of anger and frustration, James snatched up his pistol off the armchair, grabbed Deanna's shotgun, and bolted from the room, out the door by the bar and across the back deck.

Silence descended, but for Leigh's quiet crying.

RUEBEN

RUEBEN ran into the shelter of the trees, instantly grateful for the gloom and even the extra bite of cold once he was out of the weak sun. He dodged left and right, then skidded to a stop, panting. Where did he go? No way would he draw James to his treehouse, even though the safety of that place was dubious at best.

"What are you doing, child?" Grandma Molly asked from the shadows beside him. "You got a plan?"

"I just have to get him away from them," Rueben whispered, hands trembling, voice weak and shaking. "Maybe I can draw him in, then double back and free them. We take a car? It's only James now, right?"

He remembered the cajoling of that thing in the night. Whatever it was that had awakened out there, that drew him to the horrible ground behind the low fence, it spoke to James as well, that much was obvious. There was another possibility. There was power to be used here. What about he and James find out who it might favour more?

The walkie hissed in his hand, made him jump. "Who are you, huh?" James's voice sounded almost amused, like he'd decided this was a game, and one he planned to enjoy playing. "Where have you been all this time?"

Rueben lifted the walkie.

"Careful, champ," Simon said.

Rueben licked his lips. "You any good at hunting, James?"

"Oh, this *is* a turn up. How exciting. You sound like a kid. Are you a kid?"

"I'm old enough to fuck you up."

James's laughter broke up in an electronic crackle. "Is that so? I like you already. What's the plan?"

Rueben turned and ran deeper into the trees, thinking frantically.

That low, hissing whisper tickled past his ears again. *Cooooommmmme...*

Rueben's heart stuttered, appalled at the oily presence, but instantly drawn to it as well. The voice was weaker, and Rueben somehow knew that was down to the daylight, but he didn't care. He remembered the loose ground and all the weird trees, the slope going down, down. He hated it now, its power to hypnotize him would never work again, he promised himself. Yet he was hardly able to resist the drag of it. And surely it had at least as strong a hold over James. Maybe stronger, because James was clearly mad. He could use that.

"You explored far into the forest?" he asked into the walkie as he moved, ducking left and right around dark trunks.

"Why? Are you in league with it?" James asked. He sounded suddenly affronted. Jealous? "The thing out there? Is that how you've hid from me all this time?"

Rueben slid to a halt, turned to look back. Through the thick forest he picked out bits and pieces of the hotel and lawns, a glimpse here and there, but the place was mostly obscured. Then he saw a movement. Brief, just a flicker, as someone moved left to right. Not into the trees.

"You scared, you pussy ass bitch?" Rueben asked. "You have to come in to find me. To find *us*!"

"Come in, eh? You think I haven't been in already? You haven't seen my work back there?"

"I don't know. Have you? Or did you chicken out?"

James's broken laughter again. "Oh, I'm no chicken, little kid. Oh no. We have talks, me and that thing out there. Ideas have been floated, yeah? Promises made."

Rueben frowned, moved deeper into the trees again. What the hell did that mean? But he had no other cards to play. "I wonder if they're similar promises to the ones it made me?"

There was static hiss for a moment. James had pressed the talk button, but was saying nothing. Had Rueben put him on the back foot? Got him thinking? It didn't matter as long as the ~~bastard came~~ for him.

"One, two, Jimmy's coming for you!" James said, singsong and cracked. Then there was a howl, a human parody of a wolf, but through the air, not the walkie talkie. From the lawns behind the hotel. Rueben pictured the lunatic tipping his head up to the cold clouds as he bayed.

Rueben had only gone about a hundred metres back into the trees, but he heard the sudden crash and thrash of someone running haphazardly in behind him. He turned and bolted.

CLAY

"WE have to help him!" Leigh's voice cracked with barely contained emotion. "Clay? Are you shot? What can we do?"

Clay took long, deep breaths, trying to still the myriad pains snaking through his body. And trying to quell the adrenaline pumping, making his heart hammer, his eyes flicker, seeing double.

"Clay? It's just us now." Leigh sobbed, the sounds escaping despite her obvious effort to keep it in. "Rueben is alone out there with that lunatic. Oh, Clay, we can't let him get my baby!"

Clay winced, her words like daggers. He'd watched Grant die horribly, he knew the pain of losing a son, but his son was at least a grown man. Rueben was a child, barely into his teens. Clay couldn't imagine how terrified the poor boy must be, but he was so damn proud of how brave Rueben was being. "Hang on," he gasped. "Give me a second."

"Clay? Are you shot?"

He heard Leigh twisting and writhing against her bonds, presumably trying to get a look at him. He laughed, the absurdity of everything pushing him dangerously close to snapping. "Little bit," he said, slowly gaining his breath. His hip, lower back, and knee were their usual fire of age and arthritis, but new pains existed too. His left shoulder and upper arm, and a patch across the top left of his chest. He managed to twist his head to see. Scarlet flowers bloomed across the shoulder and front of his shirt, small holes in the thin canvas material of it. Not too many, he must have only caught the very edge of Deanna's blast. Most of her shot had splintered the wood of the column. If Marcus had still been alive, tied to the other side, he would have caught the full blast of it, been blown to smithereens.

"I'm okay," he said. "For a given value of okay, anyway. Just caught a few stray bits of shot."

"Are you bleeding?"

"A bit, yeah."

"Shit, Clay!"

He licked his lips, he was so damned thirsty. "I know, I know." He looked down at his shoulder again, saw the stain of blood in a couple of places further down his sleeve where it had trickled down inside. He twisted to see his hand tied back against the side of the column and grimaced. There was blood there too, a couple of small rivulets over the back of his hand, drops on the floor beneath. It would be enough, he knew that from what had happened to Grant. The way those questing worms of night had appeared up through the blood on the floor, then found their way over Grant's body, absorbing blood as they went, and then into him through the rent skin. If night came around again, the same would happen to Clay, through the wounds from the few small balls of shot that had pierced him. He didn't want to go like that, better that Deanna's shot had blown him away. But then Leigh would be left alone in all this, and that was unimaginable.

His eye caught something else. It took him a moment to get past the fog in his brain and figure out what he was looking at, then a slow smile crept across his face. Was this the first bit of luck they'd had? The shotgun had blasted a large chunk of the column away on the far side, right by where Marcus had been sitting, and stray edges of it had caught Clay. But some had also caught the rope, tied as it was low down, close against the floor, the shot had almost missed it, but not quite. In several places the rope was frayed and split. Not all the way through, but in a couple of places, only a few strands still held it together.

Clay twisted his arm and hand, ignored the burning pain in his shoulder as he moved the small holes from the shotgun, and managed to get his fingers around a part of the rope right by one of the most extensive pieces of damage. He hauled against it, cried out as his muscles cramped and his wounds flared.

"Clay? Are you okay?"

"The shotgun blast damaged the rope. I'm trying… to…break…" He grunted with effort as he shifted to get a better grip, pulled again. His muscles burned, the wounds opened from where they'd begun to coagulate and fresh blood trickled down his arm and across his chest. A grunt that was almost all sob escaped as his fingers quit and slipped free. "Fuck this aging carcass!" he yelled, head tipped back to cast his fury at the heavens. "I used to be strong!"

"Clay, you're still strong!" Leigh said. "I know you're getting old, you're not as strong as you once were, sure. But you are *not* weak. You're still strong. Come on, try again. You can do this!"

He heard the desperation in her voice, the sudden hope. She saw a chance here to go to Rueben's aid. And she was right, this was a chance. The best they'd had. The best they were going to get. The only one. He sat still for a moment, took several long, deep breaths. Leigh must have heard him, chose to hold her tongue for a moment, but he felt the need emanating from her. He nodded once. "Okay."

Moving more slowly this time he shifted his butt first, suppressing a yelp against the shards of agony through his hip. He only managed to turn slightly, a couple of inches, but it changed the angle of his chest and shoulder just a little, and that gave him a different position for his arm. He shifted his hand under rope, right beside where the shot had almost severed it. It was the thinnest section he could see. He drew in a long breath, wrapped his hand tightly into the rope, then braced himself and pulled.

He grit his teeth, let a low growl grow into a shout of fury as every muscle in his body tensed and strained against a few fibres of man-made material. He refused to quit, as agony lanced back and forth through every limb, as his heart slammed his ribs, his vision crossed and threatened to black out.

"Come on, Clay!" Leigh's voice was high. Desperate, yes, but full of belief too. She genuinely believed he could do this. He had to believe it too.

"Come on, Clay! You're not too old yet. You're an angry, powerful son of a bitch! Don't let this beat you!"

Clay roared and hauled with all his might. Something in his chest tore with a red-hot streak of pain, the skin of his fingers split and he was sure his bones would separate any moment. His shoulder flamed, his head pounded, his heart threatened to burst. He screamed, let all his frustration fly with his voice.

And the rope snapped.

Clay shot back as it gave way, yanked to a stop as his bonds on the other side stopped his body from going over. He cried out, every part of him alive with pain, and tears poured over his cheeks. He sobbed and gasped, blackness sweeping in from every side. His sight reduced to two swiftly narrowing tunnels. He was dizzy. Pain arced along his left arm, fire at his wrist, slamming in front of his shoulder.

"Clay? Did you get it? Clay!"

Leigh's voice was distant, like he heard her from under water. He imagined her standing on the edge of a pool looking down as he sank inexorably. His chest tight, breath refusing to come, his heart stuttering, like an old car about to break down.

Everything went black.

RUEBEN

JAMES was somewhere behind him, but not close. Not yet. Rueben knew this bush well, had played for hours and hours, made all kinds of discoveries. Animal tracks that led under thick brush, trees easy to climb to gain great height, creeks and rivulets with ice cold, clear, fresh water that could provide a drink or turn an unwary ankle. But what use was any of that?

Bring him to meee…

The voice had gained strength and clarity. It hissed through his mind, oily and slick. But clearer than ever, more compelling than ever. Still not really words, but its intent was as powerful as language. Rueben grit his teeth, the drag on his mind hard to resist. It took a huge force of will to stay away from the sloping, loose ground, the dead and blackened trees. In all the years of visiting, he'd happily avoided that entire area, stayed on the good side of the low fence. With so much bush to explore, he didn't spare a second thought for the place too dangerous to play in. Some things were easily accepted as law. As gospel. But then, whatever resided there had slept. It hadn't called to him. Now, awake, it persisted, cajoled, begged him to come.

And he would. Why not? If James could make deals with it, so could Rueben. To save his mother and grandfather, he would pay its price. Whatever that might be.

"No, child!"

Grandma Molly stood before him, under the shadow of a low branch. He looked at her for a moment, then couldn't stop a tear from breaching, rolling over his chilled cheek. "I'm so tired, Grandma. And I'm scared."

She reached for him, the pain of not being able to gather him into a hug evident in her eyes. "I know. I know. But you have to save yourself. You have to get away."

"Loop around. Go back to the hotel and free your mum and Clay, then get away." Simon stood beside Molly, and she cast him a sudden glare.

"He can't go back in there!"

"He has to!"

"No, he most certainly does not. The boy needs to save himself."

Simon shook his head, lost for words for a moment. "He can't just leave Leigh and Clay in there to die! He wouldn't be able to live with himself."

"If it means he survives, of course he can. What if he tries to free them and that lunatic comes back? What then? They all die!"

A howl burst out, startling them all. It sounded close, and was without a doubt James. He's coming for me, Rueben thought. And he'll get me if I just stand around like this.

Bring him to meeeee…

James howled again.

"You hear that?" Molly demanded of Simon. "You hear that monster out there?"

"He's not the only monster, Moll. You know that. I know it." Simon pointed at his nephew. "Rueben knows it."

"Stop it! Both of you!" Rueben's voice was a hissed whisper, harsh but suppressed. James could be anywhere out there. "There are monsters, and it's up to me to save Mum and Grandpa Clay. I will not leave without them."

Simon nodded, Molly frowned.

"But I need to buy us time," Rueben said. "I need to lead James further in first." Then he had to convince whatever that thing was to favour him and not James. He could do that.

To meee..!

"Did you hear that?" Rueben asked. "Can you hear the thing out there?"

"I only hear James howling like a mad dog," Simon said.

"Me too. What do *you* hear, child?"

Rueben licked his lips, shook his head. If they couldn't hear the oily voice, he didn't want to discuss it with them. But James heard it, he'd admitted that. Was it telling James the same things? Was it exhorting James to bring Rueben in as well? Playing them against each other in order to have them both?

Reuben saw himself in a sea of blood. Delivering blood, by bringing more people here.

He looked around himself, the sensation clearer and stronger than ever. "Why?" His voice wavered, not loud, but desperate. And was it suggesting the same thing to James?

"Who do you hear, child?"

And then Rueben knew, without a doubt he understood its need. Human blood. Animals came this way and kept it alive when occasionally their blood was spilled. Tiny, almost inconsequential hints. But human blood was nectar to it, empowered it. Once before it had tasted and almost risen, but it wasn't enough. Now it had a taste again.

Rueben stood, indecisive, trying to understand. He remembered all the bodies, drained to husks. And animals wouldn't do. People weren't rare... But *here* they were. Its concept of the population would be mightily skewed.

He understood more as it pushed its will into him. He saw how the sun hurt it, but the night was its domain. He understood the power it could give him when it had regained its own strength. *Would* give him, if only he kept up the supply.

How could he believe this thing? Would anything so awful ever tell the truth? But if he could lure James to it, then promise it more, it would let him go in order to fulfill that obligation. He just had to convince it to rely on him, not that madman. He didn't need to ever come back once he was away.

Surely the thing was telling James exactly the same. Rueben wasn't green enough to think that wouldn't be case. Surely James was hearing the same promises, the same exhortations. It only needed one of them. But Rueben knew this bush and James didn't. Rueben could surely prove to this thing that he was of sounder mind, more trustworthy. He had family who owned the hotel, who could bring people right to it. They never would, of course, but he could make that case. What did James have? Only lunacy.

"Don't do it, child! Whatever you're thinking, don't. Save yourself."

"And your mum and Clay!" Simon glanced at Molly, his eyes angry, then back at Rueben. "You can get around, into the kitchen, grab a knife and cut their ropes. Then all three of you are up and away. It'll only take moments. Let James run around lost out here."

Rueben licked his lips, nodded. "I have to make sure he's far enough in."

"Child, please–"

"No, Grandma, this is my choice. I won't just save myself. I won't leave Mum and Clay behind."

Squinting, trying to push the slick voice from his mind and operate under his own volition alone, Rueben turned and headed around past the back of his treehouse, aiming to come to the eastern side of the deep, dangerous loose depression in the forest. He keyed the walkie as he ran.

"You hear me, fucker?"

The hiss of returning static was instant. "Oh, I hear you! I'm coming for you!"

"Come on then!" Feed James to this thing, then promise it more. Simple. Rueben yelled, and tipped his head back to mimic James earlier howl. It echoed up through the trees. He keyed the walkie again. "Hear me? Come on, fucker!"

He ran on.

LEIGH

FOR fifteen minutes after Clay collapsed, Leigh screamed herself hoarse, yelling his name. If she twisted in her bonds and craned her neck to one side, she could just make him out, hanging limply against the ropes still looped around the column. But one arm had flopped over and to the floor beside him, free of the ropes. He had done it, he'd broken the rope, and now lay as if dead. Had the effort finished him? A heart attack? It wasn't fair!

After she'd stopped yelling, Leigh had sat and cried. She'd never felt so powerless, so impotent. And she had never hated anyone like she hated James Glenn. She didn't know it was possible to hate another human being with the radiant passion with which she loathed that man.

Still Clay lay insensate.

Where was Rueben? Had he got away? If he'd managed to escape, James would have come back. If James had caught Rueben, he would have come back too, surely. Were they still out there, playing cat and mouse? Empty, desperate, she waited.

As a little girl, she had been ordered to attend church and Sunday school. Her parents were proud Christians, and not the evangelical modern type who seemed to shout about Christian values to anyone who would listen while acting in every way contradictory to those ideals. No, her folks had been what people might call good Christians. They'd attended church regularly, taken her and Simon along. They did good works in the community, always there when a natural disaster like a storm or flood meant people needed help. Leigh remembered dozens of times when strangers had walked around her house, being made tea, being fed, offered a place to rest.

Her mother always made things—jam, linen shopping bags, crocheted clothes and toys, and more—and those things were always donated to school fairs, to sales, to church picnics. Her father was recognized throughout the area as a man people could rely on. He would drive fifty kilometres to help with a breakdown, he would climb a roof and fix a chimney, he would give up a weekend to help paint a fence. Leigh's parents were good people, good Christians, good neighbours.

They struggled a little with Simon's sexuality. He came out to Leigh first, asked for her help. She wasn't surprised, of course. She'd known since she knew what gay was. *Oh, that's how Simon is!* she remembered thinking, and she couldn't have been more than 8 or 9 at the time. Together they went to their parents, and Leigh held Simon's hand while he came out to them. Her father had gone quiet, looked away. Her mother had gathered Simon into a hug. Bizarrely, it seemed to Leigh, the news came as a complete surprise to both of them. But within a day, they had processed the information and both made great pains to assure Simon they were okay with it. It took a long time more for them to actually be okay with it, to show through their actions they had accepted and understood, but they did eventually.

They were good people. None better. And they both died in terror and burning pain in a car wreck when Leigh was just 19. Two young men, out of their heads on ice, had T-boned her parents car through a red light and both vehicles became one tangled mess of metal and glass wrapped around a lamp post on the corner of the junction. Both cars were engulfed in flames in a matter of seconds and her parents and both ice-heads had burned to death in the wreckage as horrified bystanders watched, unable to do a thing. By the time emergency services arrived, only blackened twists of metal remained. All four had been formally identified by dental records. The young men's friends had confirmed the two boys were wasted when they'd driven away from a party only minutes before the crash.

And when her parents went like that, so did any vestige of belief in any kind of benevolent god. Leigh and Simon both sat stunned at the joint funeral, held with great reverence at their parent's church, and they admitted to each other later that surely no god would allow such a thing to happen to such people. The priest made platitudes like how god wanted those fine people to be at his side, how they'd done more good in their short life than many achieved even living into great old age, but that was all so much bullshit to Leigh. She needed her parents. Simon needed them. So many in the community loved and needed them. And her parents needed to see Leigh and Simon grow and achieve. Both were barely even adults yet and her parents had only been in their forties. There was no justice to it.

Alone in the family home after the wake, sitting together on the back porch sharing a joint, Leigh and Simon had talked and agreed that there were three possibilities. Either there was no god, or there was a god but he couldn't prevent the accident, or there was a god and he didn't *want* to prevent the accident. Option two and three made both of them less than inclined to care about, let alone worship, any such capricious monster. So Leigh had settled for the most likely answer. The most obvious. There was no god.

Now, with Simon dead, Grant dead, Marcus dead, Rueben lost and alone, maybe Clay dead too, while that piece of shit James Glenn ran around alive and well, she had never been more convinced there wasn't the possibility of any god. And yet, whatever was happening, whatever had killed Grant, proved there most definitely were monsters beyond the monstrous humans she'd always been aware of. And that terrified her more than anything. There were real monsters out there preying on people, but there was no god protecting them. The world was black and filled with blood. She couldn't exhort god to save Clay, because there was no god.

There was no hope.

But she would be damned if she'd quit on her son.

She decided that when James came back, hopefully without having found Rueben, he would want to do terrible things to her. She could use that. He would have to untie her to make the most of that opportunity. She would appeal to his disgusting need. She would offer trades, favours, and she would make damn sure he paid the price when he loosened her bonds. It was the only hope keeping her sane, that Rueben would evade James, and James would come back for her.

The afternoon darkened towards dusk, and James didn't return. Neither did Rueben.

Then Clay made a sound.

Leigh lurched up from her fugue state, the ropes biting into her. "Clay! Clay, wake up!"

He groaned again, softly, almost too quietly to hear, but it was definitely him. She twisted and strained her neck to see in the mirror and sure enough, he moved slightly from side to side.

"Clay!"

He jerked slightly, sucked in a ragged breath.

"Clay, please, wake up!"

"Whaaaa…"

Leigh drew a deep breath, blew it out slowly to calm herself. "Clay, you have to wake up. We still have time. It's nearly dark, but James hasn't come back. Think of Rueben, Clay! Think of Roo and how we can help him. I refuse to believe he's dead!"

"Okay," Clay muttered, quiet, weak. Then a little stronger, "He's… okay… kinda. Molly… says…"

"She's here? Molly's here?"

"Uh huh."

Leigh looked up, around. Did the woman's ghost float around or stand somewhere? It didn't matter. "Molly, please get him up. Help him!"

"All right," Clay said, voice a little stronger again. "The pair of you… cut it out." A half smile tweaked his lips and he used his free hand against the ground to push himself up a little. He made an awful sound of pain, a pitiful cry.

Leigh winced to hear it. "Move slowly! Move slow, but keep moving. You broke the rope, remember?"

"I remember. Give me a minute here."

Leigh had never felt such relief in her life, such soul-rinsing respite. Did they really have a chance now? She kept her neck craned, watched as Clay pulled himself into a better sitting position, no longer hanging in the ropes. He grit his teeth as he moved, but still involuntary sounds of pain escaped him. His face twisted in a grimace, but he reached around, out of Leigh's field of vision. She had to look back to the front before her neck cramped and seized up, but she listened to his grunts and gasping breath. And she heard the rope hissing against itself, and against the column, as he pulled it free. He was doing it. He was getting free.

Come on, Clay! Come on. This is the bit where James comes back just as we're escaping.

Clay cried out again and she twisted once more to see him on his hands and knees beside the wooden column, free of all ropes. His back arched and fell as he gasped in agonized breaths. She clenched her teeth, wanting him to hurry but not wanting to hurry him. He was doing his best, she knew that.

"I know, I know," he said, glancing up at nothing to his right.

No, not nothing. At Molly. Were there really ghosts? Did ghosts mean there was more, after death? Leigh shook the thought away. At best, it might mean that there was a god, but in that case options two and three of her realization with Simon that night still applied. Either this god couldn't or wouldn't protect her family. So fuck him. It was down to them, ghosts or not.

Clay hauled himself to his feet, face still scrunched in agony. He leaned against the column and sucked in quick, pained gasps. Tears trickled over his cheeks, but he was unaware, or ignored them.

"Okay," he said at last. "Okay." He hobbled over to Leigh and let out more noises of pain as he crouched beside her. She leaned toward him and he smiled, took her cheeks between his dry, rough palms and kissed her forehead. Then he began searching her ropes, pulling and frowning.

After a moment he grunted in frustration. "I can't do it, these old hands too numb. The knots are too tight. Wait, I'll get a knife."

Leigh tipped her head back against the column in frustration as Clay slowly rose and hobbled away. *Come on, come on!*

She envisioned the back door bursting open and James running in, the pistol waving in front of him. Unable to resist, she looked across past the bar and saw night falling out there in the bush. Where were they? Why had it been so quiet for so long?

"This was fortuitous."

She whipped her head back to see Clay, moving a little more easily. He had a large kitchen carving knife in one hand, and a shotgun in the other. "One of the idiots left this behind."

He grinned as he moved slowly back to his knees. He put the shotgun down and set to work sawing with the knife. Leigh and Marcus kept the kitchen tools in good condition, the knives razor sharp. It went through the thick nylon with ease. The moment the pressure slackened she began pulling and dragging herself free, relief surging through her. Adrenaline spiked in her system and she let out a laugh that was half-crazed, and she didn't care. Clay looked at her, head on one side. His lips twitched in a smile.

Leigh grabbed up the shotgun and Clay stood, the large, sharp knife still held tightly in his hand.

"Let's go and save Rueben," Leigh said. "Which way?"

Clay looked slightly past her for a moment, then nodded. "Molly will show us," he said. "Come on."

Limping heavily on his bad leg, but exuding sheer grit, he went for the back door. Leigh gripped the shotgun tight and followed.

RUEBEN

IT TIME slipped and blurred like taffy, minutes stretching to hours, hours whipping by like seconds. Grandma Molly and Uncle Simon tried again and again to convince him to turn away, to run back to the hotel. They exhorted Rueben to give up the chase. But he couldn't. He'd played cat and mouse with James for hours, while the thing down there rejoiced in their fear. It had taken a while to find his way around to the dead, dark hole in the forest. He'd looped back and forth, tried to keep track of James, but inevitably they had slowly closed in on the ground he had thus far spent a lifetime avoiding. Sometime previously his walkie had gone dark, the battery spent. Whether or not the same applied to the one James carried he couldn't know. But it didn't matter. Like animals, they yelped and howled to each other through the trees. Molly and Simon tried time and again to tell him the thing down there had him hypnotised, it was controlling him and James, toying with them, waiting for dark. He knew it to be true as well, but that was okay. He had his plan.

As he'd moved, Rueben had found a good, solid, straight stick and he would pause, use the knife from Bob Hickman to whittle at it for a few moments, then move on. Over time he'd created a wickedly sharp point on it. Now he carried a strong spear some four feet long in one hand and the small knife in the other. Both ready to bleed James with when the moment came. Now it grew dark, and the time was at hand.

Rueben felt exultant as they neared the blackened land. He shared the joy of the thing down there as he and James toyed with each other.

Something strange had happened inside his mind the closer he got to the huge crater in the forest. He remembered his previous visit, called back from the brink by Molly and Simon. As soon as he came near to the blackened, loamy ground, with its cloying fungal aromas, memory had flooded back. And the voice came clearer and more promising than ever. The Entity, he had decided to call it. He didn't know if that was the right word, but it seemed to fit. He needed to call it something, give it more form than a simple disembodied sensation. As soon as he'd thought that, the Entity had agreed.

It chilled Rueben to his marrow, but the thought was irresistible too. He needed to see more, to understand more. It didn't mean he needed to serve the thing, not if he chose not to. He might only be a kid, but he was strong of mind and body. He would resist it. James might be too far gone, unable to resist the directives of the Entity, but not Rueben. He had strength, didn't he? He would feed James to it, promise it more, but then never return. Simple as that.

"I bet James is thinking exactly the same about you, champ," Simon said, leaning close so Rueben could not avoid his gaze. "Think about it. This isn't you. This is *it*. The Entity. It's making you think these things. And it's making James think the same. Don't you reckon?"

Rueben shook his head. "I don't know," Rueben muttered. Whether he was answering Simon or the Entity, he wasn't sure.

The ground underfoot was loose and uncertain, shards of shale and slate-like stone, slipping over each other like fish. Rueben couldn't stand still, constantly adjusting his balance against the slick ground, as the black and stunted trees twisted and reached around him. He hid against the dark trunk of one slightly larger tree, looked out for James. He needed to spot him, then sneak around and stick him with the spear. The Entity revelled in the thought of more blood nearby.

Simon leaned close again. "Roo, sport, you gotta go. Run, buddy. Get up and away from here, now! You've done enough, James is all the way back here. Now you can go."

"They're free!" Molly stepped up beside Simon, her face split in a grin.

Rueben frowned. "What?"

"Your mum, your Grandpa Clay, they're free. They got out of the ropes. They're coming this way, but don't let them come this far. Go back, child! Go meet them, stay ahead of James. Get away!"

"They're free?"

Shadow like an oil slick swept up through Rueben, made him cry out and shudder as he was drenched in hate and malevolence. The Entity seemed to grip hold of him with its will.

A howl split the darkened air and Rueben jumped. James was close. Too close. He spun around, squinting through the almost-night. Clouds shifted and the moon shone down, the entire area softly lit in a wan, silvery glow, and there he was. James stood across the slope, maybe a hundred metres away. He was stripped entirely naked, his body smudged and darkened with dirt, his hair dishevelled. In the moonlight, his broad grin was savage, teeth and the whites of his eyes bright, his gaze insane.

He tipped his head back, his leanly muscled body glistening with sweat, and howled again. "AAAAWWOOOOOOOO!"

He held a pistol in one hand, gleaming grey-silver in the night, and a shotgun in the other. Rueben looked down at his spear and penknife in dismay.

That black malevolence through Rueben's body pulsed and washed like a tide, like a tidal wave, and he hissed in fury. "No more!"

He wasn't even sure what he meant by that. No more obeying this thing? No more killing? Whatever, it didn't matter. Finally seeing James standing there, like he was the one in charge, like he dictated events, filled Rueben with a blind rage. Leaving Molly and Simon calling desperately behind, he ran hard up the slope for the cover of trees to circle around behind the man responsible for so much pain.

The Entity exulted, a rippling laughter emanating through the land. Rueben gained the shadows of the healthier trees, ran as low and quiet as he could.

"Where is he?" James yelled. "You said he was here!"

Rueben's heart hammered, his breath burned in his chest. He gripped his spear with both hands, one hand gripping the penknife against it. The sharp length of wood preceded him, braced against his body. He saw James's sweat-slick back, limned in moonlight, as he stood on the edge of the hollow ground. The murderer howled again, face to the moon, as Rueben tucked low into his run and sprinted as hard as he could, planning to plant his spear right through the bastard.

James's howl morphed into a maniacal laugh as he turned and tipped his head back down just in time to see Rueben close the distance between them. His eyes popped wider still and Rueben barrelled into him, driving his spear ahead. James simultaneously dropped the shotgun to grab at the spear and brought the pistol up in his other hand. He yelped in surprise as the sharp wooden point punctured the flesh above his left hip, Rueben's speed too much for him to deflect it completely. The shotgun he'd dropped slipped away down into the crater and the pistol fired, its sharp report an ear-splitting crack in the night right by Rueben's head, but no bullet hit him.

James roared in pain as they went down and rolled over each other, sliding back into the huge, wide crater. Rueben didn't let go of the spear, tried to twist it as they tumbled. Pain sang through him as they fell, then slowed and James muscled himself up and sat astride Rueben's chest. The spear stuck right through his side, Rueben saw the blood-soaked point sticking out of his back, glistening in the night, but it hadn't killed him. Didn't even seem to slow him, despite the man's face twisted in pain.

The Entity had driven him to this idiot attack and now he would pay for it. What had he been thinking? He was a thirteen year old boy, he couldn't fight a crazed, full-grown man like James Glenn. James brought the pistol around.

The Entity just needed a little more. It was so close.

A little more what? So close to what? The blood dripping from James's wound seemed to swell in the night, glistening black and glowing red inside, and it scurried away into the depths of the crater, flickering with dozens of tendril protuberances. The ground heaved.

Panic threatened to overwhelm Rueben. James's eyes were gleeful as he reared back and howled again. Rueben thrashed underneath him, but James shifted his weight and pinned Rueben's arms with his knees.

"It doesn't matter who, did you not realise that?" James asked, laughing. "It was always about the strongest, that's all. The one most able to bring the blood, to *keep* bringing the blood. That was never going to be you, you stupid kid! You think you're stronger than *me*?" He tipped his head to one side, staring down. "There was one before. Oh, so long ago. He did very well, but lost his mind when he ran out of family. Too far, you see, too far away to fetch more people. And no one came, and slowly he went mad and the pain became too much and he ended himself. So fucking weak. But not me. Oh no, not me. I am not weak. I can bring so many, yes?" He pressed the pistol to Rueben's head and Rueben quailed, squeezed his eyes shut. "I can wash this fucking place in blood, all for *its* glory."

"Let's start with yours, you fucking animal."

Something cast a shadow over the moon and Rueben saw his Mum as she leaned forward and pressed the thick barrel of a shotgun into James's chest. His mouth opened, his gun hand swung upwards, then everything exploded in noise and fire, and the Entity revelled.

LEIGH

"MUM!" Rueben's face was shocked as James's blood sprayed and the animal who'd terrorized and murdered her family flew backwards off her son.

Leigh's teeth creaked together, she clenched her jaw so hard. James hit the loose scree of the wide crater and slid on his back further down its slope. His face wide in shock, his torso wider in blood and bone. Shattered ribs stood up like broken teeth from a gaping mouth, his organs shining in the moonlight, Rueben's spear still in him, sticking out at an angle as he slid. Black tendrils glowing red inside quested desperately upwards as James's corpse was sucked dry.

Rueben scrambled to his feet and Leigh dropped the shotgun, grabbed him into her arms. She held him tightly to her, felt his face pressed into her shoulder as he hitched with wracking sobs. "Oh, Mum! Mum!"

His arms wrapped around her and he squeezed and she had never felt anything so good. She pressed her face to the top of his head, smelled dirt and fear and blood, but she smelled Rueben too. Her mind flooded with memories, of his tiny form soon after birth and that new life smell. His hair as it came in, his skin after a bath. The slow devolution into a teenage funk, but always that scent of pure Rueben underneath. If he came home dirty and sweaty from a sports game, she still smelled it. It would never leave, the power of that scent memory stronger than any other trigger. And now she smelled it again. She sucked it up, tears breaching. He was here, in her arms.

He was safe. The monster who'd tried to kill them all hadn't succeeded. She still had her Rueben.

"Leigh, Roo. We gotta go!" Clay's voice was tight with fear. Surely that bastard hadn't survived having his chest blown wide open, the blood sucked from him. She imagined him rising from the dark ground, bleeding and capacious, his face wrenched asunder in hate and rage.

She looked up and saw something worse.

Those same writhing, scintillating blobs of night, glowing red from the inside, alive with tiny flickering tendrils, swarmed all over James, climbed out of him, and in a procession they hurried on rippling limbs down into the crater. Down to where something else moved. Something massive flexed and heaved.

James's corpse shrank rapidly, sucked empty in seconds, and those scurrying black creatures flowed down and gathered together. In the lowest depth of the crater, where nothing lived, not even the twisted, blackened trees, the ground rose and fell like a giant breathing.

It rose again, dark earth splitting and flexing, sank only a little, then rose higher still. Like some giant bug, some gargantuan grub, finally emerging after an eternity of waiting. Those rippling black parts from James, his blood, each alive with a deep red glow, coalesced and sank in. Leigh stared, momentarily dumbfounded. She remembered the same things from Grant's violent death, flooding out of the back door of the hotel and off across the grass. They had gone in this direction. Had they come all this way? Drawn here? Soaked in here?

"It finally has enough!" Rueben cried, his voice cracked with panic.

"Enough what?" Leigh asked. "Enough *for* what?"

"It's still weak, but it has enough blood rise!"

"What does?"

The thing itself answered her. The ground rose once more, bucking upwards and splitting apart, and something emerged. A black, glistening curve rose, like polished leather, as if the carapace of some giant beetle were pressing out from a thousand years of slumber. Then angles hitched up either side and Leigh realised with horror they were jointed limbs. Giant, thick and corded, yet the jet black skin somehow still loose, undulating. Huge hands, each half a metre across, pressed into the rocky ground and the thing heaved again. With a slap of air, wide, twisted, featherless wings, heavy black flesh stretched between bony phalanxes, burst free, scattering rock and shale. And then the creature's giant head came up, elongated, wide at the brow, the forehead high and hairless, the chin long, the mouth wide, capacious. Teeth bristled in there like black diamonds and two protruded well beyond the others, those needle sharp canines each as long as Leigh's hand or more.

The creature shuddered and flexed as it rose, its long body straightening, more limbs appearing. *Legs?* Leigh wondered, but they had an extra joint, double-kneed and not entirely certain yet against the ground. And too many arms, she realised, as a second pair flexed out from beneath the first. Each arm ended in those giant hands, the fingers each tipped with a long, black curving claw. All four arms had extra joints too, the fingers had too many knuckles as they writhed and raked at the ground as the thing pushed itself free, first to those crooked knees, then slowly upright. It stood so tall, more than three metres, then more than four as it rose but still hadn't straightened.

The flesh of its long thin body pulsed as it drew itself up, then it turned dark red eyes on them. The rippling scillae, like those that had carried all the blood to this place, burst up from its skin, licked at the air and retracted again, over and over, a bristling forest surging all over its body and limbs relentlessly.

That deep wide mouth split open and it howled, ear-shattering in triumph and, Leigh thought, a desperate hunger.

Forms pushed and twisted through the skin of its enormous body, and Leigh cried out when she saw Grant's face, made all from shining black undulating flesh, his mouth stretched wide in a scream of horror. Other forms flexed and squirmed from the body of the thing. She saw Marcus and that bastard's brother, Paul. Several others she would never recognize.

Previous victims? The family from the hotel's bloody history? They pulsed in and out of it, a parody of their living selves, faces contorted in tormented agony, surrounded by those rippling tendrils.

It took one stagger-step forward, uncertain still but desperate, and its face split in a grin, those red eyes staring at them. Even from deep in the crater, it looked directly at them, tall as it was. Its body a pulsing, shining, slick mass shifting with shapes that rose and thrashed, only to be absorbed back in and reappear elsewhere, a constant reformation in a sickening rhythmic pulse, as its too many arms flexed, those huge wings stretched and beat, sagging but gaining structure, gaining tension. Its double-kneed legs pushed straighter and it stumbled forward once more.

The creature's maw yawned, deep red glowed within, those glittering black diamond teeth disappearing down a seemingly bottomless throat that defied physical space, from which a deep and sonorous howl echoed.

"Run!" Clay yelled and Leigh shuddered, realised she'd been mesmerized by it.

"Come on, Roo!" She dragged at her son as he stared open-mouthed, dumbstruck.

Fifty metres from them, and down a slope, yet they still had to look up to take it all in as it stagger-stumbled up the loose surface.

Rueben ran and pulled on Leigh as much as she pulled on him and they hauled each other to the side of the crater and finally to firmer ground between the healthier trees at its edge.

"Come on, come on!" Clay said, gesturing wildly with one hand. The other hand was pressed against his hip, his face twisted in a grimace. Leigh had run ahead of him to get here and the old man had caught up, but at what cost to his health. He looked to be in agony, his face white as the moon, his arm and chest red with blood.

At the lip of the crater she chanced a glance back. The thing stretched up, rising its mass high into the air. It paused, stretched up again, shuddered at the top of its extension. It reminded her of a cat, arching into the sun on waking from a nap. How long had this thing slept?

Again, it began to move, both legs and four arms gripped and flexed into the soft ground and the creature dragged itself along, animal-like despite its clear ability to stand tall on two legs. It made its way up the slope towards them, rippling with uncanny grace.

"I'll do it!" Rueben yelled, startling Leigh. "I'll bring more! Let us go and I'll bring more!"

"You can communicate with it?" Leigh asked, stunned.

"Don't listen, Roo!" Clay said. He crouched, crying out tightly in pain, then held Rueben's shoulders. He still held that large knife in one hand. "It's a liar, a trickster. It's a monster and will kill us all."

Rueben shook his head. "No, no. It needs more blood. It's awake, but its weak. It needs blood, so it needs us to *bring* it blood. It'll let us live."

"You maybe," Clay said. "Not your mother. Not me. It only needs one."

They stared at each other for a moment and Leigh trembled with shock and frustration. "Come on, we have to go!"

"You know it's true," Clay said. "I feel it too. Go, Roo. Run! Save your mum."

Relief washed through Leigh when her son nodded.

"Don't look back," Clay said. "And don't listen to its lies."

He stood up and stepped past them. Leigh glanced back to see the monster halfway up the slope, sinking and rising as it forced itself against gravity, sometimes down on all its limbs, other times rising like it was learning again how to walk.

"What are *you* doing?" Leigh asked.

Clay smiled. "Buying you time."

"What?"

"Grandpa, no!"

"Look at me. I'm an old man. I'm broken and I can't run. But I can help you. It won't be able to resist stopping for me, and that buys you time." He looked down at Rueben. "You live for me, son. Save your mother, and you *live*!"

Rueben looked from his grandfather to a space right beside the old man. "You'll take care of him?"

Leigh realised her son had to be talking to Molly. Clay reached a hand out into the air, his smile soft and full of love. "I've missed you so much."

"I love you both!" Rueben said.

Clay glanced down. "We love you too."

They both looked into the air again, nodded. "I will!" Rueben said.

"Here I come, Moll," Clay said. He turned to Leigh. "Go!"

Tears poured over Rueben's cheeks and Leigh realised she was crying too. But the cold centre of her knew he was right. The part of her that would do anything to protect her son recognised his words as necessary. And she loved him then more than she ever thought possible. She nodded, throat too tight to speak. The three of them hugged tightly, then Clay pushed them away.

"You run and you don't look back!" Clay said, then turned to face the creature.

Leigh and Rueben ran, ducking between the trees. Leigh chanced a glance back and saw Clay's back, silhouetted against the edge of the crater. His arm still raised, fingers curled like he held someone else's hand. Clay lifted the knife and drew it against the flesh of that arm. "I'm bleeding, you fucker!" he yelled. "Come and get it!"

The monstrous thing, standing taller and stronger than ever, reached the top and towered over Clay, dwarfed him. It paused, looked down at him and that wide mouth stretched open, those two long canine teeth, dagger-like, seemed to flex forward like a snake's fangs. Then its head darted down and engulfed Clay, closed hard over his torso and the thing's neck pulsed, its back flexed, as it sucked and sucked.

Leigh hauled Reuben with her into the trees.

RUEBEN

LOSS howled through him, another one he loved gone. The creature's howl of ecstasy was proof enough that his grandfather had been correct. It paused down there, sucking up everything Clay had to offer, heedless of the source, while Rueben and his mum ran. It would do the same to his mother and leave Rueben alone in the world, with nothing to love and no purpose but to serve its ravening appetite. He refused to accept that fate and he refused to let Clay's sacrifice be wasted.

"Where do we go?" he yelled as they raced through the dark trees.

Enough moonlight came through to guide their way, but roots dragged at them, unseen obstacles in the shadows caused them to trip and stumble. They held onto each other, dragged each other along. At least the thick trees would surely hamper the thing's progress too.

"We get to the hotel," his mum said, gasping for breath.

"And then what?"

"We take the ute." She glanced down. "Can we outrun that thing, do you think? In a car?"

"Maybe. I think so. It's not strong yet, it needs more."

Leigh tripped and nearly went down, but staggered overlong steps to save herself. Rueben pulled her up with him, realised he was almost her height now. Before long he'd be taller, maybe he'd even grow taller than his dad. Than his dad had been. He pushed the grief down and let his anger rise. Let it fuel his legs to run. To survive. To live long enough to grow taller than his dad.

"Okay," Leigh said.

"It's coming!" Rueben yelped, his voice high, cracking with fear. "It's finished with Grandpa and it's coming."

Leigh's face was set hard as stone as she ran. "He gave us a head start. It's enough."

They ran on, heads down. Rueben's legs burned with the effort, his lungs tight with fatigue. Simon stood between two trees up ahead, a slightly brighter glow in the night.

"Hurry!" he said. "You've got this, champ! You've got a lead. Use it."

Rueben nodded as he and his mum bolted right past. They burst out onto the wide lawns behind the hotel, the moonlight brighter than ever free of the trees. Not pausing for breath, they sprinted across and his mum dragged him over the back deck and into the doors of the lounge.

"The key's in the ute!" Rueben said.

"I know." The fire crackled in the hearth, its warmth almost smothering after the frosty chill of the woods. As they ran, his mum let go of his hand and bent to pick up one corner of a rug.

"Mum, what are you doing?"

"Help me!"

Not understanding, but doing as he was told, he helped Leigh grab the rug and drag it out from under a couch. She hauled it across to the fireplace and dumped one end into the flames. It immediately began to smoulder.

Then he understood.

"Come on!" Leigh said, and ran through the dining room.

They took hold of a runner rug that led towards the toilets and pulled on it, felt it tear away from the sticky backing that stopped it slipping on the floorboards. His mum was done with this place, and wanted to make sure no one else came and was tempted into the same deadly activity. It felt right, to destroy everything that had led to the destruction of his family. His dad dead, and his uncles and his grandpa. The arseholes who'd brought that death down upon them too. If James hadn't come here and started spilling so much blood, the thing out there, whatever it was, would never have awoken.

But it had tempted someone once before and nearly had its way. And it had tempted Rueben too, and more successfully tempted James once he ventured close enough. It was clearly a thing that could never be risked again.

Its presence was distant, but powerful. And Reuben knew it would win. It had the blood it needed to rise once more. The work was done. What point was there in trying to stop it now?

"Rueben!"

He jumped, startled by the strength of the voice snapping his name like a gunshot. Simon stood there, his face clouded with anger. Rueben had never seen him like that before.

"Don't listen to its lies, remember?" Simon's face softened. "You hear me? You don't listen! It's up now, sure, but it's weak. Without more blood, it can't stay strong. And in the day, it has to hide, it can't bear the sun."

Rueben stared. Simon's face implored him. His mum needed him. They threw the end of the rug into the fireplace. It caught immediately, began to burn, and they pushed on into the kitchen. His mum grabbed the curtains, wrenched them down to lay over the gas cooker, and turned on all the burners. The curtains caught, the wall behind the hob blackened and the paint bubbled.

They ran together across the driveway and into the garage. His mum jumped into the driver's seat of the old ute and Rueben clambered in beside her. She turned the key. The engine coughed, the car jerked, then stilled. They heard crashing and the breaking of tree limbs out across the lawns.

"Come on, come on!" Leigh said through gritted teeth.

She turned the key again and the car coughed and juddered, fired and backfired. She revved it and the engine roared and died.

"Fuck! Come on!"

Rueben closed his eyes and sucked in a deep breath. *Come on*, he thought. *Don't let all this be for nothing! Not Mum too.*

Leigh turned the key again and the old truck revved and roared into life, black exhaust billowing up behind them. She gunned the engine once, twice, then pushed it into gear and floored it. They both yelled out wordlessly as the ute smashed through the wooden doors of the garage, splintered wood bouncing off the bonnet and windscreen. The great black monster, striding now on its long legs, four arms raised, wings stretched wide behind it, came rapidly across the lawns towards them. Its eyes glowed bright red, its mouth wide in an ear-splitting howl. Cadaverous forms twisted and pulsed in and out of its mass.

Rueben and Leigh both winced as the creature's howl pierced their ears, then Leigh turned the car towards it.

"Mum, what are you doing!?"

She didn't answer, just crouched low over the wheel, teeth clenched in a grimace, and roared across the driveway, out onto the grass. The monster paused, stretched itself high, and lifted its four arms higher, like a huge spider displaying threat. Rueben imagined those massive, glistening limbs punching down into the vehicle, spearing it like the car was a bug on a corkboard.

Then his mum swerved left and right, pressing the accelerator to the floor. She was a good driver, she controlled the vehicle as it slipped and slid on the dew-damp grass, then she hauled up the handbrake and slid broadside into one of the creature's legs. The car rattled and shuddered with the impact, the window on the driver's side burst in with a rain of glittering cubes, but the leg Leigh had targeted buckled with a loud crack and the Entity roared in pain.

Giant arms stabbed down and back, but Leigh floored the accelerator again and was already tearing away from it.

"Go, Mum!" Rueben yelled, almost laughing with the terrified joy of it.

Leigh drove in a fast, tight circle and came in hard behind the monster, aiming for the back of the other leg. The heavy bull bar on the ute slammed into the back of its lowest knee joint and the creature howled and fell backwards. Leigh slewed the car sideways, drove hard as the creature turned and grabbed for them again. One hand scraped the side of the ute, black claws curling up rolls of metal door skin, Rueben and his mum yelling as the car rocked, then she was driving hard once more.

"Time to go, I think!" Leigh said and accelerated harder still. "That should slow it down." The old truck roared and bounced across the lawn, skidded as the wheels bit into the gravel of the driveway. At furious speed, Leigh swerved around between the hotel and the cottage, flames already licking out of the kitchen door they'd left open.

Rueben twisted around, looked out through the rear screen. The horror from the crater came after them. It limped and staggered, used its arms to assist its damaged legs. Those huge wings flapped and beat at the night, lifting and dropping the thing as it came. Maybe when it was strong enough it would fly like a huge bat, but right now the wings only took some weight from the limbs as it chased them. Yet weak as it was, injured as it was, it still managed to move terrifyingly fast.

"Mum, it's still coming!"

Leigh growled, an animal sound of determination through her clenched teeth, and drove harder. The truck fishtailed on the loose driveway, the creature in a stumbling roll behind them, loping on all its limbs. Its mouth wide, those two long teeth glittering in the moonlight. Its red eyes burned bright like fire.

Leigh swerved and hit the brakes. Rueben looked forward to see why and saw they had reached the road, his mum slowing but still turning onto it dangerously fast. The car skidded across the asphalt, Rueben's side slamming into a roadside tree. He yelled in shock and anticipated pain as his window shattered in across his lap. His mother wrestled control of the car again, and drove. One massive, glistening, black hand stabbed down into the asphalt, splitting the surface and burying itself right where the car had been a fraction of a second before. Then Leigh was driving hard and fast, the road in their favour, the tyres gripping well.

The creature came after them, but began to quickly fall behind.

It's cajoling was plaintive now, almost pathetic. Its need desperate.

"I'll bring you nothing!" Rueben said, and he meant it. Wind whistled in, cold and wonderful, through the missing windows. Over the trees, behind the bulk of the horrific thing as it shrank in the distance, he saw the orange glow of the hotel burning.

LEIGH

"YOU should sleep, Roo."

"I don't know if I'll ever sleep again."

She smiled despite the deep spike of pain that gave her. "I know what you mean."

How would they ever recover from this? How would they explain it? As dawn smudged the sky pink and grey, she guided the ute down the mountain. All she had to do was get them out of there. Anything else could wait until after that.

"Uncle Simon says the thing has gone back to ground. Back in the crater. It can't stand the daylight."

She glanced over, saw her son as a man now, dirty and hurt but brave and strong and powerful. So different from the kid in the back seat driving up here only a few days before. "You really talking to Si?" Grief pulsed hard in her chest.

"Yeah. Dad could never see the dead. Grandma Molly says Auntie Cindy can, but she won't. She doesn't like it. And I can. I do like it. It's a family thing."

"Okay." Given everything else she'd recently seen, how could she ignore the truth of her son's words now? "Tell him I love him."

Rueben smiled. "He says he loves you too."

Leigh tried and failed to suppress a sob. She nodded. "So it hates the light?" Anything to change the subject.

"Yeah. Maybe it'll never get far from the bush up there, it's so remote. Simon says it needs more blood, so if it doesn't get any, it'll have to sleep again. Hopefully forever. I guess we can't know."

"We have to make sure we never sell the land. Not sure how we'll afford that, but we can worry about it later, I suppose."

"I'll help, Mum."

"I know you will, love. Can you see your dad?"

Rueben's face fell and he shook his head. "Not everyone stays," he said quietly. "Simon says he'll go soon too, he thinks. He can feel something pulling and he hopes it's Uncle Marcus. He says Grandma Molly went with Grandpa Clay. I could see her before, but she's not here now." Rueben sniffed. "But Uncle Simon says I'll always be able to see dead people who *are* still around, and sometimes talk to them. He says to not be afraid of them but to always trust my feelings."

Leigh nodded, lips pursed. "I guess that's good advice for all of us."

Swallowing down her grief as well as she could, she put an arm around her son and drew him close. Whatever else, she had Rueben. He had survived, and she was still here to look after him for as long as he needed her. He leaned against her shoulder. She kissed the top of his head and drove on into the dawn.

ACKNOWLEDGEMENTS

DESPITE the solitary nature of writing, no book happens alone. I want to thank Kevin Lucia, Dan Franklin, Lisa Lebel and Richard Chizmar plus all the other hardworking staff at Cemetery Dance Publications for making this novel happen. Thank you all for your faith in me.

I especially want to thank my good friends Joanne Anderton and Philip Fracassi for their invaluable feedback on early drafts of this book. You guys made the novel so much better than it would otherwise have been.

Huge thanks to my agent, Becky LeJeune, and thanks also to that great Aussie, Alex Adsett. I wouldn't be where I am today without you.

Beyond this I won't name people in particular, because I'm terrified of missing someone, but every friend in writing and publishing, you know who you are and you are beyond valuable to me. Every friend outside the writing world who supports me in any way, I love you. Thank you all.

In this age of digital theft in the form of so-called "AI" and language learning models, I absolutely do *not* want to thank everyone pushing the "AI is inevitable" agenda. It's just another tech grift where people without skills try to cannibalise everything good and creative in the world. Art has always been and will always be a human endeavour. The innate humanity of artistic creation is the soul of everything we enjoy. No form of "AI" will ever be used in my writing or in the production of my books, in writing or covers or recording. I can't believe we're in a position where that has to be stated, but I can't in good conscience stand by and not say something. At the very least this stuff needs to be trained with consent and compensation. Until then, it's simply stealing. On a brighter note, I want to thank my amazing family, who support me in every way. Thank you for your unwavering belief.

And to everyone reading this book, I thank you in particular. I really hope you enjoy the ride. Just… don't spill any blood, okay?

—Alan Baxter, NSW, May 2024

Printed in Poland
by Amazon Fulfillment
Poland Sp. z o.o., Wrocław